Richard Laymon was born in Chicago in 1947. He grew up in California and took a BA in English Literature from Williamette University, Oregon, and an MA from Loyola University, Los Angeles. He worked as a school-teacher, a librarian and as a report writer for a law firm before becoming a full-time writer. Apart from his novels, he published more than sixty short stories in magazines such as *Ellery Queen, Alfred Hitchcock* and *Cavalier* and in anthologies, including *Modern Masters of Horror, The Second Black Lizard Anthology of Crime* and *Night Visions 7*. His novel *Flesh* was named Best Horror novel of 1988 by *Science Fiction Chronicle* and also listed for the prestigious Bram Stoker Award, as was *Funland*. Richard Laymon wrote more than twenty acclaimed novels, including *The Cellar, The Stake, Savage, Quake, Island, Bite, Body Rides, Fiends* and *After Midnight*. He Died in February 2001.

For up-to-date cyberspace news of Richard Laymon's books, contact Richard Laymon Kills! at: http://rlk.cjb.net

D1638692

Alarums

Richard Laymon

headline

First published in 1993
by HEADLINE BOOK PUBLISHING

First published in paperback in 1994
by HEADLINE BOOK PUBLISHING

A HEADLINE FEATURE paperback

1

ISBN 978 0 7472 4130 0

Printed and bound in Great Britain by
Mackays of Chatham PLC, Chatham, Kent

HEADLINE PUBLISHING GROUP
A division of Hodder Headline PLC
338 Euston Road
London NW1 3BH

TO KATHLEEN AND KELLY LAYMON,
MY MOM AND DAD,
WHO BROUGHT ME INTO THE WORLD
AND RAISED ME WITH LOVE
AND HAVE ALWAYS STOOD BESIDE ME
– FROM ME WITH LOVE –

E'en the Daws and Jackals trembled with Afright
As strange Alarums, crying Chaos, bruited through the Night.

'The Portent'
Henry Loveworth

CHAPTER ONE

Bodie fidgeted, trying to find a comfortable way to sit on the straight-backed chair. It was impossible. The chair had been designed by a sadist.

The music, too.

He could be at a movie right now. Or back at his apartment, sprawled in his lounge chair, reading a book. Instead, here he was in Wesley Hall on a chair grinding his butt bones to powder, listening to a string quartet.

The music fairly lilted.

Boring as hell. Doug Kershaw or Charlie Daniels, now those are a couple of guys who know how to treat a violin.

Melanie, of course, wouldn't be caught dead stomping her foot and sawing out a lively number.

She sat there as stately as a mortician, stiff-backed and prim, playing what sounded like the background score of 'Four Wimps at Tea-Time'.

Melancholy Melanie.

She looked like a poet contemplating suicide. Thin, almost cadaverous. Glossy black hair hanging to her shoulders. Big, gloomy eyes set in a face so white it seemed nearly translucent. A very long, pale, vulnerable neck. And the choker, of course – one of those velvet bands around her neck.

Bodie found her chokers very erotic. Especially when that was all she had on.

'If I unfasten that,' he had once asked, 'will your head fall off?'

'Perhaps.'

Straddling Melanie, he'd reached behind her neck to remove the narrow ribbon.

She'd whispered, 'Not yet,' held onto her ears, then said, 'Now.'

Sensitive and haunted, but not without a sense of humor.

Bodie shifted his position on the chair. Crossing his legs helped a little. He'd been smart enough, this time, to take a front row seat. At the last concert, he'd been so boxed in that even the small relief of crossing his legs had been impossible. He checked his wristwatch. Ten till nine. Fifty minutes down, seventy to go. He wondered if he could survive that long.

A number ended to quiet applause, and Bodie clapped harder than anyone.

They'll think I'm truly appreciative, he thought. They'll be right. I appreciate the fact that it's over.

Melanie looked at him. Her expression didn't change. Distant, solemn and rather haughty, befitting the occasion. Bodie winked.

Melanie quickly turned her eyes away, but blushed. The color suffused her creamy neck and face. She squirmed just a bit, then stiffened her back even more than before, tucked down her chin firmly against the violin and waited, rigid, for the music to resume.

The new tune sounded much like the last one.

Here we go again.

Bodie glanced at his wristwatch again. Only two minutes had passed.

Don't worry, he told himself. This *will* end. Eventually. Then freedom. Stretch. Get the kinks out. A nice long walk to Sparkey's. A salami pizza, a pitcher of beer. Relief.

All you've got to do is hold on until ten o'clock.

Does anyone really *enjoy* this music? he wondered. The hall was pretty crowded. Everyone here couldn't possibly be the lover, relative, or friend of a performer. Well, plenty of them were students and teachers from the music department. They probably eat it up, the same way Melanie . . .

She jerked as if she'd been kicked in the back, but nobody was behind her. She flung her arms across her face. The violin fell to her lap. The cello player to her left dodged the tip of her flying bow. She made strangled, gasping sounds. The violin dropped to the floor as tremors jolted her body.

Bodie leaped up and ran to her.

A seizure?

Heart attack? Epileptic fit?

He lurched to a stop in front of Melanie, careful not to step on the violin, and grabbed her wrists. Her rigid arms jumped and twitched in his grip as if an electric current were sizzling through them.

'Melanie!' His voice had no effect.

He forced her arms down and pinned them to the sides of her thrashing body. Her face was inches from his – twisted and gray, eyes rolled back so that only the whites showed. Her tongue lolled out. Spittle dribbled down her chin. Her wheezing breath was hot on Bodie's face.

Somebody bumped into him. He realized they were surrounded by a crowd. People murmured to each other, some asked questions, some called out advice.

'Get back!' he snapped.

He was scared. He'd never been so scared. Melanie looked as if she were being killed – ripped apart inside or electrocuted.

'Paramedics,' said a voice behind him. 'I'll call the paramedics.'

'Yeah, quick!' Bodie yelled.

Melanie's chair suddenly tipped back as she rammed her feet against the floor. Bodie tugged her arms. The chair thumped down and she lurched against him. Bodie, off balance, staggered backward. Someone tried to catch him, but failed. He tumbled to the floor, Melanie on top. Her forehead smashed his nose.

Suddenly, the quaking stopped and the stiffness went out of her. She lay motionless. Bodie tasted blood, felt it trickling down his throat and dribbling along his upper lip and cheeks. 'Are you okay?' he asked.

Melanie shook her head. 'I have to go home,' she muttered. She looked up at the crowd clustered around them. 'I'm sorry,' she said, and burst into tears.

They assured everyone that they were both all right. The paramedics hadn't been called yet. Bodie turned down an offered ride to the hospital. Handkerchief pressed to his nose, he explained that he would take Melanie to the hospital himself, for a checkup. She nodded in agreement, red-eyed but no longer crying.

4

'We'll be fine,' she said. 'Thank you. Thank you all for your concern.'

A member of the quartet brought Melanie's instrument case to her. 'Everything's in there,' the girl told her. 'Your violin's fine.'

Some of the group stayed with them as they left the auditorium – offering sympathy or encouragement, asking questions, ready to help in case of a relapse. Professor Trueblood, head of the music department, preceded them and opened doors. 'My car's just around in back,' he said. 'I'll drive you to the emergency room, I insist.'

'Really, I'm fine,' Melanie told him. 'Thank you, anyway. I'm fine.'

'I'll take care of her,' Bodie said through his sodden handkerchief.

'You're in some need of attention yourself, young man.'

'I'll be all right.'

Professor Trueblood watched from the door of Wesley Hall as they hurried down the concrete stairs. Once away from him, they walked slowly side by side.

They walked through the warm night in silence. Then Melanie asked, 'How's your nose?'

'It'll live.' He sniffed. 'I think the bleeding's stopped.'

'I'm sorry I hurt you.'

'It's nothing.' He looked at her. 'Are you going to tell me what happened?'

'Oh, Bodie,' she whispered. Her arm slipped around his back, her small hand warm on his hip. 'It's something terrible.'

'I know. I saw.'

'Not that. I mean . . . *what I saw.*'

'What you saw?'

5

'My dad. It must've been Dad. Or my sister.' Her hand tightened on Bodie's hip. 'God. He . . . he must be dead. One of them, anyway. I . . . damn it.' She sobbed. 'I don't know which one. But Dad, I think. When it happened last time, it was Mom.'

Bodie stopped. He turned and stared down into her glistening eyes. Her sorrow made a thickness in his throat and a tight hurt in his chest. But her words . . . What was she saying?

He tucked the handkerchief into his pocket and gently took hold of her shoulders. Too late, he realized he had blood on his fingers. 'I want to understand,' he said.

Melanie stiffened. She lowered her head and wiped her nose with a cuff. 'There was something coming at me,' she said in a shaky voice. 'Only not at *me*. It was dark and noisy and running at me and I knew I had to get out of the way or it would kill me, but I didn't have time, it was too fast and it got me. It got me.'

Bodie pulled her gently against him. She lowered her face against the side of his neck. He felt its wetness, the tickle of her eyelashes. 'That's what happened in your mind?' he whispered. 'While you were . . . shaking and stuff?'

He felt her nod. 'Jesus,' he muttered.

'When it happened before, I was eleven and at summer camp. It was Mom that time.'

She had told Bodie about the loss of her mother, the woman slipping in the bathtub, smashing her head and drowning. 'You had a vision or whatever then – like tonight?' he asked.

'Not exactly like tonight. But yes. That's why I know Dad's dead.'

'You don't *know* it,' Bodie said. 'Not for sure.'

She didn't answer.

'Come on. Let's get back to the apartment. You can call home. Maybe everything's fine.'

In their apartment two blocks from campus, Bodie stood in silence behind Melanie while she dialed. Her head was down. On the shoulders of her white blouse were the rust-colored marks left by his fingers.

She listened to the phone for a long time, then hung up and turned to him. 'Nobody answered.'

Bodie looked at his wristwatch. Nine-thirty. It would be eight-thirty, Pacific time. 'Maybe they went out for dinner or something. Why don't you try again in an hour or so?'

'It won't do any good.'

'You can't be sure,' he said. 'How many times have you had these . . . visions?'

'Only once like this. Strong like this. When Mom was killed.'

'How come you never told me about it?'

She was silent for a moment. Her arms tightened around him. 'I didn't want you thinking I'm a weirdo.'

'Hell, I already knew that.'

'I love you, Bodie.'

'See? That proves you're a weirdo.'

'Yeah.'

'Look, what do you want to do?'

'Go home.'

'Right now?'

'Yeah. I've got to. I can't stand it.'

'Do you want me to go with you?'

'Do you mind?'

7

'No, of course not.'

'You can drive back in time for your Monday classes, and I can just stay there until . . .' She shrugged.

'Maybe we'll find out everything's all right.'

She didn't answer.

As they held each other, Bodie thought about the trip. Her father's home in Brentwood, California, was probably more than eight hours from Phoenix. If they got away by ten, they would reach the house around six in the morning, five o'clock Pacific time.

A long drive, especially going without sleep. But Bodie felt a stir of excitement about making the trip – a journey through the desert night, Melanie at his side, maybe stopping along the way at a diner for coffee. It would be like a little adventure, even though the occasion for it was anything but joyful.

'Let's pack up,' he said, 'and get going.'

CHAPTER TWO

'He set fire to house. He think, "Ha ha, I burn up body, no body." He think, "Me clever fella." Not so clever. Take more than house on fire to dispose of corpse. All he do, he cook it like side of beef.'

The Los Angeles County Medical Examiner grinned and nodded sagely as his remark brought a few chuckles and moans from his audience. Pen looked around. The dapper little oriental, a cross between Quincy and Charlie Chan, had his listeners spellbound. They were eating it up.

She was glad she'd finally worked up the courage to come to one of these meetings. Even though she had sold only one story so far, she felt special to be sitting among so many mystery writers.

Gary Beatty leaned sideways on his seat, shoulder brushing against her. He took a thin cigar from his mouth. 'The man's got good patter,' he said, twitching his lip like Sam Spade. 'Too bad he don't talk English.'

Gary was the first person she'd met here tonight. She had arrived early, found a parking place on a sidestreet beside the Greater Los Angeles Press Club, rushed with her umbrella through the rain, and barely gotten seated at the Press Club bar before he climbed onto the stool beside her.

'Heyyy, Allen,' he greeted the bartender.

'Gary, how are you?' Allen, an oriental, spoke with a voice like Paul McCartney. 'What can I get you, eh? Coors or Bud?'

'Make it a Coors.'

Allen finished preparing Pen's vodka-tonic and set it in front of her. Pen unsnapped her handbag. Gary shook his head. 'It's on me,' he said.

'No, really . . .'

'Never look a gift-drink in the mouth.'

'Well . . .'

'Don't make me twist your arm, babe. We both might enjoy it too much.'

She'd stayed with Gary, talking and drinking, for twenty minutes. Then he'd led her up to the meeting room.

'This'll separate the men from the sissies,' Gary said as the overhead lights went out.

'Do you think he'll show bodies?' Pen asked.

Gary tipped back his head and blew out a smoke ring. 'I wouldn't be at all surprised.'

The first slides showed the Los Angeles Medical Examiner's headquarters building and fleet of golden vans. As they appeared on the screen, the coroner gave statistics about the size of his department, its annual budget, the number of bodies handled during the previous year, the previous month. Gary, Pen noticed, was taking notes. 'We do booming business,' the coroner said. Rather gleefully.

Then it started getting bad.

A slide of the autopsy room. Stainless steel operating tables. Trays of surgical instruments. Scales for weighing excised organs. Slanted tables with drains at their lower ends to catch the run-off.

Pen realized she was holding her breath. She let it out, inhaled deeply, and took a drink of the vodka-tonic she'd brought up with her from the bar.

The next slide showed a sunlit field. One of the golden vans was near a couple of police cars. Several men stood in knee-high weeds near the top of the picture. 'Nice spot for picnic, but we have customer.' The projector clicked and hummed. The customer appeared.

A woman. She was sprawled face-down. Her skin looked bluish-gray and puffy. The bottoms of her feet were dirty. Surrounding her were the shoes and ankles of men from the previous shot. 'She not be here long. Overnight, maybe.'

A close-up of her buttocks. What had looked in the longer view like a dark smudge was now obviously the contusion surrounding a bite. 'Our killer make big mistake. Love bites. Teeth marks not fingerprints, but almost. Good for us, bad for him. Maybe we get saliva sample. If he secreter, we get blood type from saliva. Pin him down good.'

The picture changed.

A different naked woman. Heavier than the other one. She was face-down on a table in the autopsy room. The little man stepped close to the screen and pointed a finger at her rump. Both buttocks were a deep, grayish purple. 'Post-mortem lividity. When heart stop pumping, gravity act on blood. Blood sink.' He pointed out other blotches on her shoulder-blades and the backs of

11

her legs. 'Look like world's worst hickey. But we know she supine after death. Can't fool Mother Nature.'

Gary groaned. 'What a wit,' he muttered.

Pen took a deep, shaky breath. She felt light-headed and a little weak. Something's wrong, she thought. Too much vodka? She wanted to take another sip, but she didn't dare.

The next slide showed a man.

He was stretched out on a table. A blue cloth covered his face. He was naked. His skin was red. 'This not post-mortem lividity, this not sunburn, this cyanosis.' He went on. Pen kept glancing at the corpse's limp penis, and forcing her eyes away from it, and looking again.

She shut her eyes. Her face felt cold and numb. She rubbed it with her hand. It was wet.

This, she thought, is what they call a cold sweat.

Christ.

What am I doing here?

Then came a close-up of a gaunt, dead face. A man with whiskers. And a white speck of something in the hair of his left nostril. 'Nature always at work,' said the chipper coroner.

Pen's ears were ringing.

He pointed at the speck. 'Fly eggs. Fly eggs like little clocks, very handy. We know they left after death, so . . .'

Pen set her drink on the floor and picked up her umbrella and handbag. She rose on wobbly legs, side-stepped past Gary's knees, and made her way along the side of the room until she reached the head of the stairs. The narrow staircase looked steep. She paused, wondering if she dare try to descend. Damn well better, she thought. Gotta get out of here before I toss my cookies.

Hooking the umbrella handle over her left wrist, she clutched the wooden hand-rail and started down.

Her mouth kept filling with saliva. The staircase looked darker than it should. When she blinked, it had an electric blue aura. She clung to the railing, sliding her hand down it, prepared to grip it firmly if her legs should give out.

You're gonna faint or barf, she thought. One or the other.

God, what a disaster.

Fly eggs.

She gagged, her throat straining and tears coming to her eyes.

Then she was at the bottom of the staircase, breathing deeply of the fresh, cool breeze. It helped. The rain sounded pleasant spattering the courtyard in front of her. It seemed to be coming down harder than before.

She still felt shaky, but her vision was better and the cold tightness in her stomach seemed to be easing. She pursed her lips and stretched her mouth wide. The numbness had left her cheeks.

Opening her umbrella, she wondered what to do. One thing was certain, she couldn't go back upstairs. That left two alternatives: either cross the courtyard to the Press Club bar and wait there for the meeting to end, or go home.

Gary might stop by the bar after the meeting ended. But there was no guarantee of that. And if he should show up, it might lead to trouble.

Probably end up trying to fend him off.

Better just leave.

She stepped out of the entryway. The rain drummed

on her umbrella as she hurried through the courtyard and down the concrete steps to the parking lot.

Twenty minutes later, she closed the apartment door behind her and hooked the dripping umbrella over its knob. Rump against the door to steady herself, she pulled off her boots. She carried them into the bedroom, turning on lights as she went.

It felt good to get out of her clothes. She hung up the damp skirt in the closet, slipped her feet into an old pair of moccasins, and put on her robe. The robe was soft against her skin.

In the bathroom, she switched on the heat light. Then she went to the kitchen and removed a bottle of Burgundy from the refrigerator.

A glass of wine, a good book, a long hot bath – the life of luxury. Worth coming home for.

The cork came out with a low, ringing pop.

She carried the bottle into the dining area and took a crystal glass from the cabinet. Back in the bathroom, she filled the glass. She took a drink, the wine cool and tart in her mouth, warm after she swallowed. Its heat flowed downward, spreading.

Nice, she thought.

This will be very nice, far superior to sitting in the Press Club bar.

Something might have developed with Gary.

Forget it.

He just would've tried to pull something. They all do. If you don't come across, they try to force you. The hell with them.

She set down the glass and bottle beside the tub – near the far end so they would be easy to reach once she

14

was in. Kneeling, she stoppered the drain and turned the water on. She got the temperature right, almost too hot to bear, then dried her hands and went to get a book.

Her loosely belted robe hung open. She left it that way, feeling too lazy and comfortable to bother closing it.

She switched on the light in the spare bedroom, her office. Resting on the corner of her desk was the new Dean R. Koontz book. It was getting good, but it was a hardbound. No risking a hardbound in the bath.

She started toward her bookshelves and yelped in pain as a corner of the desk gouged her thigh. Clutching herself, she whirled around and dropped onto the chair.

'Jesus,' she hissed.

When the pain subsided, she lifted her hand. No blood on her leg, but a layer of skin was peeled back, ruffled and white, leaving a patch of shiny pink flesh.

She let out a trembling breath.

Damn it, why didn't I look where I was going? It'll feel great when the hot water hits it.

From where she sat, she could hear the bath water.

She started to stand up.

And noticed the telephone answering machine beside her typewriter. Its red light was on. She looked more closely.

Four calls while she was gone? A busy night.

She rewound the tape, pressed the playback button, then turned away and headed for the bookshelves.

'Hello, honey.' Pen didn't recognize the man's voice. 'Sorry you're away. I wanted to talk to you about my big hard cock and your hot juicy cunt.'

The words pounded her breath away. She spun

around, stared at the brown plastic recorder.

'How'd you like me to fuck your brains out, huh? Yeah, I'll stick it right up . . .'

She lunged at the desk, arm out, stiff finger set to jab the voice to silence. The machine beat her to it, a quiet beep signaling the end of the message.

Pen's legs felt weak. She braced herself over the desk, elbows locked, hands flat on the cool wood.

Second message.

Same voice.

'How'd you like it if I stuck my tongue up . . .'

She stabbed the stop button.

Shut her eyes. Lowered her head. Took deep breaths as her heart slammed.

Goddamn demented sicko. Good thing I *wasn't* home. Better fly eggs than . . .

Pen opened her eyes. Glimpsed the blond tuft between her legs. Jerked the robe shut and pulled its belt tight. Looked at the machine.

Maybe the bastard quit after two calls.

She pressed the fast forward button, watching the counter turn. Okay, third message. '. . . come in your mouth. I want to shoot my load down . . .'

She shoved the eject control. The cassette flipped up. She tore it from the machine and threw it.

CHAPTER THREE

They were heading west on Highway 10, an hour out of Phoenix, the headbeams of the VW van pushing ahead of them through the darkness and lighting more than Bodie cared to see beyond the breakdown lane.

The fencing over there had snagged a lot of tumbleweed. That seemed to be its sole purpose.

Beyond the fence was nothing.

Nada.

Hell, there's plenty out there, he thought. Plenty of rocks and sand and cacti and tarantulas and scorpions. And tumbleweed.

He remembered an old episode of *Thriller* or *Outer Limits* (hard to keep the two shows straight) where a couple got stuck in an area very much like this and the goddamn tumbleweeds got them. Surrounded them, closed in, and . . .

A pale shape the size of a trashcan scooted into the path of his headlights. Bodie's foot jumped to the brake pedal. Before he could ram it down, the thing had already blown past his lane.

A tumbleweed, must've hopped the fence.

It looked like a giant hairball of dead sticks.

Skeletal.

The back of his neck tingled.

'It's coming for us,' he said – quoting his favorite line from *The Night of the Living Dead*. He tried to smile.

Melanie turned toward him. Her face was a pale oval with dark smudges for eyes and lips. 'Just a joke,' he said. She didn't answer. 'Remember that old *Thriller*? Maybe it was *The Outer Limits*. This couple was . . . Hey, would you say something?'

'I was so awful to him. I never stopped blaming him for . . . what happened to Mom. I know it wasn't his fault, but he was right there in the house. If he'd only heard her fall . . . If *I'd* been there, instead of away at camp.'

'Who sent you to the camp?' Bodie asked.

'They did. Mom and Dad. I didn't even want to go, but they said it would be a growth experience. They felt I was too dependent and introverted, that camp would help "bring me out". I didn't have any choice about going. I know I shouldn't hold myself responsible for Mom's accident. Dad either. It wasn't his fault any more than mine. But what you know and what you feel don't always match up. So things were never right between Dad and me after that. I tried . . . I just couldn't forgive him, or myself. Then he went and remarried.'

'Right away?'

'No. I was a sophomore in high school. That really broke it. I mean, here he was pushing sixty and Joyce was like twenty-six. It was disgusting. I couldn't handle it. I moved in with my sister and lived with her till I finished high school. I just couldn't . . .' Her voice trembled. 'Now he's dead, and I'll never . . .' She began to weep.

'You don't know for sure he's dead,' Bodie told her.

'I know. I know.'

'We'll find a gas station. There's got to be one around here someplace. I want you to call again.'

'It won't do any good.'

'You've sure got a lot of faith in that vision of yours. You might just have it all wrong.'

She sniffed and didn't answer.

'You admitted, yourself, that you weren't sure who the victim was. You thought it might be your father *or* your sister.'

'It was Dad.'

'*Now* you're sure?'

'Yes.'

'You know, maybe this is one of those things where a person sees into the future. Precognition? If it is, then maybe going there might be part of some design to prevent it from happening. Possible?'

'I don't know,' Melanie muttered.

Not a flat-out denial. Bodie felt that he had made a breakthrough . . . at least opened a crack in her certainty. 'When you had the vision about your mother, was it before or after her accident?'

'Right at the same time. I had it while she was drowning.'

'Okay, that's your one major experience with this kind of thing. This time could be entirely different. In fact, when you start thinking about it, the second time with anything is almost never the same as the first. Think about it. Your first drink, your first date with a guy. Look at the first time you had sex. I know for a fact it was different the second time around – a whole new ball game, so to speak.'

'I'm glad you find this amusing.'

'I'm just trying to help, Mel. You're all upset about this thing, but it's possible that your vision wasn't what you think. I'm just saying that maybe your father – or whoever – is still okay. Maybe this was a warning, and you're meant to get there in time to prevent whatever you saw.'

'I guess it's possible,' she admitted. But there was no conviction in her voice.

It *is* possible, he told himself.

Hell, it's possible that the whole damned episode was a figment of her imagination. All that guilt revolving around her father, probably a subconscious wish for him to croak, God only knows what other hang-ups are ticking away in her head. An emotional time-bomb that finally blew.

He decided to keep that theory to himself.

The last thing she needed right now was Bodie suggesting she'd flipped her gourd.

We'll find out soon enough, he thought. If it turns out that her father got his ticket canceled tonight . . .

Bodie saw an oasis ahead. Lights, buildings, a Shell sign high atop a pole. Coming up fast.

He eased his van onto the exit ramp, a single lane curving away toward the Shell station, a second station across from it with a lighted wooden sign announcing 'Bargain Gas', a Denny's restaurant, and a squat adobe building decorated with blinking blue neon that read, 'Bingo's Bar and Grill'.

Melanie leaned across the seat for a look at the gas gauge. 'You've got half a tank,' she said.

'Better safe than sorry.'

'I guess I might as well call while we're stopped,' she

said. She didn't sound eager.

Bodie stopped beside the self-service pumps at the Shell station. Straight ahead, at the edge of the lot, stood a pair of public telephones. 'Do you want to call while I fill her up?'

'I have to use the john.'

They both climbed out of the van. Bodie stepped to the pump, unhooked the nozzle and shoved down the start lever. He watched Melanie. She was walking with her head down, looking depressed and vulnerable. Not much different from the way she usually looked, a way that made Bodie want to hold and comfort her. He found his eyes lingering on the seat of her corduroys, loose-fitting pants that almost but not quite hid the moving curves of her buttocks. He imagined slipping his hands down the waistband. The cool smoothness. He wondered if she was wearing panties.

She's probably wearing them tonight, he thought. Sex would've been the furthest thing from her mind when she'd changed clothes for the trip.

She vanished around a corner of the building. Bodie took off the gas cap and thrust the spout into the neck of his tank.

It's these balmy Arizona nights, he thought. A guy can't help getting a little horny.

If she phones and everyone is fine, maybe he would pull off the highway . . .

Cut it out.

It's always terrific in the back of the van. A certain risk of exposure that adds to the whole . . .

The nozzle shut off. He hooked it back onto the pump, capped his tank, and headed for the office. He was nearly there when Melanie appeared, striding past the corner of the building, rubbing her hands on her cords.

'No towels?' he asked.

'One of those stupid blower machines.'

'I'll move the van over by the phones.'

She nodded, and kept on walking. Bodie continued to the office. He paid for the gas, and came out.

Melanie was standing at one of the phones, searching inside her purse.

The filling station was deserted except for Bodie's van. He decided not to move it, after all, and headed for Melanie. She looked up at him. 'Problem?' he called.

'I've only got a quarter.'

He took out his wallet. 'Make it a card call,' he told her. 'Mine's here somewhere.' By the time he reached her, he had found his calling card.

'Thanks,' she said.

He explained how to use it.

Melanie turned away and dropped her quarter into the slot. As she dialed, Bodie stepped close against her back. He held her shoulders gently. 'It'll be all right,' he said. She nodded, her hair caressing his chin and mouth.

She read off the card numbers to the operator.

He felt her body tighten.

'It's ringing,' she said.

He rubbed her shoulders, felt the bra straps under the crisp fabric of her blouse.

'Nobody's answering,' she said.

'Give it some time.' Bodie pressed his lips to the back of her head. Her hair had a faint, pleasant aroma of lemons.

'It's no use. Nobody's home.'

She hung up. A quarter clanked and skidded into the coin return. She fingered it out, turned around, and looked up at Bodie with her wide, hurt eyes.

'I wish I could make everything all right,' he said.

'I know.'

'Look, maybe there's someone else you could call. A neighbor?'

She bit down on her lower lip, frowned.

And suddenly started digging in her purse. Her hand came out with a small, red booklet.

Pen's eyes moved across the page, following the lines of words. She thought she was reading the paperback novel. Her eyes traced over its sentences, and she wasn't aware that none of their meaning reached her mind.

Sorry you're away, I wanted to talk to you.

What if he calls again?

My big hard cock . . . your hot juicy cunt.

He's out there somewhere, a sicko, and he's thinking about *me*.

Maybe right now reaching for his phone.

Pen turned a page of the book. Her eyes followed the words and she listened, expecting to hear the distant jangle of her telephone. All she heard was a slow drip of water near her feet.

He might never call again.

Oh, he will. He will.

Four calls already tonight.

Probably four, though she'd only listened to three of them.

He likes the sound of my voice.

Four times, she had talked to him. *Hello. I'm sorry, but I'm unable to answer your call at this time. If you'd like to leave me your name and . . .'* Four times, her voice had traveled the wires and come out close to his ear like an intimate whisper. She saw him alone in a room with her voice. The lights were off so he could pretend that more than her voice was there – that his hand was Pen's hand stroking him in the darkness, or Pen's mouth sucking him, or . . .

That's it for the answering machine.

He won't get another chance to use my voice.

Give it away. Give it to Dad. 'I don't want the damn thing,' he would say. 'Do the world a favor and deep-six it.' Good joke, though. Gift-wrap it and watch his face when he tears open the package. Pen smiled as she imagined his reaction.

Hey, she thought. Congratulations, you're thinking about Dad, not that . . .

How'd you like it if I stuck my tongue up . . .

Damn it.

Her thighs jumped shut, sweeping up a wave of hot water that lapped the undersides of her breasts. She turned a page and continued reading. 'Penny squirmed under the bed . . .' Hey, this gal has my name! She turned back a few pages. The name Penny popped out at her from almost every paragraph. Who's Penny? What's going on? Scanning what she had read so far, she realized that none of it had registered.

With a sigh, she sat up, reached over the side of the tub, and set the book on the floor beside the wine bottle. Her glass, resting on the edge of the tub, was empty. She picked it up, brought the bottle in with her, and filled the glass.

Ought to get myself smashed real good, she thought.

She drank half the wine in the glass, then poured to

24

the top and set the bottle down carefully on the rim of the tub.

Get good and polluted, maybe you'll crack your head getting out, and . . . like mother like daughter. No more worries about your friendly neighborhood pervert.

Being careful not to spill, she eased down again into the liquid heat. Lower this time. Her head sank against the air-filled backrest. She held the glass close to her face and stared through the clear purple Burgundy.

The color of post-mortem lividity.

Mom . . .

Christ, don't start thinking about her.

This has certainly turned into a banner night.

Some creep I don't even know . . .

How do I know I don't know him?

The voice.

He could've changed his voice, disguised it.

These kinds of guys, though, don't they usually call strangers? Open the phone book, pick a name, any name, as long as it isn't a man's. Not much to be said for the old ploy of using your initial. He sees P. Conway, he knows it's not a Peter.

'No Peter here,' she mumbled. 'No, indeed.'

She tried for a drink.

Too late, she realized she should have sat up for it.

The rim was almost to her lips before the base of the glass met her chest. A quick tip. Wine sloshed into her mouth, spilled down her chin. Choking, she lurched up. She tried to hold her mouthful of wine, realized it would spurt out her nose if she didn't get rid of it, and coughed it out. The wine turned the water pink between her legs.

She coughed, sniffed, took a deep breath that made her lungs ache.

25

Neat play.

She blinked tears out of her eyes.

Go Mom one better, drown on a mouthful of Charles Krug.

Death, where is thy sting?

The pink cloud spread out and vanished, but the sweet aroma of the wine filled Pen's nostrils.

She drank what was left in her glass, then set the glass aside.

Sliding her feet up the bottom of the tub, she raised her knees out of the water. Leaned foward. Sniffed them. A pleasant odor, but if she did nothing about it she might be sorry. It would stick with her like spilled perfume, cloying after a while, even nauseating.

A banner night. Star-spangled.

She spread her knees wide, leaned between them, and tugged the chain of the drain stopper. The rubber disk came up with a belch. A small whirlpool appeared on the water's surface, and the level began to drop.

A quick shower.

She hated showers.

You can't hear a damn thing.

The Manson family could break down your door, Norman Bates could waltz in singing 'Mammy', the telephone . . .

You could fall down and split your skull.

Especially after you've had a few snorts.

She hated showers.

What're you gonna do, you smell like a guided tour of wine country?

She turned her head. The empty glass and the half-empty bottle of wine stood on the tub's rim. She would have to move them out of the way. The book on the floor, too. Showers could be very messy.

She reached for the bottle.

The telephone rang.

Her whole body lurched. Her hand struck the bottle's neck. With a quick grab, she caught the teetering bottle and held it steady.

The phone rang again.

YOU BASTARD, YOU HAVE NO RIGHT!

Each jangle was a blow smashing against Pen's heart, pounding her breath away.

She saw herself climb from the tub and rush, streaming water, into her office. Snatching up the phone. *You rotten degenerate shit, if you ever call me again . . .*

No, that's what he wants. My voice, my fear.

Give him a blast with your whistle.

The police whistle was on her key ring. The key ring was in her purse. In the living room. On the coffee table.

Grab it and blast his ear off.

That'll wilt your big, hard cock you goddamn . . .

The ringing finally stopped.

She let go of the wine bottle.

She listened. She heard her thumping heart, her quick shaky breaths, the water gurgling down the drain, silence beyond the locked bathroom door.

He knows I'm home, now. The tape didn't talk to him, he knows I'm home.

The tub emptied. The drain went quiet.

Pen sat there. Wet. The wet turned cold. She was shivering.

She sat there, hunched over, knees up, breasts against her legs, arms hugging her shins. Teeth clamped shut to keep them from clicking.

Droplets of water squirmed down her skin.

27

The thing to do now is . . . is what?

Make it so he can't call back.

She squeezed her legs harder.

Right now.

Pen let go, unhuddled, lost the comfort of warm firm legs tight together and tight to her breasts.

She felt very naked, very vulnerable as she stood up and lifted a leg over the side of the tub.

It rings now, she thought, I fall, crack my head open.

She swung her other leg over.

Both feet on the bathmat.

Your timing's off, you creep.

She felt as if she had tricked him, won a small victory.

Then there was the soft dry warmth of her towel. It rubbed the wetness away. It eased the chill. It calmed the shivers. Her teeth unclenched, and she noticed the ache in her jaw muscles.

When she finished, the towel smelled of Burgundy.

She wrapped it snugly around her breasts and tucked in a corner to hold it in place.

At the door, she gripped the knob and hesitated.

Don't clutch up again, she told herself. He's not out there. It's perfectly safe.

She turned the knob. The lock button popped with a loud, springy ping. She pulled the door open and stared through a gap the width of her head. Lights from the living room, her office, and her bedroom glowed through the hallway. Nothing looked wrong. But it all looked wrong, strangely mutated and alien.

A voice on a tape, and the world shifts.

She listened. .

There was the faint hum of her refrigerator, nothing else.

A drop of water trickled off her rump and skidded down the back of her leg. Reaching a hand around, she smeared it away.

Wait a while longer, why don't you? Stand here till he calls again.

She stepped into the hallway. Glanced into her bedroom as she passed its door.

Nobody jumped out at her.

Of course not. I've got a bad case of the willies, that's all.

She stopped at her office door. Saw the cassette on the carpet, the answering machine beside the typewriter.

First things first.

At the end of the hallway, she made a quick scan of the living room. Her eyes swept to the door. The guard chain hung in place.

Satisfied?

Pen wasn't satisfied, but she felt her shoulders ease down a bit.

She stepped into the kitchen. From the hallway came enough light for her purposes, but she flicked the kitchen switch anyway to kill the shadows.

Just above the switch panel, her telephone was fixed to the wall. She wrapped a hand around it and pulled. The metal plate stayed on the wall, its jack hole empty. She placed the disconnected phone on top of her refrigerator.

One down, one to go.

With swift long strides, she returned to her office. She carefully avoided the desk corner that had earlier gouged her leg.

The answering machine. The phone. Their cords dropped off the edge of the desk, hung nearly straight down the gap between the side of the desk and the bookshelves, then curved upward and vanished behind the books.

Pen sidestepped. She dropped to a squat, held herself steady with one hand on the desk corner, and reached into the gap with her left hand. Her fingertips found the cords. She followed them, twisting sideways, slipping her hand over the book tops. Her towel fell. The phone blared, jolting her heart and ripping her breath away. With a cry of fright and rage, she hurled herself forward. Her right shoulder rammed the desk, shoving it, turning it. Another blast from the phone. Her knees hit the carpet. She squirmed, wedging herself into the gap, shelves digging into her hip and ribs, the desk edge scraping across her right breast. The phone shrieked in her ear. She writhed, teeth bared, whimpering, and her fingers found the phone jack. She yanked it from the wall.

Silence.

She eased herself free.

Her trembling fingers grasped the towel. She dragged it with her as she moved backward on her knees.

Eyes fixed on the phone.

The next best thing to being there.

CHAPTER FOUR

'This *is* Friday night,' Bodie said. 'People go out.'

'I know,' Melanie muttered. She was slumped in the passenger seat, knees up, feet against the dash. She had been like that since they left the service station. Staring straight ahead, but too low to see out the windshield. 'Maybe it was Pen it happened to,' she said.

Maybe it's no one, Bodie thought. 'Worrying about it won't do any good. Why don't you go in back and try to get some sleep?'

She didn't answer. She didn't move. She stayed curled up, head pushed forward by the seat back. Bodie wondered how she could breathe in that position.

'Doesn't your sister go out on dates?' he asked.

'No.'

'No?'

'Well, sometimes, I suppose. Hardly ever.'

'What is she, fat and ugly?'

Melanie turned her head. In the dim light, her face was a blur. Bodie couldn't read her expression, but he guessed that she wasn't amused.

'Just trying to cheer you up,' he explained.

'She's beautiful,' Melanie said.

'As beautiful as you?'

'Yeah, I'm a regular Bo Derek.'

'You look great to me.'

'You haven't seen Pen.' There was no admiration in Melanie's voice. Her monotone sounded just slightly resentful.

'She sure has a terrible name,' Bodie said.

'Who notices?'

'Me.'

'You haven't seen her yet.'

'What does she look like?'

'The Playmate of the Year.'

'Which year?'

'Any year.'

'I can't wait to meet her.'

'I'll bet.'

Bodie reached over. He patted the back of Melanie's upraised leg. When she didn't protest, he slid his hand down the soft corduroy and caressed her rump. 'I'm not big on Playmates,' he said.

'You . . .'

'I know, I haven't seen Pen yet. Her favorite books must be *The Prophet* and *Jonathan Livingston Seagull*.'

Melanie humphed.

'So why doesn't she go out with guys?'

'She's got a problem with them.'

'Ah.'

'Not "ah". It's not like that. It's just that they're always hitting on her. They've been hitting on her since she was – God only knows – twelve or thirteen. She got tired of it, that's all.'

'That's some problem.'

'It can be. I suppose. I wouldn't know.'

Bodie leaned closer to Melanie. His fingertips found the center seam of her corduroys. He stroked along it, feeling her heat through the fabric. He pressed harder, rubbed. Melanie caught her breath.

'Not now,' she said.

He took his hand away.

Melanie lowered her feet to the floor and sat up straight. 'I'm sorry,' she muttered.

'No, I understand.'

'It's my *family*. Dad or Pen . . .'

'I know. I'd be upset, too. But it is Friday night. Just because nobody answered their phones, you shouldn't jump to conclusions. All you've really got to go on is that vision or whatever it was.'

'You think it was just my imagination.'

'I didn't say that.'

'It's what you're thinking.'

'No, but I do think that's possible. You're carrying around all this resentment and guilt about your father – about your sister, too, apparently. I'm no shrink, but –'

'That's right, you're not.'

'I'm just trying to help.'

'I'm not a mental case.'

'Melanie . . .'

'If you didn't believe me, you should've said so in the first place. I could've come by myself.' Her voice climbed higher, trembling. 'I don't need this. It's hard enough . . .' She inhaled with a sob. 'Forget it.'

'Hey, come on,' Bodie said softly.

She got up, squeezed between the two seats, and disappeared into the rear of the van.

Good work, Bodie thought. He sighed.

Christ, you can't win.

You'd think she would jump at the possibility that her vision was a false alarm. Does she *want* it to be true?

We're talking about her father or sister biting it, for Christsake.

Yeah, maybe she does want it true. In the back of her mind. Wishful thinking. All right for *you*, Dad. You had it coming – let Mom drown, then married a tramp young enough to be your daughter. Take *that*, Pen. That'll teach you – think you can get away with looking like a goddamn Playmate of the Year?

I've gotta see this Pen.

I'll bet you do, Melanie said, her voice bitter in his mind.

She wants them to pay.

Vengeance is sweet, and a whole lot sweeter if you're there to see it happen, arrange for a little telepathic connection so you can feel their agony as their bodies get smashed.

Bodies smashed. Now that's convenient, isn't it? What did she say? It was noisy and running at her, and too fast for her to get out of the way. Like a car or a train. Some kind of vehicle.

That'll smash you up pretty good. Disfigurement. The gorgeous sister who always got the guys – maybe some guys *you* wanted for yourself – gets nailed by a car. The Playmate of the Year body turned to a broken pile of gore. Take *that*, you bitch. *Now* who's the pretty one?

Bodie didn't like the way his thoughts were going. He turned the radio on. Dolly Parton, 'Singles Bars and Single Women'. He left the volume low to keep the sound from disturbing Melanie.

Maybe she'll fall asleep back there. Sleep, that knits

the raveled sleeve of care. She could use it. A couple of hours of forgetting about her damned vision.

Maybe we shouldn't have called.

Especially her sister.

That made it a whole lot worse, finding out that Pen wasn't home, either.

Where was she? Maybe out at a movie or something. But maybe Pen had been notified of her father's accident and she'd left her place to be with him. At the hospital. At the morgue.

Or the reverse: Pen the victim, her father the one called away from home.

One way or the other. That's why nobody answered.

I'm as bad as she is, Bodie thought. Face it, I'm half expecting the vision to turn out real.

If it wasn't telepathy or something, it was a mental blowout and Melanie's running on a flat.

For her sake, it better be real.

You don't want that, either.

What you've got here, old pal, is one of your basic no-win situations.

Heads you've lost your dad or sister, tails you've lost your mind.

Not me, Melanie. I'm just along for the ride.

Don't you wish.

She's part of me, like it or not. Her problems are my problems. It got that way, somehow.

When he first saw Melanie, she was walking toward him with her books clutched to her chest, her head down, a frown on her face. It was a sunny Friday, late enough in the afternoon so that most classes were over and everyone around the campus seemed cheerful and

35

relaxed. Everyone except this girl mourning over the cracks in the walkway.

Bodie felt sorry for her. He also felt intrigued. She looked lovely, fragile – ethereal – and quite obviously down in the dumps.

Badly in need of rescue.

She was still several yards ahead of him, still gazing at the walk, and he knew she would pass him without looking up.

So he fished a quarter out of his pocket. He gave it an underhand toss. It clinked on the concrete, bounced, landed on its edge and rolled in a crazy zig-zag toward the girl. Bodie knew, from the slight side-to-side motions of her head, that she was watching the quarter's approach. As it took a swerve to the right, she lengthened her stride. Her sandal slapped it flat. Her frown was gone when she raised her face and met Bodie's eyes. She looked rather satisfied with herself – pleased that she had succeeded in halting the runaway coin.

'Thanks,' he said. 'It got away from me.'

She didn't say a word. She was now looking edgy. Maybe feeling intimidated because she was a freshman – so obviously a freshman – and he was old enough to be a grad student or even an instructor. She took one step backward.

Bodie crouched to pick up the quarter.

She wore a knee-length skirt. She had slim, pale legs. They had no tan at all. Their whiteness made them seem blatantly naked.

Bodie had a difficult time forcing his gaze away from them.

He peeled the quarter off the sidewalk, and stood.

The girl's face was red. One of her fine, black eyebrows was curled upward in a pretty good imitation of a question mark. Bodie guessed that she had noticed the inspection of her legs.

I'm done for, he thought.

The girl sidestepped, ready to be on her way.

Bodie sidestepped, too.

'Excuse me,' she said. Her voice trembled. 'Please, I'm in a hurry.' She stepped the other way. Again, Bodie blocked her.

She gave up trying to dodge past him. Standing still, she looked into his eyes and caught her lower lip between her teeth.

'I'm sorry if I upset you,' he said.

'I'm not upset.'

'And I was *not* staring at your legs,' he added.

'There's nothing *wrong* with my legs,' she said.

'Really?' He didn't know why he said that. He could think of nothing else to say.

'My legs are fine,' she insisted.

'And dandy,' Bodie said. 'They're a couple of the dandiest legs I've seen in a long time.'

'Yeah, I'll bet.' She watched him with narrowed eyes.

Either she has a leg problem that I didn't notice, Bodie thought, or her self-image needs an overhaul.

'In fact,' he said, 'I couldn't help wondering what the rest of them looked like.'

'I've only got the two.'

'That isn't what I . . .' He realized she had made a joke. Taken totally by surprise, he burst out laughing. The girl didn't laugh, but a corner of her mouth turned up in a rather wry half-smile.

'I've got this-here quarter,' Bodie said. He flipped it in

the air and caught it. 'What-say we mosey over to the student union and I'll buy you a Dr Pepper?'

She accepted the offer.

It started that way: a tossed coin, a look at her legs, a misunderstanding, and a joke that made things right.

Melanie seemed perplexed that he found her attractive. She made nervous jokes about being skinny and plain.

The next night at the drive-in, when he fumbled under the back of her blouse to unhook her bra, she said, 'You'll be sorry.' He said, 'Don't be ridiculous.' He got it open and reached around to the front and she grabbed his wrist. 'Don't,' she said. She was weeping, her tears making silver slicks down her face in the light from the movie screen. 'It's padded,' she sobbed. 'So?' She let go of his hand. He moved it to her breast. 'See?' she asked. And Bodie said, 'That's not so bad, Herman.' She laughed through her sobs, and elbowed him. The breast was warm and smooth. It wasn't large, but it filled his hand. The nipple felt very big. The other breast was the same. His hand wandered from one to the other. He wanted them in his mouth, but when he tried to unbutton her blouse, Melanie stopped him. 'Not here,' she gasped. They left the drive-in and Bodie drove to his apartment.

When he opened the door, she stood rigid and gazed into the dark room with wide, frightened eyes. Bodie took her hand. It felt like ice. It trembled. 'Nothing to worry about,' he said, and led her inside. He turned on the lights.

'I don't know about this,' she said. Her voice sounded high and tight.

'Neither do I,' Bodie said to calm her down. 'Let's just watch some TV.'

A quick, jerking nod.

'We don't have to do anything,' he told her.

'Okay.'

He turned on the television. Leaving Melanie on the sofa, he went into the kitchen and poured wine. Then he sat down beside her. She used both hands on her glass, trying to hold it steady. As she took a sip, she watched Bodie raise his glass. They both saw the surface of his wine shimmer. He was shaking a little, himself.

'What are *you* so nervous about?' Melanie asked.

'Who, me?'

'Yeah, you.'

They stared into each other's eyes. For a long time.

'We *don't* have to do anything,' she told him. Smiling, she set her glass on the table.

Bodie put down his glass.

They kissed. They held each other. She was trembling, but she was the one who eased *him* down onto the sofa. They lay on their sides, their bodies together. She still trembled, but she untucked his shirt and unbuttoned it and spread it open and caressed his chest. Bodie followed her lead. Soon, they were both bare to the waist. Bodie kissed her mouth, her eyes, her long neck with its black velvet choker. He stroked and held and squeezed her breasts while her hands roamed his back.

Her hands didn't venture below Bodie's belt. He abided by the unspoken rule, and kept his own hands from straying lower on Melanie.

He realized, soon, that this was as far as Melanie was willing to take it. The lower half was out of bounds. Squirm and rub, but hands off and clothes on.

He realized something else.

Melanie was a virgin.

She had to be.

The lower half wasn't just out of bounds, it was not even on the map.

Bodie would be her first.

If he could just get her pants off . . . That might not be easy, though.

Better not try it.

Maybe tomorrow night, or . . .

Melanie's hand pushed under his belt. Her cool fingers curled around his penis.

My God, he thought.

As her fingers slid, he opened the waist of her corduroys.

The corduroys ended up beneath her. Bodie didn't know it. He didn't know much of anything. He was dazed above her, inside her at last but only partway, holding back, aching with the feel of her slick tightness hugging him, needing in all the way but holding back, not wanting to hurt her though her fingers dug into his buttocks, urging him deeper and she panted, 'Harder . . . In . . . Push!' And, at last, he pushed. Flinching rigid, Melanie gasped, 'Oh!' in a high hurt voice and thrust up against him. He went deep. All the way. All of him inside and it was past bearing and he erupted, throbbing and pumping.

She held him. She stroked his hair. She wouldn't let him up. He mumbled lazily about not wanting to crush her, but she told him not to worry about it.

Bodie fell asleep. When he woke up, he was still on top of Melanie. He was still inside her. He felt *glued* to her. 'I think we're stuck,' he said.

'Good.' She smiled and kissed the tip of his nose.

'I think we really *are* stuck.'

'Something must've dried.'

He pulled free as gently as he could, but it hurt her. Her lips peeled back with pain.

Bodie looked down. 'Not a pretty sight.'

Melanie sat up. She looked. 'Yuck.'

'I guess we'd better take a shower.'

They took a shower. Bodie, Melanie, and Melanie's corduroy pants. When they were finished, only the cords were still bloodstained. 'They'll never be the same,' Bodie said.

Melanie smiled. 'Neither will I.'

She's part of me, like it or not. Her problems are my problems. It got that way very fast and maybe not on purpose, but that's how it is and that's why I'm driving through the desert night with a psychic or a nut case in the back of the van.

'I'm sorry,' she said near his ear.

He felt a rush of affection.

'Forgive me?' she asked.

'You had every right to be upset.'

She eased forward between the seats and rested a hand on Bodie's thigh. He looked at her. The bare arm led to a bare shoulder. Below the shoulder was the mound of a breast. A small breast, its nipple large and dark. 'Why don't you find a place to pull off the freeway?' she suggested.

'Are you sure?'

The answer was Melanie's hand sliding to his groin.

Bodie started looking for an off-ramp.

CHAPTER FIVE

After a quick shower to get rid of the wine smell, Pen dried herself with a fresh towel. She put a bandage on her scraped thigh, slipped into her moccasins, and put her robe on. Then she picked up the empty glass and the wine bottle.

Polish it off, she thought, and maybe you'll be able to sleep.

You'll sleep, all right. You'll be dead to the world, and maybe that's not such a grand plan.

You might even have a visitor.

Don't even *think* about that.

I'd damn well better think about that. He has my phone number, so he must have my address. It's right there in the directory for him. The answering machine is off, so he knows I'm here. What if he decides to come over?

They don't do that, she told herself, and opened the bathroom door. She walked quickly to the kitchen and put the wine bottle into the refrigerator. Then she rinsed out her glass at the sink.

Crank callers don't pay visits.

Who says so?

Fictional cops. In books, on TV, in the movies. *He's just a crank caller, ma'am. No reason to be alarmed. These guys who get their jollies phoning up women, they're timid mice afraid of their own shadows. That's how come they use the phone, 'cause it's anonymous and safe. You've got nothing to worry about.*

That's what they say, those fictional cops. And the next thing you know, the caller who's a timid mouse is sneaking through the gal's house with a butcher knife, intent upon carving her up.

Pen turned off the faucet. She set the glass in the sink. As she dried her hands, she looked across the kitchen. In the dining area stood her table surrounded by four sturdy, straight-backed chairs.

She carried one of them into the living room, moved her umbrella aside, and tilted the chair backward, wedging its top rail under the doorknob.

'That'll slow him down,' she muttered.

She didn't need to check the windows; they'd been closed and latched since last weekend. With dowel rods in the runners to keep the windows from being slid open, they were secure.

Real secure, she thought. Glass.

If he wants in badly enough . . .

He would have to be crazy. There are fifteen other apartments in this complex, all with windows facing the courtyard and pool. If he smashes a window – if I scream – someone will hear.

Would anyone come to help?

Probably. Manny Hammond, for instance. There's a guy would jump at the chance to rush to my rescue. Wouldn't that be wonderful. Better him than nobody, I suppose. By a small margin.

Pen returned to the kitchen. The butcher block on her counter held eight knives. She took the two largest knives into her bedroom. She placed one on the night-stand. Crouching, she set the other on the carpet just beneath the edge of her bed.

In case we end up on the floor . . .

Are you serious? she wondered.

Must be, I'm doing it.

She realized that she didn't want to leave the night-stand knife in plain sight. She took a copy of *Publishers Weekly* from her magazine stand and spread it open on top of the weapon.

Okay, you're in good shape now.

You're in good shape, all right, if paranoia's good shape. You're acting totally bonkers.

Yeah? Better safe than – her mind flashed a picture of the coroner's slide, the naked woman face-down on the autopsy table, buttocks purple. *World's worst hickey*.

One more knife, she decided, and returned to the kitchen for it. She placed this knife on the floor beneath the other side of the bed.

Back in the living room, she unplugged her stereo and removed its extension cord. Kneeling in her bedroom entryway, she ran an end of the cord through the gap between the door and the frame, over the top of the lower hinge. She brought the plug back through under the hinge, made a knot, and yanked. The cord held firm. She drew it across the doorway and tied its other end around the rear leg of her dresser.

Standing, she admired her work.

'Have a nice trip,' she said.

What else might she . . . ?

Isn't this *enough*? I'm certifiable.

This is enough, she decided.

She turned off the bedroom lights.

Other lights in her apartment were still on. She had intended to leave them on. But the dark line of her trip cord was plainly visible across the bottom of the doorway.

It won't do much good if he can see it.

Pen stepped over the cord and made her way through the apartment.

She wished she could leave all the rooms bright. But darkness would work against him in more ways than just hiding the cord.

You really are expecting him to show up?

No, not really. All right, yes. Yes, I think he'll show up. Maybe.

She'd been raped once. She didn't intend to let it ever happen again.

Maybe I should get the hell out of here.

She stepped over the cord. She sat on the edge of her bed.

I could drive over to Dad's house and spend the night there. Or go over to a friend's. Abby or Jane or Loretta — any one of them would be glad to let me stay. I can't just barge in, though. I'd have to call first. Plug in a phone, call, get dressed, go out in the rain.

What'll that solve? she asked herself.

It'll get me through the night.

But what about tomorrow night and the night after that?

'Fuck it,' she muttered.

If he's going to come, let him come.

She got up and turned off the lights. She took off her

robe, draped it over a chair, slipped out of her moccasins, and climbed into bed. The cool, smooth sheets felt wonderful. The heat of her body warmed them. Snuggling, she buried her face in her pillow.

You're *really* planning to sleep in the raw?

I always do.

This isn't always. You want to be starkers when he jumps you?

If. *If.*

Pen felt cozy. She didn't want to leave the comfort of the bed. But she forced herself to sit up, turn on the bedside lamp, and swing her feet to the floor.

There was a naked woman in the mirror, walking toward Pen. Her face made a mocking snarl, a lip curling up, baring teeth.

'Yeah, I know, it's all your fault.'

The rotten bastard doesn't even know what I look like, she thought. He probably picked my name at random. I could be a refugee from the ugly farm, he'd still be giving me grief.

I'm a woman, that's all he cares about.

A pair of breasts and a vagina.

I want to talk to you . . .

A chill squirmed up her body.

She bent and tugged open a drawer. She pulled out a pair of powder blue silk pajamas. She put them on, the cool fabric sliding over her skin like oil. Clinging, revealing.

Better than her nightgowns, though.

A lot better than nothing at all.

She rubbed her arms, feeling the goosebumps through the slick fabric.

The woman in the mirror sneered at her, obviously

47

disgusted with the whole situation.

Pen took off the pajamas and put them back into the drawer. She opened the top drawer, saw that she was down to her last four pairs of good panties, and searched near the back of the drawer until she found some old ones. They were ragged and the elastic was limp. Perfect.

She found an old, frayed bra and put it on. Then a pair of jeans. Calvins. The tightest jeans she owned.

So tight they peeled the bandage off her thigh.

She fastened them.

The woman in the mirror rolled her eyes upward. *You're a clown.*

Okay, I'm a clown.

She put on a baggy blue sweatshirt.

Her tightly encased legs made it hard to bend over, but she managed, and put on socks. Then she crossed to her closet and took out a pair of cowboy boots. She put them on. They had pointed toes. Great for kicking.

Looking down at herself, she shook her head.

Thank God I'm alone. Bad enough that *I* know I've flipped out.

Dressed like this, she wasn't about to get inside her sheets. She remade her bed, leaving the pillow out, then turned off the lights and lay down. On her back.

Great. Like taking a nap on the couch.

Bonkers.

So what's the alternative? Pretend nothing's wrong? *Don't* brace the front door, *don't* booby-trap the bedroom entrance, *don't* arm myself? Curl up naked and cozy under the sheets as if there isn't a guy out there who maybe wants to rape me?

She closed her eyes. Her lids felt spring-loaded. Keeping them shut took an effort. She pulled the pillow over her face. Folded her hands on her belly.

I'll never fall asleep this way, she thought.

Maybe that's best.

I can catch up on my sleep tomorrow after sunrise. I'll be safe once it's daylight. Just lie here and relax. Try to think pleasant thoughts, fat chance.

Instead of pleasant thoughts, Pen found herself wondering whether there were any other precautions she might take. Call the police? They'd probably tell her to get an unlisted number. But that wouldn't stop the creep from dropping by when he got the urge.

If I just had a gun.

Well, you don't.

Maybe pick one up tomorrow.

There's a waiting period for handguns, she knew from story research. About two weeks.

But I could walk out of a store tomorrow with a shotgun. I think. Yeah, the waiting period only applies to pistols, doesn't it?

So buy a shotgun.

Then what? Sleep with it?

Yeah . . .

Pen opened her eyes. She was curled on her side, legs spread out as if she were running. The leg on the bottom was numb. The tight jeans had cut off its circulation.

She didn't remember turning onto her side. Had she fallen asleep? Opening her eyes, she squinted at the lighted face of the alarm clock. Three-thirty.

Asleep, all right, but not for long enough.

Her leg tingled painfully as she rolled onto her back.

She shut her eyes again.

And heard a footstep. Her heart slammed her breath away. She lay rigid, listening. She heard only the thud of her heart. Then another quiet, scraping step. Not inside the apartment, but on the concrete walkway just outside her window.

The window was above her face.

She rolled, dropped her knees to the floor, and slid the knife out from under the magazine. Still on her knees, she crept away from the bed. She rose to her feet and leaned against the wall at the far end of the window.

With one finger, she eased out the edge of the curtain a fraction of an inch. No face. She widened the gap enough to see out with both eyes.

Someone was there, all right.

She took a breath so deep that her chest strained against her bra and she heard a quiet ripping sound from somewhere along the back of the garment. She let the air out slowly. Very tired all of a sudden, she leaned her shoulder against the wall. She continued to peer out the window.

So much for your lurking degenerate, she thought.

At the door of the corner apartment, only a couple of yards beyond the end of Pen's long window, Alicia Bonner was wrapped around her boyfriend. The eighteen-year-old girl, who apparently took her fashion cues from the *Mad Max* movies, wore boots that made quiet, shuffling sounds on the walkway as she adjusted her stance against the apartment door.

The overhang of the roof sheltered Alicia and her friend from the rain.

One of Alicia's hands shoved under the belt at the

rear of the guy's jeans. She squirmed, her thighs hugging his upthrust leg.

My big hard cock and your hot juicy cunt . . .

There should be a way to erase your mind, Pen thought. Rewind, press a button, and erase the voice as easily as you might remove it from magnetic tape.

Patent it, you'd make a bundle.

She heard whispers through her window.

How long are they going to be at it?

As long as it takes. Right.

Pen put the knife on the table, lay down on her bed, drew the pillow down over her face, and sighed.

As long as they stay out there, she realized, I don't need to worry about my friend.

Friend?

Go to sleep.

In spite of the pillow over her head, she could hear the rain, sometimes a shuffling boot, sometimes a whisper.

Thanks for the sentry duty, kids.

She found herself relaxing, easing toward sleep.

Gotta pee.

Not too badly yet. But better get it over with.

Moaning, she forced herself to climb out of bed. She unbuttoned her jeans as she crossed the dark room, and was pulling the zipper down when her boot stopped in mid-stride.

Oh, yeah.

The trip cord.

Oh, shit.

Her other foot flew forward to catch her, but the cord hooked it back.

Both feet snagged, she yelped and threw out her arms as she dived through the doorway. The far wall of the

51

corridor pounded a forearm aside and smashed the top of her head.

Stars. A galaxy. Whirling bright.

Ringing. Pen heard ringing.

I'd better get the phone.

But somebody was digging a fork into her brain through a neat round hole in her skull. Prodding around, prying out bite-size chunks of gray matter.

I'd better get the phone while I still have enough brains left to . . .

Wait. I killed the phones.

Him.

How does he make the phones ring when they're not plugged in?

It's not the phones, it's the doorbell.

Her stomach clenched. Her heart hammered, shooting bolts of pain through her head.

Groaning, she clutched the top of her head.

No hole there. A tender lump the size of a split golf ball.

The ringing stopped.

Pen opened her eyes. The hallway was dim with the vague blue-gray gloom of early morning.

She was sprawled belly-down on the floor, her cheek itchy against the carpet. She pushed herself up to her hands and knees, squeezing her eyes tight as pain surged through her head.

You're lucky you didn't kill yourself, the way . . .

Sounds from the front door. Someone trying the knob? A scrape and click of metal against metal.

Pen unhooked her feet from the trip cord and thrust herself up. She leaped it, rushed across her room and snatched the knife off the nightstand. Her head pounded. The back of her neck had burning steel rods that rammed into the base of her brain with each step as she ran, jumped the cord, and sprinted down the corridor to the living room.

The front door was open!

Only a few inches, but enough to admit the hand.

The hand was clutching the back of the chair, shaking it, trying to work it out from under the knob.

CHAPTER SIX

'Hurry!'

'I'm trying.'

'Let me try.'

'I'm getting it.'

'Come *on*.'

With his left hand on the outside knob, Bodie pulled the door tight against his right arm. The chair inside slipped down a bit. He tugged at it. He was pretty sure he could get it out of the way, but he wondered what Melanie would ask him to do about the security chain. Kick the door open and rip its mounting from the wall?

Then came a thud of footfalls. Someone charging toward the other side of the door.

'You bastard!'

He lurched back against Melanie, jerked his arm from the gap. A long blade jabbed out. He stumbled backward as fast as the blade approached him. Almost. Its point nicked his side.

His feet tangled with Melanie's. He fell against her. The bars of the balcony's guard rail rang as Melanie hit them.

An arm in the blue sleeve of a sweatshirt waved the

knife, blindly slicing the air.

'Pen!' Melanie blurted.

The arm stopped. The blade tilted upward. The arm withdrew from the opening. A moment later, half a face appeared in the gap, a single eye staring out through strands of blond hair. And lower, one breast in the same blue sweatshirt worn by the knife-wielding arm.

'Melanie?'

The half-face and breast went away. The door shut. Bodie heard the chair bump the door, heard the security chain rattle. Then the door swung open wide.

This is the Playmate of the Year? Bodie thought. This is the Weird Sister. Double, double toil and trouble . . .

At least she had put down the knife. Trembling fingers parted the hair away from her face. She muttered, 'My God, I could've killed you.'

'Just a flesh wound, ma'am,' he drawled. Holding his side, he got to his feet.

Pen bent forward and looked around as if to see whether anyone had witnessed the assault. 'Come in,' she whispered.

Bodie held back and let Melanie enter first. Pen shut the door behind him. She leaned against it. She looked haggard, distracted. 'I don't . . . I'm so sorry. I don't know what to say.'

'What's going on?' Melanie asked.

She shrugged. Her jeans were open, smooth skin showing above a triangle of white panties. She seemed to realize this at the same moment as Bodie. She raised the zipper and buttoned the waist. 'I had some trouble,' she murmured. She rubbed the back of her neck. 'Come on, we'd better get a bandage.'

They followed her into a short corridor. Passing a

bedroom, Bodie saw an electrical cord stretched across the bottom of the doorway.

What the hell is going on? he thought.

In the bathroom, she asked him to sit down and take off his shirt. He lowered the toilet cover and sat on it. As he removed his shirt, Pen took disinfectant and a tin of Band-aids out of the medicine cabinet. She moistened a washcloth at the sink.

'I'll do that,' Melanie said.

Crouching beside him, she cleaned away the blood and pressed the balled cloth to his cut. With his arm raised, Bodie watched. She took the cloth away. There was a quarter-inch gash below his last rib. Blood welled out. Melanie covered it again.

Pen unwrapped a Band-aid. 'I don't understand,' she said in a haggard voice. 'What are you doing here?'

'I had a vision,' Melanie explained.

Pen frowned. 'Of me?'

'I'm not sure.' She lifted the washcloth and squirted disinfectant onto the wound. The cool spray made Bodie flinch. As blood began to trickle out again, she took the bandage from her sister and pressed it firmly in place. 'There,' she said.

'Thanks.'

'You came all the way from Phoenix . . . because of a *vision*?'

'That's right.' Melanie stood up. 'This is Bodie, by the way.'

'I'm sorry I hurt you, Bodie,' she said, looking so sorry that he feared she might begin to cry.

'No sweat.'

'I thought you were . . . someone else.'

'Who?' Melanie asked.

'I don't know. I got these calls last night. Obscene calls.' She turned away. She reached into the medicine cabinet, took down a bottle of prescription pills, apparently realized her mistake, put that bottle back and slipped her fingers around the plastic bottle beside it. Aspirin. After filling a cup with water, she swallowed four of the tablets. 'I'm such a wreck,' she muttered. 'I smashed my head up.'

Melanie met Bodie's eyes. 'See? Didn't I tell you?' She turned to Pen. 'I knew you were in some kind of terrible trouble. My vision – it was like the one I had when Mom drowned.'

'Well, I'm not dead, anyway. Though that might be preferable, the way I feel right now.' She made a smile that was very much like a grimace. Rubbing her face, she said, 'Have you two eaten?'

'We drove straight through,' Bodie said. Except for an hour parked on a desolate road – a stop, he suspected, that had to do with Melanie wanting him properly satisfied before his encounter with the gorgeous sister.

'Why don't I get us some breakfast?'

As they headed for the kitchen, Melanie noticed the cord across the bedroom entrance. 'What's that?' she asked.

'A precaution. I was . . . I managed to convince myself he'd break in. Last night.'

'The caller?'

'Yeah.'

'Was it someone you know?'

'I don't think so.'

They entered the kitchen.

'Just an anonymous obscene phone caller?'

'*Just?*'

58

'They're usually harmless,' Melanie pointed out.

'So I've heard.'

'How did you get hurt?' Bodie asked.

'I tripped on the wire. Hoist on my own petard,' she added, a wry smile lifting a corner of her mouth. 'Bacon and eggs?'

'Great. I'm starving.'

Melanie nodded, crouched, and took a pan out of the cupboard.

Pen took out a coffee filter.

'I can make the coffee,' Bodie told her. 'Why don't you sit down and relax?'

'Sitting down won't help, I'm afraid. What I need is about twelve hours of sleep.' Her trembling hand spilled some coffee grounds onto the counter as she dumped scoopsful into the filter. 'I'm so wasted.' She frowned. '*You* two must be exhausted. You drove all night, and . . .' Her voice just stopped as if the rest of her sentence wasn't worth the effort.

'Let's get some food in us first,' Melanie said. She started peeling off strips of bacon and arranging them in the skillet. 'Why don't you tell us what happened?'

Pen emptied a container of water into the top of her coffee machine. Then she leaned against the counter. She rubbed the back of her neck again. 'Like I said, I got these obscene phone calls.'

'What did the guy say?' Melanie asked.

Pen glanced at Bodie, and lowered her eyes. 'Never mind what he said. It was pretty bad.'

'What did *you* say?'

'Nothing. He was on my answering machine.'

Melanie lit up. 'You've got him on tape?'

'Yeah.'

'Fabulous. Let's hear what he had to say.'

Pen shook her head.

Bodie frowned. '*We* called you last night. Mel did.' He looked at Melanie. 'You didn't get the answering machine, did you?'

'No.'

'What time was that?' Pen asked.

'Around ten, your time.'

'Ten?' She moaned. 'That was you? I'd turned off the answering machine by then. I was taking a bath. I thought you were *him*. So I got out and disconnected the . . .' She frowned. 'Did you call twice?'

'Just once,' Melanie said.

Pen's lip curled up.

Melanie turned on the burner under the skillet. 'So what happened after you disconnected the phones?'

'That's when I got to thinking he might come over.'

'What made you think that?'

'Why *shouldn't* I think that? He made it pretty plain that he wanted to . . . mess with me.'

'But that kind of guy almost never . . .'

'*Almost*. I know. But maybe this guy is the exception. I mean, he had my phone number so he obviously had my address. Anyway, I decided to be ready for him. That's why I blocked the door and strung that damn cord. Just to be ready, you know? Just in case. That's why I had the knife. So in the middle of the night I forgot about the cord and took a header into the wall.'

She looked sideways at the coffee machine. The glass pot was full. She took mugs down from a cupboard. Her hand trembled badly as she filled them. She gave a mug to Bodie.

'Do you still think the guy might come over?' he asked.

She shrugged. 'What's to stop him?'

'We're here now. I guess Mel's vision paid off.'

'Yeah,' Pen said. 'It was right on target this time.'

'We'll keep watch for you,' Melanie said. 'You can sleep all day if you want.'

'I may have to.'

When breakfast was done, Melanie and her friend both insisted that she get some sleep. She went into the bathroom and drank a glassful of Alka-Seltzer. When she came out, Bodie was kneeling in her bedroom doorway, removing the cord.

'Don't worry about anything,' he told her.

She thanked him. Then she turned to Melanie and hugged her tightly. 'It's great to see you again, kiddo.' She ruffled Melanie's hair.

Alone in her room with the door shut, she turned back the covers of her bed. The sheets looked wonderful. There was no need any more for the confining, protective clothes. She took them off. Because of Bodie being in the apartment, however, she put on pajamas before crawling into bed.

She eased the pillow over her eyes to block out the morning light. Her neck felt stiff, but her head no longer ached badly. The food and aspirin had helped. She took a deep breath. She felt pretty good, considering.

Her ordeal was over, at least for now. Maybe it was over for good.

She had over-reacted, that's for sure.

Damn near cracked her skull. Damn near broke her neck. Damn near stabbed Bodie.

I *did* stab him.

He was very nice about it.

Nice guy.

Lucky Mel.

Lucky me, having them both here.

But how long would they stay? She hadn't asked. They'd have to go back to school soon, maybe even tomorrow.

Don't worry about that now.

Nothing to worry about now.

She rolled over, the pajamas sliding against her skin, the covers up around her neck, and fell asleep.

'Do you think we can both fit on the couch?' Bodie asked.

'Who can sleep?'

'Me,' he said. 'I'm beat. *I* didn't sack out in the van for the last half of the trip, remember?'

'I don't know about you, but I want to hear the tape.'

'I don't think Pen would want us to.'

'She doesn't have to find out.'

Bodie sat on the couch. He patted the cushion beside him. 'I'll talk dirty to you.'

'Not funny. Whatever the guy said, it scared the hell out of her. I've never seen her like this.'

'I thought maybe she was *always* maniacal.'

'Come on.'

Bodie stood up. His heart pounded fast and he stood motionless, waiting for a light-headed feeling to pass.

'You okay?'

'My body's telling me to sack out.'

'So sack out,' Melanie told him, sounding a trifle

annoyed. 'I'll listen to the tape alone.'

'That's all right. I'm up.'

He followed her. She wandered around the apartment, searching for the machine. Apparently, Pen hadn't owned it when Melanie was living with her. Finally, she led the way into an office next to Pen's bedroom. The answering machine was on the desk. Empty.

Melanie scowled at it. 'The cassette's gotta be around here someplace,' she whispered.

She searched the waste basket.

Bodie found the cassette on the carpet at the far end of the room. He turned it in his hand. It didn't look damaged.

'Close the door,' Melanie whispered.

He quietly shut the door and returned to the desk. Melanie slipped the cassette into the up-tilted holder and snapped it into place. She rewound the tape. And played it.

'Hello, honey. Sorry you're away . . .'

Melanie turned the volume lower.

The voice sounded nasty. It would've sounded nasty reading a McDonalds menu, Bodie thought. But the things it said . . . He pictured Pen listening, imagined how she must have felt. Alone in the apartment. Exposed to the sick mind of a stranger, violated and scared.

The tape only permitted a brief message. But the bastard had time to tell her what he wanted to do before a beep cut him off mid-sentence.

'I don't see what she was so upset about,' Melanie muttered. 'Just your standard obscene . . .'

'How'd you like it if I stuck my . . .'

'This is really sick,' Bodie whispered over the continuing voice.

'It's not *that* bad,' Melanie said. 'Pen's gotta be nuts to let this stuff upset her so much. I've had some bad calls. They never freaked *me* out like that.'

The guy's time ran out, but he called again. 'Suck me, honey. Open up wide. Suck me off. I want to come in your mouth. I want to shoot my load down your throat. Come on, open up. Open wide, you whore. Yes, yes. Take me in, swallow my cock and – *beeeeep.*'

Three down, one to go.

Bodie took a deep breath.

The fourth message started.

'Pen, it's Joyce. Your father's been in a terrible accident. I'm at the emergency room of the Beverlywood Medical Center on Pico. You'd better get here as soon as you can.'

CHAPTER SEVEN

Pen struggled awake. Someone was knocking on her door. Why was her door shut, and who . . . ? She remembered. Melanie's here. And her boyfriend, Bodie. The guy I stabbed.

What if I'd killed him?

She seemed to shrink inside.

The door opened and Melanie's face appeared in the gap. She looked hurt and confused. 'You'd better get dressed.'

'What's wrong?'

'We listened to the tape.'

Pen's throat went tight. 'Well, damn it, thanks a bunch. You and Bodie both?'

'Joyce was on it.'

'Huh?'

'On your tape. Dad's been hurt. They took him to an emergency room. Joyce didn't say how he was, just that he'd been in a terrible accident.'

'God. Oh, no.'

'We'd better get over there.'

'Yeah. Yeah. I'll just be a minute.'

The door shut.

Pen sprang from the bed. She flung her pajamas off.

An accident. Dad.

In a daze, she took panties from her drawer and stepped into them. She was still pulling them up as she rushed to her closet. She tugged a pair of white slacks off a hanger, put them on, and grabbed the nearest blouse. It was burgundy, silken, too dressy for the slacks. She didn't care. She put it on and pushed her feet into sandals while she fastened the buttons. She let the blouse hang out. She zipped her pants on the way to the door.

' . . . call her,' Bodie was saying as she entered the living room. 'She could tell you how he's doing.'

'I guess.'

'Call Joyce?' Pen asked. 'Yeah.' She turned back and went into the kitchen. Her disconnected telephone was still on top of the refrigerator. She pulled it down and plugged it into the wall. With a shaky hand, she dialed. Melanie appeared beside her.

A busy signal.

She hung up. 'It's busy.'

Melanie, closing her eyes, let out a long breath as if having the news postponed was a blessing.

Pen drew the girl gently against her. Melanie's arms went around her and she rested her forehead against the side of Pen's neck. Her breath felt hot through the blouse. 'Don't worry, okay?'

'I'm scared.'

'So am I.'

'What if he's dead?'

'He's not. Joyce would've said so.' But my phones were unplugged, Pen thought. Joyce might've tried to call back. 'Come on, Mel. Let's go.' She eased the girl away.

'Do you know where they took him?'

'The Beverlywood Medical Center.'

'Okay. It's not far.'

They hurried down to the front of the apartment building. Bodie offered to drive. His blue van was parked at the curb. Pen rode in the passenger seat and gave directions, while Melanie crouched behind the gap and hung onto the seat backs.

The numbness in Pen wouldn't pass. None of this seemed real.

'Make a right on Pico,' she said.

When Pen finally saw the hospital at the end of the next block, she felt as if she were in an elevator and its floor had dropped out from under her feet.

'That's it,' she gasped.

Bodie swung his van to the curb. 'Is this close enough?'

'Fine,' Melanie said.

It's as close as I ever want to get, Pen thought.

They climbed out. Bodie fed the meter. Melanie took his hand, and Pen led the way.

The morning sky was deep blue. The mild breeze, smelling fresh after last night's rain, drifted Pen's blouse against her skin. She noticed that it felt good, and she wondered how anything could feel good at this moment with her stomach clenched and her shaking legs barely able to hold her up – with her father in the building up ahead . . .

He has to be alive. He has to be. Please.

A woman approaching, pushing a baby stroller.

He always wanted a grandchild.

Only a week ago, he'd said, 'I'm not getting any younger, you know. Why don't you go out like a good daughter and get yourself knocked up?'

Pen's throat tightened. Her eyes started to burn.

Christ now, don't cry.

He's all right, damn it.

Don't fall apart in front of Melanie. Hold it together.

She glanced back. Melanie was holding Bodie's hand and gazing at the sidewalk. Bodie met her eyes. She wondered how he must feel, finding himself in the middle of a family tragedy. Probably wishing he'd never left Phoenix. First he gets stabbed, now this.

At the corner, Pen turned toward the crosswalk. She pushed a button on the light post to activate the WALK sign, and waited. Across Pico Boulevard was a driveway marked 'Ambulance Entrance'. A police car was parked at the curb.

The WALK sign went green. She stepped off the curb and a hand clamped her shoulder from behind. It jerked her to a halt. A red blur steaked by, roaring, hitting her with its slipstream. As she staggered backwards a step, she saw the low rear-end of a speeding Porsche.

'Asshole ran the red light,' Bodie muttered.

Pen turned to him. He took his hand off her shoulder. 'Thanks. Guess I'd better watch where I'm going.'

Melanie had a hand pressed to her heart. She looked wide-eyed and breathless as if someone had just jumped at her in the dark.

'You okay?' Pen asked her.

She nodded.

The DON'T WALK sign was already flashing, so they waited through another cycle of the traffic lights. When the WALK sign returned, Pen checked the intersection before leaving the curb.

On the other side, she headed for the ambulance

driveway, realized she shouldn't try entering there, and turned around in confusion. She shrugged, stepped past Bodie and Melanie, and spotted a doorway facing Beverly Drive.

Her numbness seemed to spread and deepen as the glass doors parted.

She stepped into a reception room. A young woman gnawing her lower lip glanced nervously at her and looked away. She was on a bench, holding the hand of a tow-head no older than five who was bent forward to peer at a black woman with a bloody rag wrapped around her arm. The black woman, on a chair along the far wall, held her arm and rocked herself back and forth, humming softly. She had a blank look in her eyes. The child stopped staring at her long enough to eye the three new arrivals, apparently checking them for injuries.

Pen turned to the office enclosure on her left. Through the glass partition, she saw two women in white uniforms. One was seated at a desk. The other, heavy and wearing her brown hair in a Prince Valiant cut, looked up from her paperwork, smiled at Pen, and approached the window.

Pen froze.

She was here – a few steps, a few words, a few moments away from learning the truth – and the weight of it paralyzed her. She couldn't move. Her legs shook. She stared at the woman and gasped for breath.

Bodie stepped around her. He leaned close to the window. 'We got word that a Whit Conway was brought here yesterday after an accident. These are his daughters. They're awfully anxious to find out how he is.'

The woman looked down at something out of sight

below the counter front. 'That's Whitman Conway?'

'Yes.'

'He was admitted via ambulance last night, accompanied by his spouse.' She stopped talking, but continued to read whatever gave the information.

Pen's stomach gave a little flip.

Melanie took hold of her hand.

'His admitting diagnosis was fracture of the patellae bilaterally . . .'

'What does that mean?' Bodie asked.

'Both kneecaps were broken. His right upper arm was also fractured,' she added, bypassing the medical jargon. She rubbed her mouth. 'He also had a severe head injury. He was unconscious when they brought him in.'

Melanie's hand flinched in Pen's grip.

'He was admitted to the hospital for surgery. I only have the ER records here, so you'll need to check the main hospital for his current condition.'

She gave directions to Bodie. He nodded, then asked, 'Does it say how he got hurt?'

'He was struck by an automobile while crossing a street in Beverly Hills. A hit and run.'

Bodie thanked her. He led the way to a door at the rear of the room. Pen and Melanie followed him into a corridor.

Hit by a car. Pen thought of her own close call on the boulevard outside, but in her mind Bodie didn't stop her and the car broke her knees back. She flew headfirst at the windshield.

Dad.

A severe head injury.

Surgery.

At least he's not dead, she told herself. At least he

wasn't dead when he left the emergency room.

The woman would've known, wouldn't she, if he'd died later on? Maybe not. Or maybe she knew, but preferred to let someone else break the news.

They came out of the corridor into a lobby. Double glass doors faced Pico. A woman was seated behind an information desk.

'I'll try to find out what's going on,' Bodie said. 'Why don't you two have a seat?'

Pen nodded. She guided Melanie to a sofa near the wall, and they sat down.

Bodie spoke to the woman at the desk. She made a telephone call, said something to Bodie. He came back and sat beside Melanie. 'A doctor's going to come out and talk to us.'

They waited.

Pen rubbed her sweaty hands on her pants.

I'm sorry, we did everything humanly possible.

A man came through a doorway at the far side of the lobby. He walked straight toward them. He was not the old, weary physician Pen had expected. He looked young, not much over thirty, handsome and energetic. He belonged in tennis whites, but he wore gray slacks and an open white jacket, a shirt of Stuart plaid and a solid green tie, loosely knotted. He carried a clipboard.

Pen tried to read his expression. It was business-like. It gave nothing away.

Bodie was already standing.

Pen forced herself up. Melanie hesitated, then stood.

'I'm Dr Gray,' he said, and shook hands with Bodie. 'I'm the neurosurgeon who operated on Mr Conway.' He had a pleasant voice, a pleasant smile.

'How is he?' Melanie asked, her voice a choked whisper.

'Your father's in a stable condition.'

His words tore the fog from Pen's mind.

Dad's all right.

The tears came and she thought, it's okay, oh my God, he's not dead, he's okay. 'Can we see him?' she asked. Blubbering. I'm blubbering. I don't care.

'Certainly. But we need to talk first. Will you step this way?'

Talk.

It's not okay.

Dr Gray led them into an office. They sat on soft chairs and he sat on the edge of his desk, facing them.

'Your father sustained what we call a subdural hematoma. The impact from the accident caused blood vessels inside his skull to rupture. We operated on him immediately after he was admitted last night to open the skull, relieve the pressure of the blood build-up inside, and stop the bleeding. The surgery went well. However, your father did sustain a certain amount of brain damage, which is almost inevitable considering the trauma he experienced.' Frowning, Dr Gray rubbed his cheek as if checking for whiskers. 'I've seen patients in worse condition than your father make full and complete recoveries. I've seen others who weren't so fortunate. But your father is in excellent physical shape for a man his age, so we can be somewhat optimistic about the outcome. At present, however, he's comatose.'

'He's in a *coma*?' Bodie asked.

'He hasn't regained consciousness since the time of the accident. He is no immediate danger, however. We have him on life support systems, and his condition is being constantly monitored. His vital signs are good.'

'You think he'll come out of it, though?' Bodie asked.

'There's just no way of knowing. He might pull out of it today or next week . . .'

'Or never,' Melanie said.

'That's also a possibility. But we're doing everything we can for him.'

CHAPTER EIGHT

Bodie stood at the foot of the bed. Melanie, beside him, stared at her father while Pen went to the man's side and took hold of his hand.

A sheet covered him to the chest. Tubes ran into his nostrils and arms. The top of his head was wrapped in bandages.

The cardiac monitor had a jagged green line and beeped regularly just as such machines did on television – which was the extent of Bodie's exposure to such things until now. The respirator made a chirping sound as it pumped air into the man's lungs. Somewhere, Bodie had heard the term 'bird respirator'. He supposed they were called that because of the noise.

All very interesting.

He wanted the hell out of there.

The doctor had made it sound pretty good, almost as if the coma was just a minor setback. But the old guy, bandaged and hooked up from every direction, looked like a Victor Frankenstein experiment on a bad day.

'Dad, it's Penny. The doctor says you're going to be fine. Melanie's here, too.'

'Hi, Dad,' Melanie said.

'You're going to be fine,' Pen repeated.

His chest rose and fell, but he didn't twitch an eyelid. The cardiac monitor beeped at the same rate as before.

Good thing this isn't a television show, Bodie thought, or the line on the screen of the heart machine would go flat about now and you'd get that long whining noise.

So far, so good.

He didn't want to be around, though, when it happened.

A long time seemed to pass before Dr Gray suggested they leave. 'You could come back this evening at eight and see him for a few minutes. Maybe his condition will have improved by then.'

Pen squeezed her father's hand. 'We'll see you tonight, Dad.' She let go and backed away.

Melanie said nothing – as if she knew there wasn't any point.

They left the room. Dr Gray led them to the elevator and tried once again to reassure them before he departed.

As the elevator doors began to close, a voice called, 'Could you hold that?' Bodie pushed the 'Doors Open' button. An orderly swung a gurney around and rolled it inside. On the gurney was a wasted, sallow-faced old woman with greasy hair. Bodie, wishing he could go back in time and let the doors shut her out, tried to hold his breath as the elevator descended.

Hospitals. Charming places.

The old crone had a bad case of impending demise, and he hoped it wasn't catching.

Finally, the doors glided open and he hurried out. The orderly and his ghastly patient stayed. They were going down. What was down in the basement? Isn't that where hospitals took their dead? She wasn't quite ready for that yet.

Dropping back, Bodie walked alongside Melanie to the lobby doors. And then he was in the sunlight, in the fresh untainted air. Well, there was a slight odor of exhaust fumes from the cars rushing by on Pico, but that was far better than the hospital air with its smells of floor wax and disinfectant and, far worse, its secret under-smell of decay and death.

'It's nice to be out of there,' Pen said.

They waited at the corner. The WALK sign came on. An RTD bus went ahead through the intersection as if traffic signals were meant only for cars. Bodie thought of the Porsche that almost nailed Pen.

A dangerous city.

If things had turned out a little differently, Dr Gray might've spent the morning inside *her* head.

I need sleep, Bodie thought as he crossed the road. 'Maybe we should check into a motel,' he said.

'Why don't you two stay at my place?' Pen suggested. Her voice was a weary monotone. 'You can use my bed. I'll use the couch.'

Bodie felt a little flip of excitement. 'Fine with me.'

'I don't know,' Melanie said. She, too, sounded tired. 'Maybe a motel.'

'There's no hurry,' Pen told her. 'You can decide later. Right now, I think we should go over and see Joyce.'

'What for?'

'She's Dad's wife.'

'Some wife. She wasn't even there. How come she wasn't there? Isn't a wife supposed to stay with her husband when he's half dead in the hospital?'

77

'He's not half dead.'

'Really? Three-quarters? Seven-eighths?'

'Cut it out, Mel.'

'*Mom* would've stayed with him.'

'They only let *us* stay for about five minutes.'

'There's a waiting room.'

'Look, for all we know Joyce could've spent the whole night there.'

'I'll just bet she did.'

'Maybe you'd better *not* see her, if you're going to act this way.'

'I've got a great idea. Why don't you go and see her without us. Give her my regards.'

'Okay.'

They reached Bodie's van and climbed in. He started the engine. 'Where to?' he asked.

'My apartment, I guess,' Pen said. 'I'll take my car over to Dad's place, and you guys can catch up on your sleep.'

'Never mind,' Melanie said from behind them. 'I want to see her, after all.'

'Are you sure?'

'Yeah, I'm sure. I've got a few questions I'd like to ask.'

Pen turned in her seat to look at her. The movement twisted her blouse slightly, opening a gap between two of its buttons. Bodie saw smooth, shadowed skin on the side of her breast. 'Such as?' Pen asked.

'Such as where was she when Dad got hit.'

'She was with him,' Bodie said. 'She was there when he was brought into the emergency room.'

'How come *she* wasn't hurt?'

'We'll find out,' Pen said. Her blouse was drawn tight

78

against her breast. The glossy fabric was molded to it, filled, rounded, puckered just a bit in the shape of a disk at the very front. Bodie looked again at the skin inside the small opening. Then he put on his safety harness. 'But let's not make it an inquisition,' Pen added. 'Joyce is Dad's wife, regardless of what you might think of her. Dad loves her, so we have to treat her with respect. Okay?'

'I guess so.'

Pen turned to the front.

'Which way do I go?' Bodie asked, looking at her face and being careful not to lower his eyes. Her face wasn't bad to look at, either.

'Make a left at the light.'

He nodded, checked the side mirror for traffic, and pulled out.

He realized that he was now feeling pretty good – a vast change from a few minutes ago.

Looking at Pen hadn't hurt any.

If we stay with her, I'll get plenty of opportunities.

He wished he hadn't mentioned a motel. It was pretty clear that Melanie would rather stay at a motel than at Pen's apartment.

It'll work out, he thought.

I'll plead penury.

Except for Pen giving occasional instructions on where to turn, the sisters were silent during the drive. Bodie imagined they must both be dwelling on the situation, wondering how their father got hit and whether he would recover. Maybe remembering times they'd spent with him.

Melanie had more than the tragedy to cope with. She

79

also had her burden of guilt.

She'd been holding a lot of grudges, blaming him for the death of her mother, apparently dumping on him with a vengeance when he married Joyce.

She was probably wishing she'd been nicer to him.

'You'd better get to the right,' Pen said.

He eased over. They were on San Vicente, and the air streaming in through the open window was cooler than it had been a few minutes ago. Bodie suspected they were approaching the ocean, though there was no sign of it ahead.

The road had a wide, grassy center strip that appeared to be a haven for joggers.

Must be great for the lungs, Bodie thought, running your little heart out down the middle of a busy street.

'You'd better slow down,' Pen said. 'It's coming up, and you really can't see the road until you're almost on top of it.'

Bodie checked the mirror, then took his foot off the gas pedal. The area over there was heavily wooded. He couldn't see the road yet.

He flicked the arm of his turn signal, eased down on the brake, spotted the side road concealed among bushes and trees, and turned onto it. He drove slowly along the single lane. Though he could see no houses, he found evidence of their presence: patches of fence visible behind shrubbery and vines, mail boxes on weathered posts, now and then a garage, an occasional driveway entrance with a gate, a few cars parked half on the road so that he had to steer carefully around them.

The cars were not slouches: a Jaguar, a Porsche, a Ferrari, a Mercedes that looked incredibly huge and alien among the sleek sports cars.

'You can pull over behind the Mercedes,' Pen told him.

Speaking of alien – his VW van in with these ritzy vehicles. Folks would figure it must belong to the help. Caterers, perhaps. A party at the Conway residence.

A wake.

He maneuvered his van over to the right as far as possible. Bushes scraped its side. It was still jutting an uncomfortable distance into the road, but no more so than the Mercedes.

He hopped down. Instead of trying to squeeze through the passenger door, Pen swung her legs onto the driver's seat and scooted across. She gripped the steering wheel to pull herself along. Bodie tried not to look at her blouse.

He held out his hand. Pen took it, and he helped her out.

'Thank you.'

He let go of her hand, perhaps a bit too quickly. Melanie had pushed the seatback forward. He moved in, gently gripped her upper arm, and steadied her as she stepped down.

They walked past the gray Mercedes. Melanie frowned at it.

Near the front of the car stood a mailbox like the others along the road. This one bore the name CONWAY in black metal letters.

A gap in the bushes revealed a wooden gate. Farther up the road, a break in the foliage made way for a garage. The closed garage door was only a yard off the road. Must be dicey backing out, Bodie thought.

Pen, leading the way, unlatched the front gate and swung it open. She stepped through, followed by

Melanie. Bodie went next and closed the gate.

The lawn was a trim carpet of grass. Most of it was shaded by trees, which blocked Bodie's view of the house's upper story. The walkway led past a small, concrete fountain. In the center of the fountain stood a pudgy cherub wearing a mischievous leer and nothing else. Water spurted from his brass penis, splashing into the pool.

Bodie wondered if Whit was responsible for that. It was the mark, he thought, of either upper class sophistication at its worst, or a nice bit of nasty wit. The latter, he hoped. He could like a guy who got a kick out of pissing statues.

The white stucco house had the look of a hacienda. An open porch ran the length of it, shadowed by a red tile roof. A dozen flower pots were suspended by rope from the porch ceiling. Beyond them were some white, wrought-iron chairs and a love seat which couldn't be very comfortable but looked cheery. There were big windows on each side of the front door.

Pen stepped onto the porch and rang the doorbell.

Bodie heard chimes inside.

The door was opened by a young woman with a grief-twisted face who gasped, 'Oh, honey,' and threw her arms around Pen. After a quick hug and a kiss on the cheek, she seemed to notice the other sister. 'Melanie?'

Melanie received a hug and kiss while she stood motionless with her arms hanging. She didn't resist, just took it like a kid being greeted by a distant, annoying relation.

Done with the hugging, Joyce shook her head. 'It's so awful. I'm so glad you're both here.'

'Melanie drove in last night,' Pen said. She looked around. 'This is her friend, Bodie.'

Bodie said, 'Nice to meet you,' and stepped forward to shake the offered hand.

Step-mom looked about the right age to be an older sister, and had the sleek features of a fashion model. Right now, she was showing a white jumpsuit belted in at her waist. It had zippered pockets at the breasts and thighs, and one long zipper down the front. Each zipper had a big, dangling golden tab for easy opening.

She wore a thin gold chain around her neck.

She had a soft tan, curving cheeks, coral eyes, and thin eyebrows that were a shade darker than her blond hair. The hair was cut in a boyish, pixie style as if meant to show off her ears. She wore big, hoop earrings.

Whit, quite obviously, had been a very lucky man before last night.

'Please,' she said. 'Come in.'

She led them across a red tile foyer. In spite of the jumpsuit's loose fit, her walking drew it taut against her buttocks.

The living room had a plush carpet of the same burgundy shade as Pen's blouse. It also had a man on the sofa, who got to his feet as they entered.

Melanie stopped short.

'Harrison,' Pen said in a low voice.

'He's been such a sweetheart through all this,' Joyce said.

'Pen,' he said. He looked and sounded somber. He took her hand and patted it. 'I'm so sorry.'

She pulled her hand from his grip.

Harrison turned to Melanie, shaking his head. He

picked up her dangling hand and squeezed it. 'A terrible thing,' he said. 'Terrible.'

Joyce said, 'This is Melanie's friend, Dobie.'

'Bodie,' he corrected, and shook hands with Harrison. The man had a firm grip. He was somewhat taller than Bodie, maybe six-two. He was slim, but he had muscles inside his polo shirt. Bodie squeezed the guy's hand a little harder than necessary. 'Harrison Donner. I'm Whit's law partner and an old friend of the family.'

The old friend of the family must've been pushing thirty.

'Nice to meet you,' Bodie said, giving his voice some extra force.

The man had a calm, self-assured quality that wasn't arrogance, but almost.

I'm sure he's a great guy, Bodie thought. A real sport.

He no doubt belonged to the Mercedes outside, though a Porsche seemed more in character.

'Why doesn't everyone sit down and make themselves comfortable?' Joyce suggested. 'I'll get us some coffee.' She went out.

Harrison returned to his place on the sofa. Pen looked around the room until he was seated, then went to the far end of the sofa. Bodie sidestepped to a stuffed chair and sat down. Melanie sat on the carpet at his feet. She rested an arm on his knee. He stroked her arm.

'Have you been to the hospital?' Harrison asked.

'We were just there,' Pen said.

'Joyce and I were there through the operation. I think she's holding up quite well under the circumstances.'

Melanie's other hand covered Bodie's hand, pressed it gently, and stayed there.

'Were you at the accident?' Pen asked.

He shook his head. 'Joyce phoned me from the emergency room. She'd called you first, but you apparently weren't home and she got your answering machine. She needed someone to be with her.'

'So naturally she called you,' Melanie said.

'*You* weren't exactly available, young lady. Joyce did, in fact, put a call through to your number in Phoenix to no avail.'

'We were probably already on our way,' Bodie said.

Harrison looked puzzled.

Joyce came in carrying a silver tray. She set it on the table in front of Harrison and began to pour coffee into china cups. When they were full, she inquired about cream and sugar. No takers. She passed out the cups. She was shaking enough to make them clitter against their saucers.

Taking one for herself, she sat in a chair near Pen's end of the sofa – about as far from Harrison as the furniture would allow.

To Bodie, her choice of seats had a guilty look.

She obviously knew how it must appear to the sisters, finding her here with Harrison.

Bodie felt a little sorry for her.

Harrison resumed his puzzled expression. He directed it at Pen. 'Let me see whether I understand the sequence of events, here. Melanie and her friend were already en route to LA at the time Joyce attempted to call her. Therefore, you telephoned her with the news of the accident last night. So tell me, where have you been since then? You didn't phone? You didn't visit the hospital until this morning? Weren't you at all concerned about your father's condition?'

'Harrison, stop it,' Joyce said.

Pen looked grateful for the support. 'The thing is,' she said, 'I didn't get your message until this morning.' She frowned at Harrison. 'I don't even know why we're discussing this. All that really counts is Dad. I mean, Mel and I don't even know how he got hit.' To Joyce, she said, 'Were you with him?'

The woman nodded.

'We'll get to that in good time,' Harrison went on. 'I'd like to find out how Melanie learned about the accident if you didn't tell her last night.'

'Why are you so concerned about it?' Melanie asked.

'Let's just say that inconsistencies trouble me. I'm an attorney, after all. A good portion of my time is devoted to hunting them out. It's how one goes about discovering the truth.'

'You want the truth?'

Harrison nodded.

'I saw it happen.'

'Oh?'

'In a vision.'

'Let me get this straight. Are we talking ESP, telepathy, that sort of thing?'

'That's right,' Melanie said.

'And this vision of yours prompted you to make the trip?'

'She called here first,' Bodie pointed out. 'Nobody was home.'

Harrison leaned forward, planting his elbows on his knees and gazing at her. 'This is amazing,' he said. 'What time did you experience this vision?'

Melanie shrugged.

'About five till nine,' Bodie answered. 'That would be five till eight, Pacific time.'

Harrison arched an eyebrow and looked at Joyce.

'That's just when it happened,' Joyce confirmed. She was looking a trifle spooked.

'What, exactly, did you see?'

'I saw Dad get run down by a car.'

'Can you describe the car?'

'I don't think so.'

'The driver?'

She shook her head.

'It's too bad your vision couldn't have been a little more detailed. Information of that kind wouldn't be admissible, of course, but if it led to establishing the identity of the driver, we might find enough evidence to pin him down. I hate the thought of someone getting away with this.'

Pen turned to Joyce. 'You were there. Didn't you see what happened?'

'Not very well. It was dark and raining. All I know for sure is that it was a sports car. I can't even be sure of the color.'

'You didn't catch the license plate?'

'It all happened so fast.'

'How *did* it happen?' Melanie asked.

'We went out to dinner at Gerards.'

'That's in Beverly Hills,' Harrison explained. 'On Cañon.'

Pen nodded. 'I've been there. It's Dad's favorite restaurant.'

'We went there for your birthday this year,' Joyce said. 'Do you remember his parking spot?'

'The bank lot across the street.'

'That's where he parked last night. It's where he always parks when we go to Gerards.' She looked at

Harrison. 'Whit would walk blocks to avoid leaving his car in the hands of a parking attendant.'

'Don't I know,' he said.

'Destruction Derby rejects,' Pen added, apparently quoting her father.

'Anyway, since it was raining, he let me out in front of the restaurant. I told him he should just have the boy take his car. I mean, it was pouring, he was going to get soaked. But he said, "Rain'll dry. I'm not turning this buggy over to that toenail." He called the car-hop a toenail. Not to his face, but . . . Anyway, I got out and stood under the canopy to wait for him. He drove across the street and parked behind the bank. It's right on the corner, you know. The bank, not the lot. The lot's in the rear, and I guess he didn't want to go to the corner and use the crosswalk because it was out of the way. So he just cut right across the street. The light at the corner was red and there weren't any cars coming. Not from the other way, either. Then suddenly this car was hitting him.' She pressed her lips together in a tight line and stared down at the coffee cup on her lap. When she spoke again, her voice was pitched higher than before, and trembling. 'I didn't even see it till it hit him. I guess I was looking at something else. I saw him step off the curb, and there wasn't any traffic, and then I heard this awful sound and looked and he was like rolling over the top of this sports car. It never even slowed down or anything after it hit him. Whit . . . he was lying in the road and the light had turned green and all these *other* cars were starting to come at him. I ran out and . . . none of them hit him. I, you know, waved them off.'

'God Almighty,' Pen muttered.

'Did anyone in those other cars see him get hit?' Bodie asked.

'I don't know. The first cars, they just slowed down and went around me and kept going. Three or four did that. Then someone stopped, but he hadn't seen anything.'

'What about the restaurant's car-hop or doorman?' Pen asked.

'They didn't see it. The doorman was showing a party inside, and the parking guys were off parking cars. Anyway, someone called the police, I guess. They showed up and then an ambulance.' She sighed deeply. She was silent for a few moments. Staring down into her coffee cup, she said, 'It's so hard to believe something like that could happen.'

'How *could* it happen?' Melanie asked. 'That car coming out of nowhere like that.'

'It undoubtedly made a right turn onto Cañon,' Harrison said, 'and the driver didn't see him until it was too late.'

Melanie whispered, 'The bastard. He's not going to get away with it.'

CHAPTER NINE

'He . . . or she,' Harrison said, 'may lose some sleep over it, if he wasn't too drunk to know it even happened, but unless someone comes up with the license number of his car, he will get away with it. I've had any number of cases involving phantom cars. Without the license number, you're dead in the water.'

'I don't even care who did it,' Joyce confessed. 'I mean, I *care*, but . . .'

'And well you should,' Harrison told her. 'Retribution – and getting him off the streets – aside, we're talking here about a personal injury suit of rather staggering proportions. Assuming the driver was insured . . .'

'How can you even *think* about a lawsuit right now? Whit's lying in a hospital room, half . . .' She cut herself off.

Half-dead, Bodie finished for her. Or three-quarters? Seven-eighths? The phrase seemed to be making its rounds.

'I'm sorry,' Harrison told her. 'I shouldn't have brought it up. It's a moot point, anyway. We'll probably never know who the driver was.'

Joyce lifted her cup and took a sip. Apparently,

whatever remained of her coffee had grown cold. She made a face, then got up from her chair and set the cup and saucer onto the table. Returning to her seat, she managed a smile and said to Melanie, 'I hope you won't be rushing back to school.'

'Not right away,' Melanie told her. 'I want to stay around until . . .' She shrugged. 'We haven't really discussed it, but I can't go back while Dad's the way he is. Bodie may have to go back, though. He's got a teaching assistantship.'

'I can make arrangements for someone else to cover my classes,' he said. 'For a few days, at least.'

'There's plenty of room for both of you here,' Joyce said.

Bodie thought about Pen's offer. He would rather stay at her place – no question. 'I don't know,' he said.

'It wouldn't be any trouble. You can't just go off to some motel. I'm sure Whit wouldn't allow it, if he were here. So as long as you're in town, this is home. All right?'

'All right,' Melanie said. 'Thank you.'

Pen lowered her eyes. She looked as if the rejection had hurt her, but she didn't speak up.

Neat play, Mel.

'Have you eaten yet?' Joyce asked.

'Pen gave us breakfast,' Bodie said.

'Well, you two must be exhausted. Maybe you'd like to freshen up.'

'I could sure use some sleep,' Melanie told her.

'Fine. Why don't you go ahead and get some rest? Do you have your things?'

'Out in the van.'

'Fine. Harrison, why don't you give them a hand with

their luggage? I'll get out some clean sheets and towels.'

'Pen, are you staying?' Bodie asked.

'Well . . .'

'There's no need to rush off,' Joyce said. 'Besides, I'm sure you have a lot of catching up to do with your sister.'

Pen hesitated.

'You don't want to be alone,' Bodie told her.

'No, I suppose not.' She nodded to Joyce. 'If you don't mind, I could use a little rack time myself. Rough night.'

'It's all settled, then.' She bobbed her head briskly.

'I'll give you that hand with the bags,' Harrison said.

'No need,' Bodie told him. 'We haven't got much.'

'I guess I'll be on my way, then.'

Bodie expected Joyce to protest. She'd been eager enough to keep everyone else at the house. But she stood up as Harrison rose from the sofa, and said, 'Thanks so much for everything. I don't know what I would've done.'

'Just give me a call if you need me.'

'I will. Thanks again.'

'You'll be going over to see Whit tonight?' he asked.

Joyce nodded.

'Keep me posted.'

'Certainly.'

'I'm sure it'll all turn out fine. Whit's a tough old bird. He won't let a little thing like this keep him down.'

They all said goodbye, and Harrison turned away. Joyce didn't see him to the door.

Joyce poked her head through the bedroom doorway. 'I put some fresh washcloths and towels in the bathroom. If you need anything you can't find, just give a yell.'

'Thank you,' Bodie said.

She left. Bodie continued helping Melanie put clean sheets on the bed. 'Did this used to be your room?' he asked.

'It was. All new furniture, though.'

'Good thing. I bet you didn't have a bed like this.' It was a strange bed, unlike any that Bodie had seen before, a single with a space beneath it for a second bed. They had rolled out the bottom section, Joyce showing them how to raise it level with the other mattress. 'Nice that she didn't give us any grief about sleeping together.'

'She knows I live with you.'

'Still, some people . . .'

'She isn't my mother.'

'She seems nice.'

Melanie raised an eyebrow. Removing a leather toilet kit from her suitcase, she said, 'Back in a minute.'

Bodie sat on the bed. He rubbed his face. He felt vague and a little nauseous. Sleep would take care of that. And sleep would be a welcome release from having to face all this. A lot was going on. More than he wanted to think about.

Melanie came back.

'Do you have to use the john?' she asked.

'Yeah.'

'It's at the end of the hall.'

He got up slowly and crouched over his suitcase to take out his toothbrush and paste.

'When you go by,' Melanie told him, 'take a peek into the master bedroom.'

He did as she asked. In the bathroom, he brushed the fuzz off his teeth, washed his face and used the toilet. Then he returned.

Melanie shut the door. 'Did you see the bed?'

'Yeah. Something special about it?'

'It wasn't made.'

'No.' The covers and top sheet had been left in a messy heap near the foot of the bed. 'So?'

'So who used it? More to the point, when?'

'I don't know.'

'Guess.'

Bodie sat down and pulled his shoes off. Getting out of his shoes felt wonderful. He hadn't been aware of how hot and cramped his feet had been. 'It doesn't have to be that. Joyce and your father might've been using it before they took off for the restaurant.'

'I doubt it.'

He peeled off his damp socks, and sighed. 'Or maybe Joyce took a nap after she got home from the hospital.'

'She came back with Harrison. They used that bed last night. Joyce and Harrison. Dad's bed.'

Wearily, Bodie shook his head. 'And she just left the bed messed up for all to see?'

'She didn't know we'd show up.'

'She wouldn't have left it like that. Not if she'd been screwing around with Harrison. Even if she didn't make the bed right away, she would've found some excuse to get up here and fix it after we arrived. Or at least close the door.'

'Not necessarily.'

Bodie shrugged. 'If you say so,' he said, taking off his shirt. 'But I think she would've made some effort to cover up, don't you?'

'You'd think so.'

He unfastened his pants, stood and pulled them down along with his shorts. He stepped out of them and climbed between the smooth, cool sheets.

Hell, he thought, they probably did. A rotten damn thing to do, but they probably did. Maybe they'd been at each other behind Whit's back for a long time. Or Joyce just needed comfort, last night, and Harrison had obliged.

Melanie took off her blouse. She left her bra on. Her small breasts, the dark flesh of her nipples, showed through the transparent fabric.

And Bodie remembered Pen in the van, the gap between her buttonholes, the shadowy glimpse of her breast.

He felt a warm stir. The sheet began to rise between his legs, so he rolled onto his side.

Melanie unfastened her pants.

'You know,' Bodie said, 'Pen invited us to stay with *her*.'

'She doesn't have room.'

'She has a good-sized bed. She offered to use the couch.'

'Pen wouldn't be very comfortable on a couch.' Melanie draped her blouse and pants over the back of a chair. She faced Bodie. 'I suppose you wanted us to stay with her.'

'She's your sister. And I'm a little surprised you'd want to be under the same roof with Joyce, the way you feel about her.'

'Maybe I want to keep an eye on her.'

'I doubt if she'll be boffing Harrison with us in the house.'

'The bitch.' Melanie removed her bra and panties. Wearing only her velvet choker, she stepped to the foot of the bed. Bodie watched her crawl over the mattress, pull back the blanket and sheet, and cover herself. She lay on her back, staring at the ceiling.

'I think Pen really wants us to stay with her,' he said.

'Then she should've spoken up.'

'She'd already made the offer.'

'We would've been tripping over each other.'

'Haven't you forgotten something?'

'More than likely.'

'The telephone calls.'

'Big deal. A few dirty calls.'

'They were a big deal to your sister. I think she's frightened, and I don't blame her. *I'd* be nervous about staying there alone, if I were her.'

Melanie's head turned. She stared at him across the joining beds. 'You just want to see her in a nightie.'

'There's that, too,' he said, and smiled.

Melanie didn't smile.

Bodie scooted across the bed and kissed her. He whispered, 'Sleep tight,' then rolled over and shut his eyes.

Waking up, Pen lifted her face off the warm pocket of the pillow. She felt wonderful. Then she saw where she was and remembered her father. A dark heaviness spread through her.

He'll be all right, she told herself.

We'll see him tonight.

And Melanie's here. Thank God Melanie's here. Going through this alone would've been so much worse.

Maybe Dad'll be better when we see him.

She pushed herself up and sat on the edge of the bed. She had slept in her clothes. Her slick, burgundy blouse was twisted around her torso. The weight of her body had pressed wrinkles into it. She straightened it, but the wrinkles remained.

Maybe Bodie would drive her to her apartment so she could change before going to the hospital.

The apartment. The phone calls.

Fear began to knot her. She tried to push it aside.

That business doesn't count, she told herself. Not with Dad in the hospital.

But the fear grew.

Pen quickly stood up. In front of the bureau mirror, she brushed her hair. Then she left the room and hurried downstairs. The living room was empty, but voices came from the den. As she approached, she heard Bodie speaking over the quiet dialogue from the television.

'. . . a PhD in English literature. Which is probably a totally useless thing to have, but I fancy myself as a slightly eccentric professor in a patched jacket . . .' He smiled at Pen as she entered. He was slumped in an armchair, feet crossed at the ankles, one hand holding a Corona beer against his belt buckle.

Joyce, on the couch, was sipping a glass of white wine.

'Don't stop,' Pen said to Bodie.

'All through,' he told her.

'You plan to be an English professor?'

'Since I don't have any useful talents.'

Smiling, Pen sat on the couch.

'Let me get you something to drink,' Joyce offered.

'Wine would be great.'

Leaving the room, Joyce said over her shoulder, 'Pen's a writer.'

'I write mysteries,' she said. 'But I've only sold one so far. It was just a short story.'

'That's terrific. As I understand it, the world's full of would-be writers who've never had *anything* published.'

'Do you have any ambitions along those lines?'

'Nope. I'd rather spend my time reading good stuff than writing lousy stuff. Do you have a normal job?'

'I don't know how normal it is, but I'm a certified shorthand reporter. I spend most of my time trotting around to law offices to take down depositions.'

'It must be a good source for story ideas.'

She nodded. 'I've met some very strange people. The main thing, though, is that I can pick and choose assignments. I only work when I want to – which is most of the time because I *do* like to eat, pay my rent, little things like that.'

'No desire to be an attorney?'

'That'd be a full-time career. I don't have room for it.'

'Wouldn't leave you time for your writing?'

'Not enough. And I'd rather write.'

'I'd like to read your stuff.'

'It ain't Updike.'

'Ah, but is it Hammett?'

'No. It's pretty good Pen Conway, though.'

A grin spread over Bodie's face.

Joyce came in carrying a bottle of white wine and a glass. She filled the glass for Pen, gave herself a refill, and sat down. 'I guess I should start thinking about supper.'

'Don't,' Bodie said. 'I'll save you the trouble, if everyone likes pizza. I know Melanie does.'

'Where *is* Melanie?' Pen asked.

'Still asleep. I was in LA a couple of years ago and had this great pizza at some place not far from here.'

'That must have been La Barbera's,' Pen said.

99

'Right, that's the place. Is it still around?'

'Sure.'

'Why don't I drive over and pick one up?'

'Oh,' Joyce said, 'that's a lot of trouble.'

'No more trouble than you making something for all of us. Besides, I've really got a craving for that stuff. It's the best pizza I've ever tasted.'

'If you feel that strongly about it,' Joyce said. 'The least I can do is call in the order. What kind should we get?'

'Melanie doesn't like mushrooms.'

'How about salami?' Pen suggested. 'Mushrooms on half.'

'Sounds good to me.'

Joyce took a sip of wine, then left to make the call.

'Maybe you could give me directions,' Bodie said.

'I can do better than that,' Pen told him. 'I'll go with you and act as navigator.'

'I'd be glad to have you along. Maybe you'd better stay here, though. Melanie might come down while we're gone, and I don't think she'd like the idea that both of us went off without her. Besides, you might be needed as a referee.'

Pen frowned.

Bodie glanced over his shoulder as if to make sure that Joyce wasn't returning. 'Melanie wasn't too happy about finding that Harrison fellow here. She thinks there was maybe some hanky-panky going on.'

'It crossed my mind, too,' Pen admitted.

'Anyway, I don't know whether she'd say anything, but it might help the situation if you're around.'

'I suppose you're right.'

Bodie sat up straight and drank the last of his beer. 'So. How do I get to La Barbera's from here?'

'Easy.'

While she was explaining the directions, Joyce returned, opening her purse. 'They said it should be ready in half an hour.'

'This is my treat,' Bodie told her.

'No, really, I insist.' She took out a twenty-dollar bill.

Bodie waved it off. 'No way,' he said, and Joyce didn't argue.

When Bodie was gone, Joyce said, 'He seems like a very nice young man.'

'Yeah. I'd say Melanie lucked out. She's been involved with some awful twerps.'

'I wouldn't know about that.' Joyce sat down and took a sip of wine. She turned sideways, sliding a knee onto the couch and resting an arm on the back. 'I'm glad she's staying. It's awful that it took something like this to get her here, but maybe we'll finally have a chance to . . . mend fences. It would be nice if she could like me.' Joyce smiled a little sadly. 'Why couldn't she be more like you?'

'Melanie sees things differently.'

'Don't I know it? I'm young enough to be Whit's daughter, a cold-hearted gold digger and a slut.'

'That about sums it up.'

'I *love* Whit.'

'You'd have a hard time convincing Melanie of that.'

'I shouldn't have to,' Joyce said. 'But it would be such a relief if she could learn to accept me. We don't have to be buddies. Just . . . I can *feel* the chill. Even when she's trying to act pleasant, there's always this chill.'

'I know.'

'Like I'm a spider, or something, and she'd like to step on me.'

CHAPTER TEN

Pen climbed the stairs and went down the corridor to Melanie's room. She knocked lightly on the door.

'Who is it?'

'Me.' She entered and shut the door.

Melanie, on the bed, was covered to the chest. Her shoulders were bare.

'I wanted to make sure you were awake. Bodie went to get pizza. He should've been back by now, but . . .'

'Where'd he go?'

'La Barbera's. He's been gone over an hour. Hope he didn't get lost.'

'Did he go alone?'

Pen nodded. 'I offered to show him the way, but he thought I should stay here with you and Joyce.'

'Joyce,' she muttered.

'Try and be nice to her, okay?'

'Nice. Sure. What do you think Harrison was doing here?'

'I don't think you should jump to conclusions.'

'Did you happen to notice the master bedroom?'

'No.'

'Well, I did. The bed's been used.'

103

'That doesn't prove much. If she had anything to hide, don't you think she would've tidied up after herself?'

'That's what Bodie said.' Tossing the covers aside, Melanie crawled off the bed. She walked casually toward the corner of the room where her suitcase lay open on the floor. There were no tan lines on her skin. Apparently, she still believed in avoiding the sun. Areas of her back, buttocks and calves had a red hue from lying in bed.

They forced Pen to remember the coroner's slides.

Post-mortem lividity.

Dad. What if he . . .

The hospital would have called.

'You always *were* pals with that bitch,' Melanie said, squatting beside the suitcase.

'She's all right.'

Melanie found panties. She stood up, stepped into them, and turned to face Pen. She looked like a bizarre stranger: her sunless skin, her black hair, her black choker, her black lace panties. 'Harrison does get around,' she said.

'Cut it out.'

'I guess you and Joyce have quite a lot in common.'

'For God's sake, Mel.'

Melanie laughed softly. Shaking her head, she turned away and crouched over her suitcase.

The redness behind her shoulders had faded a little.

'I guess I should wear something decent for the hospital,' she said.

'Unless we make a stop by my apartment on the way over, I'm stuck with what I've got on.'

'Bodie thinks we should be staying with you.'

'The offer's still open,' Pen said.

'Do you *want* us to?' Melanie took a frilly white blouse from her suitcase and put it on.

'You'd probably be more comfortable here,' Pen admitted. 'Besides, you already told Joyce you'd stay.'

'That can be changed.'

'No. It wouldn't be nice.'

'Bodie thinks you're afraid to stay there alone.'

'How flattering.'

'Are you?'

She shrugged, but Melanie's back was to her. 'A little bit, maybe. Nothing I can't handle.'

Melanie lifted out a black skirt.

'We're not going to a funeral tonight,' Pen said.

'Not tonight.'

'You're really going to wear that?'

'Bodie likes me in black.'

'Oh. That's different.'

'You approve, then?'

'I approve.'

Bodie shook his head, rolled his eyes upward. 'What happened? Disaster. God save me from the streets of Los Angeles. It all started when I couldn't get over into the right-hand turn lane from San Vicente onto Wilshire. That resulted in quite a detour. When I finally did get to the restaurant, they didn't have our pizza. Apparently, something got screwed up with the phone order – they lost it or something. So I had to reorder and wait around while they made it.' He blew out a long breath. 'At any rate, here I am. An older man but wiser.'

As they ate the pizza, they agreed that it was well worth his trouble.

By six o'clock, they were done eating.

That left an hour and a half before time to set out for the hospital.

Joyce went upstairs to bathe and change her clothes.

In the living room, Pen sat in an armchair. Melanie and Bodie took the couch, sitting close together, Melanie's hand on his leg. They talked. But there was no talk of Joyce or Harrison or Dad, as if the subjects were taboo.

Pen's uneasiness grew as the time passed. She had difficulty sitting still, and her chest had a tightness that made breathing a struggle. Finally, she got off her chair. She lay on the floor, knees upraised. That seemed to help.

'Are you all right?' Bodie asked.

'Just nerves,' she said.

'Maybe you need a Valium or something,' Melanie said.

'Don't think so.' She rubbed her face. 'I could use a good snootful, though.'

'You've *had* a pretty good snootful.'

'Hardly. A few glasses of wine do not a snootful make.'

'Pen thinks that she can't be a writer without being a drunk.'

'I'm not a drunk. Tonight, however, I might prefer it.'

'What's stopping you?'

'I don't want to make an ass out of myself staggering into the hospital.'

Joyce entered the room. She wore a white pullover that looked like cashmere, a gray jacket and matching pleated skirt, hose and high heels.

Joyce and Melanie, both in skirts. Me in my white jeans. Great, Pen thought.

She should've asked Bodie to run her over to her

apartment after dinner so she could put on a dress.

So who cares? she asked herself. Who am I out to impress, the nurses? Dad isn't likely to notice. And if he does . . .

She pictured him awake, sitting up in bed, breathing for himself, the tubes and wires disconnected.

Don't get your hopes up.

They would've called.

'Are you feeling all right?' Joyce asked, staring down at her.

'I'm fine.'

'Too much wine,' Melanie said.

'Not enough.' Pen sat up. 'Is it about time to go?'

'Pretty soon,' Joyce said. 'I'd be glad to do the driving,' she told Bodie.

'Fine.'

Joyce slipped the Lincoln Continental into an open space of curb on Pico Boulevard, and they climbed out.

Pen, realizing they wouldn't have to walk across the road, thought about the car that had come so close to running her down that morning. A Porsche. A sports car.

A sports car had hit Dad.

The same one that almost got me?

That's crazy, she told herself. Just a coincidence. Don't try to make something out of it.

The night air chilled the material of her blouse. Shivering, she folded her arms across her chest and clamped her teeth together.

Melanie, ahead of her, walked stiffly with her shoulders hunched, but she was pressed against Bodie's side and his arm was around her back. That had to help.

107

The warmth of the hospital lobby felt good.

They entered an elevator. Bodie pushed the button for Dad's floor. The piped-in music was an orchestral version of 'Bridge Over Troubled Water'. Pen wondered if the tune had been selected for purposes of irony.

When they left the elevator, Joyce led the way to the nurses' station. A nurse guided them down the corridor and opened the door to Dad's room.

He wasn't awake, sitting up, breathing for himself.

He looked the same.

He looked dead.

Pen's eyes darted to the cardiac monitor. The line on the screen jigged with each heartbeat. Every jump of the line was accompanied by a beep.

Joyce went to the bedside and squeezed his hand.

The rhythm of his heart didn't change.

He has no idea we're even here, Pen thought.

'It's Joyce. Can you hear me? Can you understand me?' Joyce waited as if for a reply. 'Your daughters are here. Melanie came all the way from Phoenix to be with you. We're all pulling for you, Whit. You're going to be all right. You'll be just fine.' She was silent for a little while. Then she looked around at the others. 'Could I be alone with him for a few minutes?'

They went out to the hallway. Pen closed the door.

'Why doesn't she want us in there?' Melanie whispered.

'She's his wife,' Pen said. 'She wants a little privacy with him.'

'He's in a *coma*.'

'A little privacy with a gal like Joyce might pull him out of it,' Bodie suggested.

Melanie glared at him.

'Sorry,' he muttered. 'My big mouth.'

'Don't worry about it,' Pen said, more to her sister than to Bodie.

'I wonder what she is doing in there.'

'Talking to him, I should imagine,' Pen said. 'About things that don't concern you and me.'

'Maybe she's telling him to go ahead and die.'

Melanie, so prim and Victorian in her choker and frilly white blouse and black skirt, had spoken the unthinkable and was staring at Pen as if she thought Pen was dimwitted for not realizing the obvious.

'My God, Mel,' she muttered.

'If Dad dies, she gets Harrison, the insurance, the inheritance . . .'

'Have you lost your mind?'

'She might even pull the plug on him.'

'Alarms would go off,' Bodie whispered. He was frowning, shaking his head. 'I think . . . the machines are tied in to the nurses' station. If anything like that happened . . .'

'She wouldn't *do* that,' Pen said.

'Oh, no?'

'Melanie, Jesus.'

Melanie swung open the door.

Gazing past her shoulder, Pen saw Joyce turn her head in surprise. She was bent over the bed, straightening a blanket at Dad's shoulders. She pressed a hand to her chest and smiled nervously. 'You startled me.'

'Sorry,' Pen said. 'Is everything all right?'

'Fine. I was about to ask you back in.'

They entered the room.

'Did he . . . make any kind of response?'

'I'm afraid not.'

Pen followed Melanie closer to the bed and bumped her when she jerked to a rigid stop.

Melanie began to groan.

Joyce looked puzzled, then alarmed.

Melanie's back arched and she suddenly quaked. She pressed her fists to the sides of her head.

'What's she doing?' Joyce blurted. 'My God!'

Pen's mind seemed to freeze as she stood at the back of her twitching, moaning sister.

'Don't worry,' Bodie said. *He* sounded worried. 'It's like last . . .'

Melanie lurched against Pen. Bodie stopped her from falling. With Bodie at her back, Pen braced herself up and wrapped her arms around Melanie's chest. The girl's whole body jumped with spastic shudders. Pen kept her face turned away to avoid the thrashing head.

'You got her?' Bodie gasped.

'Yeah.'

'You got her? Don't let her fall.'

'Should I get help?' Joyce asked.

'No. It'll be okay.'

'What's *wrong* with her?'

Melanie's head snapped back, striking Pen's jaw just below the ear. The pain was a hot jolt. She squeezed her eyes shut, but didn't let go of Melanie.

'You okay?' Bodie asked.

Pen heard him through a ringing in her ear.

'Ease her down. Try to ease her down.'

She felt Bodie's hands on her sides, pushing at her ribcage to steady her as she sank to a crouch. The strain lessened when Melanie's rump met the floor.

Abruptly, her body went limp. Her head sagged forward. She took deep breaths.

'Are you okay?' Pen asked.

The head bobbed slightly.

Bodie's hands went away from Pen. He stepped to the front and knelt beside Melanie. 'How you doing?' he asked in a gentle voice.

'Okay, I guess.'

'Another vision?'

'I . . . I think so.'

He helped her up. Pen, rising to her feet, rubbed her sore jaw. She stretched her mouth open wide. It made her ear hurt.

'What was it?' Bodie asked.

'I don't know.'

He stroked Melanie's cheeks.

'I can't remember. Just that it was awful. But I lost it. Like sometimes when you wake up from a nightmare and it's gone.'

'Is she all right now?' Joyce asked.

It struck Pen as interesting that the question wasn't directed to Melanie – as if a more reliable opinion were required.

Nodding, Bodie put his arms around her. She clung to him, face pressed to the side of his neck. One of Bodie's hands was motionless at the center of her back. The other patted her gently.

Pen watched.

She worked her jaw from side to side.

Then she saw her father on the bed, oblivious to it all. She went to him.

'I'm sorry I made such a scene,' Melanie said when they were back in the car.

'Are you certain you're all right?' Joyce asked.

'Yeah.'

'Do those things happen often?'

'No. Hardly ever.'

'It sure scared the hell out of me.'

'I'm sorry.'

'As long as you're all right.' Joyce pulled away from the curb. She glanced toward Pen. 'Where to? Would you like to come back with us, or . . . ?'

'We're not far from my apartment.'

'You're welcome to spend the night at the house.'

'Why don't you?' Bodie suggested from the back seat.

'Pen got a couple of obscene phone calls last night,' Melanie explained. 'She's pretty frightened.'

'I'm not frightened,' Pen insisted, wishing Melanie had kept quiet about the situation. It was personal. Joyce didn't need to know about it. 'They made me a little nervous,' she said, 'but I'm okay now.'

Am I? she wondered.

She didn't look forward to being alone in the apartment.

On the other hand, getting away by herself might be a relief.

A long, hot bath. Sleep in her own bed.

How'd you like me to fuck your brains out?

She felt a hot rush of dread.

It won't get any better, she told herself, by staying somewhere else. It might even get worse.

'Why don't you go ahead and take me to my apartment?' she said.

'Are you sure?'

'It was just a voice on a phone. I can't let a little thing like that get to me.'

'Obscene phone calls,' Melanie said. 'Everybody gets them. I've had a few.'

'Me, too,' Joyce said.

'What did you do?' Melanie asked her.

'I just hung up, but I'll admit I was pretty edgy for a while.'

'They never do anything but call,' Melanie went on. 'I think they have to get their jollies over the phone because they're afraid of women. The phone is safe and anonymous. They never actually pay a visit.'

'I wouldn't say never,' Bodie told them. 'There was a story in the news a couple of months ago about a woman who was getting calls like that. The day after she got an unlisted number, she was raped and murdered. Apparently, changing number made the guy feel rejected.'

'Oh, thank you very much, Bodie,' Pen said. 'That's just what I wanted to hear.'

'I think you have a right to be worried, that's all. I didn't like the sound of that guy.'

'They all sound like that,' Melanie said.

'The calls were recorded on my answering machine,' Pen explained to Joyce.

'Whit won't let me get one of those things.'

'I've heard him on the subject,' Pen said. 'Dad likes answering machines about as much as he likes car-hops.'

Joyce turned off Pico and headed up the sidestreet toward Pen's apartment. 'You're sure you wouldn't rather stay with us?' She sounded as if she really wanted Pen to join them for the night – maybe to keep an eye on Melanie in case of another 'vision'.

'No,' she said. 'I'll be okay. Maybe I'll come by in the morning, though.'

'Do,' Joyce urged her. 'Come early, and we'll all have a nice breakfast together.'

'You've got a deal.'

Joyce eased the Lincoln to a stop across from Pen's apartment building. Pen swung her door open. For a moment, she was ready to back down.

'See you in the morning,' Melanie said.

'Right. See you then.' She started to step out.

'I'll go up with you,' Bodie said, 'and check the place out.'

She felt a surge of relief. 'Thank you. I'd like that.'

'I'll go, too,' Melanie said.

Outside the car, she put herself between Pen and Bodie, and latched onto his hand.

They walked to the iron gate, and Bodie swung it open. Pen went through first. She heard their footsteps close behind her as she cut across the courtyard toward the stairway. Party sounds of music, loud voices and laughter came from one of the apartments on the second floor. Though the pool lights were off, she spotted a couple in the whirlpool at the far end. She couldn't see who they were. She probably, in fact, wouldn't have recognized them even in light. Most of the other tenants were strangers to her. She preferred it that way.

Melanie and Bodie followed her up the stairs and along the balcony to her door. While she hunted for her keys, they caught up.

'A lot of activity around here,' Melanie said.

'Saturday night.'

'Does that guy, Manny, still live here?' Melanie asked.

'Oh yes.'

She pushed her key into the lock, twisted it, and

opened the door. Reaching inside, she flicked a light switch.

The lamp by the couch came on.

On the carpet at her feet lay a square, white envelope – the kind that birthday cards came in. She crouched over it. There was no stamp, no address. P. CONWAY was written in large, crooked letters.

Picking up the envelope, she could feel that it was empty.

'Someone must've slipped it under my door,' she muttered.

'I don't like this,' Bodie said.

She turned the envelope over, and felt her legs go weak as she read its scribbled message:

I CAME AND YOU WEREN'T HOME. TOO BAD. NEXT TIME I'LL COME WHEN YOU ARE. SEE YOU SOON.

CHAPTER ELEVEN

'Let me see.'

Pen handed the envelope to Bodie. He held it out to the side so that Melanie could read it, too.

'I guess you'd better come back with us,' Melanie said.

'Yeah,' Pen muttered. 'Let me get a few things.'

They waited in the living room.

'This is starting to look serious,' Melanie said. 'I mean, I never thought he might come after her.'

'It doesn't surprise me much,' Bodie said. 'The way that guy sounded on the phone . . . he sounded like he meant it.'

'Maybe she'd better go to the police.'

'Yeah.'

Melanie took the envelope from him and studied both sides. She pursed it open to make sure it was empty. Turning around, she stared at the place on the carpet where Pen had found it. Her shoulders rose as she took a deep breath. She sighed the breath out. Her head lowered, and she shook it slowly from side to side. 'The guy was actually here,' she said in a weary voice.

'Lucky thing Pen wasn't.'

'I feel like such a jerk.'

Bodie put a hand low on her back. Her skin was warm through the blouse. 'Don't worry about it,' he said.

'I feel like I'm in the goddamn *Twilight Zone*. Dad. This.'

'Pen almost getting hit this morning,' Bodie added.

'I'd forgotten about that.'

'I hadn't. And if you want to talk *Twilight Zone*, there're your visions. It's too bad you can't remember the one at the hospital.'

'I remember it,' she said. She turned and looked into Bodie's eyes. 'I remembered it *then*. I just didn't want to talk about it in front of the others.'

'What was it?'

'Later. I'll tell you when we're alone.'

'We're alone now.'

'Pen.'

Bodie could hear her in another room. Footsteps. Drawers opening.

'She'll be done in a minute,' Melanie said.

'Why don't you want her to know about it? Does it involve her?'

'In a way.'

'Come on, what is it?'

'No. I said later. It's just between you and me.'

'Okay,' he muttered. 'Later.'

'Don't be mad at me.'

'I'm not mad.'

'Yes you are,' she sulked.

' "True!" ' he blurted. ' "Nervous – very, very dreadfully nervous I had been and am; but why *will* you say that I am mad?" '

' "The disease had sharpened my senses," ' came Pen's voice from the other side of the room, ' "not destroyed, not dulled them." '

Bodie grinned at her.

Melanie, looking perplexed, switched her gaze from Bodie to Pen.

'*The Tell-Tale Heart*,' Pen explained.

'We oughtta take our show on the road,' Bodie said. The hurt glance from Melanie made him regret the suggestion. 'Ready to go?'

'All set.' Pen had a small suitcase at her side, a purse hanging from her shoulder. She wore the same white jeans as before, but her burgundy blouse had been replaced by a plaid flannel shirt that was neatly tucked in. She wore a suede jacket over the shirt, its front open, the dangling ends of its belt swaying as she walked.

Bodie watched her take a few steps. There was just enough difference in the look and motion of her shirt to indicate, in Bodie's judgement, that she had taken the opportunity to put on a bra.

'I'll carry that,' he said, reaching for the suitcase.

'Thank you.'

As she passed it to him, the telephone clamored. Her hand jerked and the suitcase slipped from Bodie's fingers, thumped the floor. Pen stood rigid. She flinched as the phone rang again.

'Want me to get it?' Bodie asked.

She didn't look capable of answering.

'*I* will.' Melanie rushed past him.

He hurried behind her to the kitchen and watched her snatch up the receiver. 'Hello?' Pause. 'No, this isn't Pen. May I tell her who is calling?' She listened, then covered the mouthpiece and called, 'It's some guy named Gary.'

'Okay,' Pen said. She came up beside Melanie and

took the phone. 'Hello? . . . Right, this is *the* Pen Conway . . . Of course I remember you. "Never look a gift drink in the mouth." '

Bodie felt like a snoop, listening, but Melanie hadn't left so he stayed, too. Besides, he told himself, the guy didn't know if Pen would remember him, so they couldn't be on intimate terms.

'I guess it was the slides,' she said. 'I thought I was going to barf . . . Right, I just drove home . . . I was tempted, but I didn't know for sure whether you'd come down afterwards . . . Oh, really?' Pen fooled with the top button of her shirt. She frowned slightly. 'Tonight? I really can't . . . No, it's a family situation. I really couldn't. Look, why don't you give me your number? When this situation is settled, I'll call you.' She nodded, but didn't write down his number. 'Got it . . . I will. Thanks for calling, Gary . . . Goodnight.' She hung up. 'A guy I met last night at the mystery writers meeting.' She unplugged the phone and set it on top of the refrigerator. 'We'd better go. Joyce'll think we've abandoned her.'

In the living room, Pen stopped and looked down at the envelope on the coffee table where Melanie had left it.

'Should we take it with us?' Melanie asked.

Pen picked it up and crumpled it into a ball.

'Hey, don't ruin it! That's evidence.'

'Evidence of what?' Pen asked her sister. Without waiting for a reply, she headed again for the kitchen.

'Maybe you should show it to the police,' Melanie called.

Pen didn't answer. She came back without the envelope.

'You threw it away?'

'Do you think I want it looking at me when I come back?'

'Bodie and I were talking. We think you should go to the police.'

Pen left the lamp on. They stepped outside. She pulled the door shut and rattled the knob. Walking along the balcony toward the stairs, she looked back at them. 'I'm not going to the police. First off, they've got bigger problems to worry about. Second, there's certainly not sufficient evidence to identify the creep even if they did care.' With a hand on the metal railing, she started down. 'They'd just advise me to get an unlisted number or move out. Besides, they'd want to hear the tape.'

And that, Bodie guessed, might be the real reason she didn't want the police involved. He couldn't blame her. They would insist on listening to the tape. Pen would be there with them as it played, as that piece of scum talked about fucking her, sticking his tongue in her, coming in her mouth. Hearing it again, herself, would be awful enough. But to have a couple of strangers listening, maybe wondering just how it would be to do those things to Pen . . . and they *would* wonder exactly that, Bodie thought. A man couldn't help it.

'What are you going to do?' Melanie asked.

'I don't know yet. Move out, maybe. Or buy a gun.'

'I guess I'll turn in,' Joyce said shortly after they returned to her house. 'It's early, though. Feel free to stay up as long as you want. Watch some TV, have a snack, a drink, whatever.' To Pen, she added, 'You know where everything is.'

'Would it be all right to use the jacuzzi?' Pen asked.

'Sure. That'd be nice on a night like this. I'd join you but . . . I'm the one who didn't get a nap this afternoon.'

They told her goodnight, and she went upstairs.

'You two interested?' Pen asked, looking at Melanie.

'I don't think so. But you go ahead.'

'Are you sure?'

Bodie wanted to go in the jacuzzi. Badly. He said nothing.

'We didn't bring our suits,' Melanie said.

One of Pen's shoulders rose and fell just slightly. 'Dad has some spare trunks he keeps around for guests. One of those should be fine for Bodie. You could wear your underthings or whatever,' she told Melanie.

'Or nothing,' Bodie suggested.

'Hardy har,' Melanie said.

'I'll go turn the heat on.'

Melanie dropped onto the sofa, slouched back, and folded her hands behind her head. She watched Pen walk away, then turned her eyes to Bodie.

He shrugged. With a smile to hide his disappointment, he sat beside Melanie. He put a hand on her thigh. 'I think the jacuzzi would be neat.'

'We'd freeze getting out.'

'I don't mind.'

'I'll bet.'

'What's that supposed to mean?'

'You just want to see Pen with her clothes off.'

He laughed softly, then moved his hand higher. He slid her skirt against the warm smoothness of her skin. 'I'm not interested in Pen.'

'I've seen you looking at her.'

'Of course I look at her. I do that. When people are in

my presence, I look at them. It's a defense against collisions.'

'Yeah, makes jokes.'

'Should I turn my head away when she's in the room?'

'It's not funny,' Melanie said.

'I know it's not,' he told her. 'I'm sorry. I suppose I have been looking at her. She is attractive.'

'Tell me about it.'

'But she's not you, Melanie. You're the one I love.'

He got his hand out from between her legs as she suddenly twisted around. She threw her arms around him and hugged him hard. Her face pressed the side of his neck. He lightly stroked her back.

'In spite of your weirdness,' he kidded.

'I'm so messed up.'

'You're fine.'

'No, I'm not.'

Bodie noticed a figure enter his peripheral vision. Turning his head just a bit, he saw Pen at the corner of the room. She halted, then backstepped quietly past the banister's newel post and crept up the stairs.

When she's ready to go in, Bodie thought, she'll have to come down those stairs and I'll be right here.

He felt eager, guilty.

'Have I been rotten to her?' Melanie asked.

'To Pen? I wouldn't say rotten, exactly. I know you have this rivalry or inferiority complex or something about her, but I think she could use a little more understanding from you. It isn't just *your* father who's in the hospital. He's Pen's father, too.'

'I know,' she said in a voice full of pain.

'And she also has this business of the obscene caller to deal with. Either one of those situations is pretty

123

damned traumatic, and she's had both of them dumped on her at the same time. I'm sure she'd appreciate a little support.'

Nodding, Melanie eased out of his arms. Her eyes were red and wet. She rubbed them dry with her sleeve.

Bodie stroked the back of her head. 'Are you all right?'

She sniffed. 'I don't know why you put up with me.'

'Neither do I, but what the hell.'

With a hint of a smile, she dropped back against the cushion. She let out a long sigh. Bodie leaned back, shoulder touching hers, and took hold of her hand.

'I'll try not to be such a pain in the ass,' she said.

'Me, too.' He squeezed her hand. She returned the squeeze. Later, he said, 'I would like to go in the jacuzzi.'

'Oh yeah?'

'Why don't we wait till Pen's finished? It'll be just you and me and the hot, bubbling water.'

'We'd still freeze getting out.'

'Who cares?'

Pen started down the stairway.

Bodie covered his eyes.

Melanie elbowed him.

He lowered his hands and watched Pen come down the stairs. She wore a royal blue robe that reached to mid-thigh, and had a folded towel under one arm.

'You do have a bathing suit on under that?' Melanie asked.

'Sure. I packed one tonight. I had this in mind.'

'We'll meet you in there,' Melanie said, and stood up.

'Great.'

Fabulous, Bodie thought.

At the bottom of the stairs, Pen said, 'Dad keeps those

spare trunks in the linen closet by the bathroom. No
rush, though. The water won't be good and hot for a
while yet.'

Bodie, still amazed by Melanie's decision, followed her
upstairs. She led him to the linen closet and pulled out
two swimsuits. One was striped and baggy, so he chose
the other – bikini trunks of thin, stretch nylon.

'You'll look sweet in those,' Melanie said.

'Better sweet than nerdy.'

She found two large towels, led Bodie to the bedroom.
When the trunks were on, he lifted his shirttail for
Melanie's inspection.

'Cute. Real cute.'

The clinging fabric not only bulged at his crotch, but
showed his penis in some detail. He let the shirttail fall.
'What the hell, it'll be dark out there.'

Melanie raised an eyebrow, but didn't protest.

'I'll keep my back to your sister,' he said.

'You'd *better*.' Melanie went to the door.

'Aren't you going to change?'

'Into what?'

He shrugged. This is getting better and better, he
thought. He followed her downstairs and out the back
door. Shivering, he took one of the towels and wrapped
it around his waist.

The patio was bright beneath a floodlight. Looking
around, Bodie spotted a Weber grill, an umbrella table
with chairs, and a couple of loungers. No sign of Pen or
the hot spa.

But he heard a hum of machinery off in the distance.
It made a steady, high noise like a window air-
conditioning unit.

'This way,' Melanie said.

125

He followed her off the lighted patio, into the darkness beyond. They walked on flagstones set in the grass. There were a lot of trees back here. Looking all around, Bodie could see no sign of neighboring houses.

He ducked beneath the low branches of lemon trees that hung over the walkway.

Then he spotted a gazebo with trellis walls on three sides and no top. The front side was open. Within was the elevated tub, Pen's head and shoulders visible in the moonlight.

'Welcome,' Pen said as they approached. 'I brought us some refreshments.' On the edge beside her stood a wine bottle and glass, and two bottles of beer. She had a wine glass in her hand.

Bodie dipped his fingers into the water. It felt like a hot bath.

Pen, stretching an arm out behind her, flicked a switch. A red light came on at the bottom. She wore a bikini that was probably white but looked pink in the swirling red-hued water. Bodie quickly turned to Melanie. 'Ladies first,' he said.

Melanie, standing sideways, put a hand on the wooden platform surrounding the pool and stepped out of her shoes. She took off her blouse, folded it carefully, and placed it on the platform beside the towels. She was naked from the waist up. Her skin shimmered with a rosy glow. Her nipples were stiff and jutting. Bodie, watching, felt his penis push at his flimsy, yielding swimsuit. Melanie's small breasts lifted and flattened slightly as she raised her arms to unfasten her choker. Her eyes were on him. She removed her skirt, folded it, and put it on top of the blouse. She wore brief panties of black lace. Leaving them on, she climbed the wooden stairs and stepped down into the pool. 'Oh, that feels good,' she said, and crouched until the water frothed around her shoulders. Wisps of steam circled her face.

Bodie unbuttoned his shirt. 'Can you see the house from here?' he asked, and turned his back to the women. No, he couldn't see the house through the bushes and trees. More important, the girls couldn't see his front. As he took off his shirt, he glanced down. His suit was sticking out badly.

He wished he'd picked the other trunks.

He turned around, holding the shirt low, and casually started to fold it as he climbed the stairs. He kept folding it as he looked into the water and spotted the three submerged steps. Fortunately, Pen turned away to reach for the wine bottle. He tossed the shirt onto Melanie's pile of clothes, and hurried down. The hot water covered him to the belly.

He squatted. Moving backward, he found the tile bench with his rump. He reclined and stretched out his legs in Melanie's direction. His feet touched hers. She was sitting off to his right. Pen was straight across from him.

'How do you like it?' Melanie asked.

'Fantastic.'

Pen handed a glass of wine to Melanie, then lifted a beer bottle off the ledge and leaned toward Bodie. Her bikini was the kind that tied behind the neck. Its cords looked pale against the wet glossy skin of her chest. Her breasts were below the surface, blurred by the bubbling water. Bodie took the beer bottle and thanked her.

Easing back against the wall, he took a sip. The beer was cold and good. The hot water caressed him. His suit was so skimpy and thin that he felt naked.

'The beer's great,' he said.

Pen nodded. Her blond hair was damp and straggly from the steam, and Bodie liked the way a few tendrils curled over her forehead and in front of her ears. She took a sip of wine. She was sitting up fairly straight to drink it. Her wet arm looked sleek. The tops of her breasts were just above the surface, now, lapped by moving water. Through the swirl, Bodie could see the rest of her bikini top, her tawny skin below it, the patch of pink-tinted fabric between her legs with cords stretched to her hips, the length of her legs. But the bubbling water distorted all he saw to vague, shifting blurs.

'Dad wanted to put in a swimming pool,' Melanie said. 'There wasn't room with all the trees. He didn't want any of them taken out, so he settled for this.'

'This is nice,' Bodie said.

'Especially when the weather's a little chilly,' Pen added. 'And it almost always is, at night.'

'We're only a couple of miles from the ocean,' Melanie said. She lifted her wine glass to her lips and sat up a bit more. Her breasts came out of the water. They shimmered wet in the red glow and their dark nipples stood erect.

If she's trying to steal my attention from Pen, Bodie thought, she's succeeding.

He scooted across the slick tile bench until he was directly across from her.

'Maybe you should take Bodie to the beach tomorrow,' Pen suggested. 'Over by Venice, it's a real carnival on the weekends. On Ocean Front Walk? Have you ever been there?' she asked Bodie.

'A couple of years ago. I wouldn't mind seeing it again.'

'It's a thought,' Melanie said. She looked at Pen. 'Would you like to come along if we go?'

'I think I'll start looking for a new apartment.'

'You're really going to move?'

'Probably.' Pen turned to give herself a refill.

Melanie shook her head. 'That's pretty drastic.' She lowered her wine glass. The edge of its base bent her right nipple downward. The glass eased lower. Her nipple, released, sprang up straight.

Bodie squirmed and took a drink of beer.

'I'm not sure I can stay at that place of mine any more.' Pen took a drink. Then she tilted back her head and stared at the sky. 'Would anyone mind if I turn off the lights?'

'Fine,' Melanie said.

There goes my view, Bodie thought. 'All right.'

Pen reached over the edge of the platform, and the red glow died.

The half moon was almost straight overhead. An airliner passed near it. Bodie could only see a few stars.

He looked down. The women were indistinct, pale shapes of faces and shoulders, invisible below the water's surface.

'It's peaceful this way,' Pen said.

'Dark, too,' said Bodie.

Melanie put down her glass and slipped forward. She came over to Bodie's side of the pool and eased onto the bench. Her arm slid against his. She was covered to the shoulders. The pale mounds of her breasts were barely visible through the water, and Bodie couldn't see anything below them. He put a hand on her leg.

'I'm glad we decided to come out with you,' she told Pen. 'I'd forgotten how glorious this feels.'

Bodie felt his hand being lifted off her thigh. Something was pushed against his palm. He closed his fingers around it. A small cloth of some . . . Melanie's panties.

She took them away from him and guided his hand up her leg.

'Do you still stay away from the jacuzzi at your apartment?' Melanie asked in a calm voice.

'Still do,' Pen said.

'When I was staying with her, she never went in the pool or sunbathed or anything.'

'I didn't like the idea of strangers looking at me.'

Bodie nodded. He didn't trust his voice. His hand was taken to its destination and released. His fingers slid against Melanie. His heart raced. He tried to breathe normally. He felt as if his erection might split the front of his swimsuit.

Melanie squirmed slightly against his fingers.

And suddenly it was all wrong.

What the hell was he doing?

He moved his hand to Melanie's leg. She gripped his wrist and gently urged it back, but he pulled his hand free and stood up. 'I think I'll go back in, now,' he said, trying to keep his voice steady. 'I'm starting to feel a little sick. It's probably the heat and the beer, I don't know. I'll see you two later.'

He climbed out, wrapped the towel around his shoulders, picked up his shirt, and hurried down to the concrete slab.

'So long,' Pen said. Her voice sounded strange.

'See you later,' Melanie said.

Bodie shivered all the way back to the house – but it

was Melanie that made him grit his teeth.

What in God's name went on in that mind of hers!

Be fair, he told himself. Maybe she just got horny and lost control. That'd be perfectly understandable. Hell, yes.

But he *knew* that wasn't it.

Handing her panties to him. Like a dog dropping a ball at his feet. Come on, play with me.

Play with me in front of my sister.

It'll be our little secret.

Unless, of course, she happens to notice. And that would be even better, wouldn't it?

Bodie stopped at the door, quickly wiped his legs to make sure he wouldn't drip on the floor, then entered the house.

CHAPTER TWELVE

Groggy and hot after the wine and the long time in the spa, Pen stepped into the shower. The cool water pelted her, slid down her body. She wore her bikini to rinse the chlorine from it. Then she took it off, wrung it out and draped it over the shower door.

She wondered at Melanie. The girl had actually gone into the spa topless.

No big deal, Pen thought. I would've been naked in there, myself, except for them.

Well, that's the point, isn't it? If Melanie had gone in just with Bodie, or just with me . . . but we were both in there. That's what makes it so strange.

Like she was trying to prove something. To Bodie or to me? Maybe to herself.

Pen wondered if Bodie's abrupt departure had anything to do with Melanie's behavior. She'd been sitting right next to him. Maybe put a hand inside his trunks?

Thinking about it, Pen felt a warm, trembling stir. She stopped sliding the soap over her body, set it in the dish, and turned to face the spray.

Give the girl a break, she told herself. Melanie's only trying to protect her interests – keep Bodie for herself.

It's probably worse because of Dad. Something like that throws your emotions out of whack, distorts your perspective.

I should let her know I don't have designs on Bodie.

Sure. She wouldn't believe it, though.

Pen shampooed her hair. When she was done in the shower, she stepped out and dried herself. She brushed her teeth. She used the toilet.

The cool shower hadn't been enough to take away the heat from the spa and wine, and a light film of moisture made her robe cling to her skin when she put it on.

In the hallway, she turned off the overhead lights and stepped quickly past the closed door of Joyce's room. Melanie's door was also shut. A strip of light showed through the space beneath it. Passing the door, Pen heard a radio. And Melanie.

Breathless, quick moans from Melanie not quite hidden by the smooth voice of Kenny Rogers.

Pen rushed into her room and shut the door. Wiped her sweaty face with a sleeve of her robe. The sound of music came faintly through the wall. She stood motionless, listening, but didn't hear Melanie.

Tossing her robe onto the bed, she stepped to the window and opened it. The night breeze came in, chilling her damp body.

The radio voice now sounded like Waylon Jennings and she heard a muffled outcry that gave her stomach a flip.

She hurried to her suitcase, took out her hair drier, sat at the dressing table, and turned it on. The noise of the blower obliterated the sounds of the music and Melanie.

★ ★ ★

She entered the hospital room, and the bed was empty. 'Where's Dad?' she asked. 'Did he go home?'

'Wouldn't you like to know?' the doctor said, grinning. He was short and skinny, with black hair.

'Where's Dad?' she asked.

'First show me your tits.'

'Go to hell.'

'Don't be a tease. I know you want me.' He tugged her bikini top.

I knew I should've dressed up before coming here.

The bikini tore away. She crossed her arms over her breasts.

'It's all right, I'm a doctor.' He twirled his stethoscope. 'Let me just see about your ticker.'

Pen wasn't at all sure about this. Probably a trick of some kind. But he could tell her where Dad was. She lowered her arms.

The doctor bent over and pressed the metal disk to her nipple. 'Cough,' he said.

He's no doctor. My heart isn't there. A real doctor would know that.

'I don't hear it. You'd better lie down.'

'What for?'

'So I can fuck your brains out.'

'You're *him*!'

She rammed a knife into his belly so hard it doubled him over and lifted him off his feet. He hit the floor with his hands and knees. 'Where's Dad?'

'You didn't have to kill me.'

'You're not dead, you're talking.'

'I'm gonna *get* you!'

She ran from the room and looked back when she heard rushing footsteps behind her. The man was chasing her, pulling the knife from his belly as he ran. Blood flew from his wound, spraying out, painting the floor and wall in front of him.

Pen jabbed the elevator button.

He ran closer and closer, waving the knife overhead.

Come on, elevator!

Oh shit oh shit!

Pen hopped from foot to foot. She pounded on the elevator door.

The man wore a wild grin. He started to laugh, blood exploding from his mouth and nostrils.

The elevator doors slid open. Pen jumped inside. He lunged for her, but the doors shut in time, trapping his arm at the elbow.

The elevator started down. His arm glided up to the ceiling, broke off and dropped to the floor. He kept his grip on the knife. His arm rolled. The blade lifted, pointed at Pen, made little circles. Pen backed away from it. The elevator gained speed. Plummeted.

Where is it going?

Why doesn't it slow down?

It'll stop suddenly and I'm supposed to fall on the knife, but I won't.

She sat on the elevator floor.

Outfoxed you, you bastard.

The elevator stopped smoothly without the expected jolt.

The doors parted.

Beyond them was darkness.

The lighted indicator above the elevator door read 'B'.

This is the basement. Somebody turned off the lights, that's all.

Oddly, the severed arm on the floor with the knife

twirling in its hand didn't worry Pen half so much as the darkness outside the elevator.

The basement. That's where the corpses are kept. The patients who didn't make it. Stored in drawers.

She sidestepped around the arm and stopped at the edge of the elevator floor. She peered into the pitch black.

She didn't want to go out there.

Her heart pounded with terror, and she struggled for breath.

'Hello?' she called. 'Anyone there?'

No answer came.

Of course not. The dead don't talk.

She called out again. 'Hello?'

'Help me,' came the distant, muffled voice of her father.

'I'll be right there!'

If she could just find a light switch. She reached outside the elevator, felt along the wall, and a cold hand grabbed her wrist.

'*Yyeee-ahh!!!*'

Pen lurched awake and heard the last of her outcry in the dark room. She sat up, panting.

'God almighty,' she muttered.

She drew a sleeve across her face to wipe the sweat away. Her pajamas felt glued to her skin.

One hell of a nightmare. She tried to remember it, and recalled searching for a light switch, someone clutching her hand. There must've been more to the dream, but the rest was gone.

Somewhere, she'd heard that you need to stay awake for three or four minutes – if you fall asleep any sooner, you might find yourself back in the same nightmare.

No thank you.

Besides, her mouth was dry, she had a slight head-ache, and she needed to urinate.

She got up, plucked the pajamas away from her back and buttocks, and opened her door. The hallway was dark. One of its light switches was on the wall just outside her door. She almost reached for it, but thoughts of the nightmare sent a chill crawling up her skin. She felt the tingle of gooseflesh on her thighs and forearms, the nape of her neck, her forehead. The skin of her nipples grew tight and stiff.

It was just a goddamn nightmare, she told herself.

Still, she couldn't reach for the switch.

She turned on her bedroom lamp instead. It cast a pool of light into the hallway. No one was there, waiting to grab her. Of course not.

Feeling more at ease, she walked silently to the bathroom. She used the toilet. She found Tylenol in the medicine cabinet and washed down two pills. On the way back to her room, she paused in front of Melanie's door. The strip of light at its bottom was gone. No sound came from inside. She continued to her own room, stepped through the doorway, and stopped fast.

Bodie, in a rumpled bathrobe, stood facing her window. 'Are you decent?' he asked quietly without looking around.

Pen eased the door shut. She took a shaky breath. 'I'm decent,' she said. 'What are you doing here?'

He turned around. His hands were clasped at his waist. His eyes looked nervous. He made a feeble smile that quickly died. 'I just need to talk to you for a couple of minutes. I'm sorry for barging in.'

'It's all right,' she said. Her voice sounded strangely muted and husky.

Good Christ, she thought. He came to my room. What *is* this?

She sat on the edge of her bed. Folded her trembling hands. Took a deep breath. Looked down at herself, found her top button open, fastened it, and refolded her hands.

Bodie came around to a straight-backed chair beside her dresser. His sandy brown hair was mussed. His robe was tightly shut, tied at the waist with its cloth belt. He held it together over his thighs as he sat down.

'You yelled or something,' he said.

'Yeah. A nightmare. A real winner.'

'Are you okay?'

She nodded.

'I wasn't going to come over, but I heard that, and then you walked past our door. I figured this might be the time. I was lying awake, thinking about . . .' He hesitated.

'About what?'

'Telling you.'

Telling me what? she wondered. Her heart hammered.

'Bodie,' she whispered, 'you shouldn't have come here.'

'I know, I know. Melanie'd kill me . . .'

'Could you blame her?'

'I can't keep this thing to myself.'

'You hardly know me.'

'I know I can trust you. I think we've got some real trouble about to go down.'

Pen frowned, relieved, a little disappointed, confused.

'What are you talking about?'

'Remember in the hospital room? How Melanie wigged out?'

'Remember? Are you kidding?'

'She said she didn't know what her vision was about, but that wasn't true. She remembered the whole thing. And she told me about it in the room tonight.'

Before or after you screwed her? Pen wondered, and immediately felt angry at herself for thinking it. 'What did she say?'

'It was the accident again. She saw the car speeding toward her, like before, only this time she saw the driver. She said the driver was Harrison Donner.'

'Oh, man,' Pen muttered. 'Is she sure?'

'She seemed very sure.'

'Harrison hit Dad?'

'Melanie thinks it was a conspiracy, that Harrison and Joyce planned it together.'

'Was that in her vision, too?'

'It's a theory she came up with. The way she explained it, Joyce knew in advance about their plan to eat at Gerard's – probably even called in the reservation herself. She also knew that your father always left his car in that bank parking lot, so he'd have to cross Cañon to get to the restaurant. She filled in Harrison, and he was waiting – maybe parked at the curb. When your father started across . . .' Bodie's hands lifted off his knees, hovered a moment, and dropped down again.

'What you're saying . . . Melanie thinks they conspired to murder Dad?'

'That's about it. I'm not convinced she's right, but it *could've* been set up that way. I don't see any holes in it, do you?'

140

'Harrison couldn't count on there not being any witnesses.'

'If the situation didn't look favorable, he had the option of aborting. For all we know, they used a similar set-up half a dozen times before last night, and called it off each time for one reason or another – witnesses, too much traffic, whatever.'

'You've given it a lot of thought,' Pen said.

'Two hours' worth, between the time she told me and the time I came over here.'

Pen realized she was shivering. It may have been Bodie's story. It may have been the breeze from the window chilling the nightmare sweat on her pajamas.

Bodie sat stiff in the chair, legs pressed together, hands gripping his knees.

'Are you cold?' she asked.

'A little,' he admitted.

It crossed her mind to invite him onto the bed. They could cover up.

I don't believe so, she told herself.

'I'll shut the window,' she said.

'I'll do it.'

As he went to the window, Pen dropped onto her side, reached to the foot of her bed, and sat up, dragging the knitted comforter. She held it out to Bodie when he returned.

He thanked her, wrapped it around his body, and sat on the chair. 'That's a lot better,' he said.

Pen scooted back on the mattress. She crossed her legs. She drew a blanket up behind her and draped it over her shoulders. 'So,' she said. 'What's the motive?'

'Joyce and Harrison are lovers.'

'Do you think they really are?'

Bodie shrugged. 'I don't know. It's possible. It's likely, I guess.'

'Okay. Suppose they are. That's hardly a motive for murder. Getting a divorce is a cinch in this state, and she'd come out of it with a pretty good settlement.'

'Half?'

Pen shook her head. 'They've been married almost three years. She'd probably get half of what Dad earned after the date of their marriage, plus maybe a couple of years of alimony.'

'But if she . . .' Bodie hesitated.

'Kills him.'

'Yeah. She gets it all. Plus his life insurance.'

'That'd depend on his will and on who's named as beneficiaries in the insurance policies. I imagine Melanie and I would get some of it.' Pen frowned. 'Melanie talked about all that at the hospital. Remember? She blurted out something about Joyce getting Harrison and the insurance and inheritance if Dad would die. Then she burst into the room to "save" him.'

'Thought Joyce was planning to pull the plug.'

'And that's when she had her vision,' Pen said. 'She'd barely gotten through the door when it started.'

Bodie pulled the comforter more tightly around himself. 'Are you thinking that she faked it?'

Pen considered the possibility, remembered Melanie thrashing in her arms, moaning. 'I don't think she faked the attack. But I wonder if her suspicions couldn't have triggered it somehow. She already suspected Joyce and Harrison were lovers and she thought that Joyce might want Dad to die, so it's just one more small step to the idea that Joyce and Harrison conspired to run him down. Her subconscious, maybe, took that step for her.'

'And gave her the attack,' Bodie said. 'I don't know. I had pretty much that same idea about the episode she had at the concert last night. She didn't know whether it was you or her father who got creamed, but she was carrying a real load of anger and guilt about both of you, so I got the feeling that her vision might be some kind of perverse wish-fulfillment.'

Pen gazed at him.

'I don't mean she *wanted* you dead. Just that she couldn't handle her feelings about either one of you. And her mind shorted out. Gave her the vision. But what she saw in that trance turned out to be right. Maybe this one is, too.'

'They aren't always,' Pen said, and felt a small tremor in her stomach.

'She was right about her mother, wasn't she?'

'But there were other times. Like the night of Dad and Joyce's wedding. They were flying to Hawaii for their honeymoon. Melanie and I were here at the house and she threw a pretty good fit. When she came out of it, she said the airliner had blown up in mid-air.'

Bodie pursed his lips as if to whistle, but no sound came out.

'Obviously,' Pen said, 'she was wrong on that one. No airliner at all went down that night, much less the one carrying Dad and Joyce.'

'She wasn't happy about the marriage, I know that.'

'She was outraged by it. She felt that Dad was betraying the memory of our mother, and that Joyce was a whore after Dad for his money. That's why she moved in with me before they got back from their honeymoon. She couldn't stand either of them.

'Then there was her vision about me,' Pen said. Her

143

stomach fluttered again and she suddenly felt uncomfortably warm. She shrugged the blanket off her shoulders. She took a deep breath. Talking about this, she realized, would be difficult. But Bodie needed to know.

'It was the summer before my senior year at college. I always came home for the summers. Melanie was fifteen. She'd started going with this guy, Steve Wells, who'd just graduated high school. He was seventeen or eighteen, I guess.'

'She likes older men,' Bodie said.

It forced a smile from Pen. 'Yeah, apparently so. Anyway, he spent quite a lot of time here.' She hesitated.

'And he fell for you,' Bodie said.

Pen nodded. 'Did Melanie tell you about this?'

'She didn't have to. The way she is about you, it's obvious something of that kind must've happened along the way.'

'God, it's not like I did anything to encourage him. I mean, I was nice to him. I didn't ignore him. But I never . . . flirted with him or anything like that.'

Bodie's face grew slightly red.

Pen didn't want to think about what his blush might mean. She fingered the cuff of her pajama leg. 'So he was here for dinner one night. Dad barbequed out back. After we ate, Dad had to leave. There was a meeting or something, I forget.'

'Let me guess,' Bodie said. 'The three of you went in the jacuzzi.'

Pen met his eyes.

'We didn't have the jacuzzi then.'

'Oh.'

'Melanie fell asleep on the couch. We'd had margaritas with supper, and she was pretty much looped. I went into the kitchen to make coffee, and Steve followed me. It was awful. He blurted out about how he'd lost interest in Melanie the minute he laid eyes on me, and the only reason he kept going with her was so he could come to the house and see me. I told him to forget it, I wouldn't have anything to do with him and if he'd lost interest in Melanie he should get the hell out of her life. It took him a while to get the message. But when he did, he left.

'Melanie didn't wake up for a couple more hours. In the meantime, I'd taken a bath and put on a nightgown. I was reading in bed when Melanie came into my room. She asked where Steve was, and I said he'd gone home. I didn't tell her what had gone on. I figured it was his responsibility, you know?'

'Yeah,' Bodie said. 'Why should you get stuck with breaking the news?'

'Anyway, all of a sudden Melanie threw a fit. Her eyes rolled up and she started shaking. She fell on the floor. I was scared. I didn't know what was going on. But then she came out of it and looked at me as if I were some kind of monster. She went nuts. She called me . . . some pretty awful names. She said Steve and I had made it together while she was zonked out on the couch. I told her that we hadn't done anything, but she wouldn't believe me. That's because she'd *seen* it. She'd seen it all, in glorious detail, while she was rolling around drooling on my bedroom carpet.'

Pen was shaking by the time she finished. She let out a long breath, then waited, staring at the edge of her mattress until she felt reasonably calm again. 'I denied it, and Steve denied it when she phoned him. But to this day she's convinced we both lied, that we actually . . .

screwed . . . while she was sleeping off her margaritas. She has total faith in those visions of hers.'

Bodie was frowning. The frown had started early in Pen's story, and stayed. 'It has to be terrible, getting blamed like that for something you didn't do.'

'Yeah. It almost makes you wish you'd done something to deserve it.'

A corner of Bodie's mouth curled up. 'Should've slept with the guy.'

'He wasn't my type.' Pen felt a smile come to her own face. 'At any rate, that was probably more than you wanted to hear, but . . .'

'Not at all. It tells me a lot about you and Melanie – this thing she has about you. It's been putting a certain strain on *me*, you know.'

'I can imagine. I'm sure she thinks we just can't wait to jump in the sack together.' Immediately, Pen wished she hadn't said that. She felt a heat wash over her face. 'Let's get back to her visions,' she said.

'Right. Her visions.'

'She's had at least two that were totally off: Steve and I, and the airliner that didn't blow up.'

'She doesn't believe she was wrong about you and Steve,' Bodie said, 'but you'd think the business about the airliner explosion would've shaken her faith a bit.'

'You'd think so.'

'Well, this thing tonight has her absolutely convinced that Harrison's the one who ran down your father. She's also sure that Joyce helped set it up. And she plans to do something about it.'

'Like what?' Pen asked.

'She said, "They're gonna pay." '

'She's thinking about revenge?'

'It looks that way.'

'Oh, Jesus.'

'That's why I had to talk to you. I think we need to do something.'

'Maybe you'd better take her back to Phoenix.'

'I don't think she'd go along with that.'

'What's your idea, then?' Pen asked.

'The main thing is, we need to keep an eye on her.'

'She's never been violent. That I know about.'

'Nobody ever tried to kill her father before.'

'We don't know that they . . .'

'*She* knows. She's absolutely certain. And I think there's a possibility that she's right. Those visions of hers have been on the mark more often than not.'

'I'd say they're about fifty-fifty.'

'I think she's right about those two being lovers. What do you think?'

'I'm not convinced,' Pen said, 'but I have my suspicions.'

'If they *are*, it's conceivable that they did decide to eliminate your father.'

'That's pretty hard to buy.'

'People commit murder every day.'

'I know that.'

'And the people they kill, more often than not, are friends or members of the family.'

Pen nodded. 'I've done some research on the subject.'

Bodie shrugged the comforter off his shoulders and leaned forward, elbows on knees. 'I'm not saying they're guilty. The thing is, Melanie thinks they are. She might or might not be right, but there's a strong chance she'll do something about it. I say we not only keep an eye on her, we help her.'

147

'Help her do what?'

'Nail them,' Bodie said.

'*What?*'

'Only we control Melanie, we channel her. First, we convince her that the vision isn't enough. Then we offer to help investigate. I think she'll go along with that.'

'And *do* we investigate?'

'Just some minor-league snooping. Who knows? We might actually turn up some evidence.'

'Fat chance.'

'If we do, we take it to the police. If we turn up zilch, at least we've kept Melanie out of trouble for a while, and maybe she'll even end up convinced they had nothing to do with it.'

'One problem. I'm not supposed to know about this vision she had, and I don't imagine she'd be overjoyed to find out you snuck into my bedroom to fill me in.'

'Tell her that you're suspicious. Right now, she thinks you'd take Joyce's side.'

'Did she say that?'

Bodie nodded.

'I guess I can't blame her.'

'But if you let her know that you have doubts of your own about Joyce, I think she'll see you as an ally and confide in you.'

'It's like conspiring against her.'

'Joyce?'

'Melanie.' She sighed. 'I don't know. If we start looking for clues or whatever, we might just end up feeding her delusion.'

'If it *is* a delusion.'

'Yeah, if. And if she's right, I'd be as anxious as anyone to see those two get what's coming to them.'

'Tell Melanie that.'

'Maybe I'd better.'

'I think she'll be glad to know you're with her.'

'Maybe.'

Bodie stood up. 'I'd better get out of here.' He lifted the comforter and carried it to the foot of Pen's bed. 'Talk about feeding delusions . . . if she woke up and found out I was over here . . .' He put the comforter on the bed. 'She'd never, no way, believe it was innocent.'

'I don't know how innocent it was.'

Bodie's eyes widened.

'I didn't mean *that*.' Again, she felt herself blush. 'I meant the way we're plotting against her.'

Bodie nodded and went to the door. He paused with a hand on the knob, and looked back at Pen. 'The times are out of joint,' he said.

'I think that should be Melanie's line.'

He smiled. 'Goodnight, Pen.'

'Goodnight.'

CHAPTER THIRTEEN

Melanie was not in the room.

Bodie snuggled down and shut his eyes again. The bed felt too warm and cozy to leave. Briefly, he wondered where Melanie had gone.

Then he pictured Pen in her room last night sitting cross-legged on her bed: her mussed golden hair, her blue eyes, the light sprinkle of freckles across her nose. He saw the shiny blue pajama shirt open at her throat, the way it lay smooth over the mounds of her breasts and how it draped her lap. The pants legs were stretched taut to her knees. Her ankles were slim and bare.

Bodie ached as he lingered on the image of her. If only . . . If only what?

Maybe if she had started to cry. She hadn't been close to it, though. But if she *had* cried, he could've comforted her – moved to the bed and put an arm around her, and she would've turned to him. He could've held her gently as she wept. Kissed her.

God, to kiss her. Just to hold and kiss her.

Thinking about it made a hollow ache in his chest.

Don't worry, Melanie, he thought, it'll never happen.

If Whit dies . . .

Nice thought. Damn.

But to hold her, to kiss her.

He remembered his shock of alarm when Pen had asked, last night, if he was cold. For just an instant he'd feared – and hoped – that she would ask him to come to the bed. No funny stuff, she would've said. Promise? Oh, yes.

It didn't happen.

Nothing happened.

Not quite nothing. She hadn't told him to go away. They'd sat for a long time, alone in her room, she in her pajamas and he in his robe, and they'd talked. She'd told him things, shared secrets. There had been an intimacy to it all.

Thank God for Melanie's vision. Without that for an excuse . . . It was not an excuse, he told himself. It was his *reason* for going to her room.

His intentions had been entirely honorable.

But God, what if something *had* happened!

It didn't. It won't. Don't even think about it.

Suppose she'd said, 'Bodie, I've been lying awake thinking about you, wishing you were here with me. I love you. I can't help myself.'

With a moan, he tossed his covers aside and got out of bed. When he was dressed, he stepped into the hallway. The bathroom door was shut. He heard water running – someone about to take a bath? So he combed his hair in the bedroom, then went downstairs.

From the silence, he guessed that nobody else was around. Someone had been in the kitchen, though. He poured himself a mug of hot coffee.

On the center of the kitchen table was a note folded in

half to make it stand like a tent. Bodie picked it up.

Hi!
I've gone to Mass and I have some errands to run.
Expect me when you see me. Make yourselfs at
home. Their's bacon and eggs in the fridge as well
as coffee cake in the freezer. So help yourselfs.

Love,
Joyce

Good speller, Bodie thought, and put the note down.

Gone to mass? That would mean she's Catholic. Will
you be confessing today, Joyce? And what sort of sins
will you be whispering in the Father's ear? Adultery?
Attempted murder?

Beyond the glass door, the patio was bright with
sunlight. Bodie stepped to the door. He gripped its
handle. He saw Pen off to the left, reclined on a lounger
and reading a paperback. She wore a blue and yellow
plaid blouse and white shorts. Her legs were stretched
out, long and slender, her bare feet crossed at the
ankles. She had a coffee mug in one hand.

Bodie wanted to go out there and pull up a chair
beside her.

What could it hurt?

He didn't know what it could hurt, but maybe she
wanted time to herself and maybe Melanie would put in
an appearance full of suspicion and maybe he had just
damn well not find himself alone with Pen first thing in
the morning.

So he backed away from the door.

He carried his coffee mug into the living room. The
Sunday *Los Angeles Times* was on a lamp table. He

153

searched through it until he found the book section, then sat on the couch to read it while he drank his coffee and waited.

When his mug was empty, he returned to the kitchen. He filled it. He stepped to the door and looked out again. Pen was still on the lounger. Her knees were drawn up, and she held the book open against her thighs. Her hair glinted in the sunlight.

With a sigh, he turned away. He took his coffee back to the living room and sat down. This is crazy, he thought, and I'm a rat. She's Melanie's sister, for Godsake.

I haven't done anything.

And I'd better not.

It would probably blow up in my face, anyway. Even if Pen were interested in me (a damn big if), she's loyal to Melanie. Look what happened when that Steve character put moves on her.

Bodie found the newspaper's 'Calendar' section and began to look at the movie ads.

Then Melanie came down the stairs. She wore her tan corduroys and a gray sleeveless sweatshirt with the neck stretched out so it hung below one shoulder. Her choker was black.

'Where is everyone?' she asked as she approached him.

Bodie stood up. 'I don't know where your sister is. Joyce went to mass.'

'Mass?' She smirked.

'All squeaky clean?' he asked, and stroked the back of her head. Her thick black hair felt damp. She moved against him, and they kissed. Her hands slipped into the rear pockets of his pants. As they rubbed him, Bodie eased his own hands under her sweatshirt. Her skin felt smooth. There were no straps. He ran his hands up and down her back. Velvety. Warm. Bare. She felt wonderful and she was his and he was nuts to want Pen when he already had Melanie. He pushed a hand beneath the waistband of her cords.

'Aren't you ever *not* horny?' she whispered against his lips.

'Not when you're around.'

She smiled slightly. She kissed him again, then eased away. 'I wonder if the bitch left us something to eat.'

'Bacon and eggs in the fridge, coffee cake in the freezer.'

They headed for the kitchen.

'She sure got out of here early,' Melanie said.

'Think she's avoiding us?'

'I'd avoid us, if I were her.' Melanie lifted the note off the kitchen table. 'Mass. That's rich. Wants us to think she went off to pray for Dad?'

'Maybe she did.'

'Yeah, to pray he dies.'

Bodie stepped over to the door. 'Oh, there's Pen. I wonder if she's eaten yet.'

'Ask her.'

He slid open the door. The sound made her look around. 'Good morning,' he said.

'Hi, Bodie.'

His heart beat a little faster. 'Are you hungry?'

Nodding, she swung her legs off the lounger and stood up. Bodie caught himself staring at her legs as she walked toward him. He turned away.

'It's wonderful out there,' she said and entered the kitchen. 'I never sit out at my place.'

155

'Maybe you can find a new apartment with a private patio,' Melanie said.

'I should try. Sleep well?' she asked.

'Fine,' Melanie answered.

'Me, too,' said Bodie. 'Zonked right out.'

'The jacuzzi will do that to you. That and the booze.' She met Bodie's gaze and looked away. 'I was out like a light.'

'Did you see Joyce's note?' Bodie asked.

'Guess she's making herself scarce. Who could blame her?'

'What do you mean?' Bodie asked.

'Just that she can't be very comfortable around Dad's family. She's obviously sleeping with Harrison, after all.'

'I thought you didn't believe that,' Melanie said. 'What changed your mind?'

'Being around her, I guess. I can't even put my finger on it, but there's something about her. Maybe the way she's been acting – I don't know – ingratiating. It's as if she has a guilty conscience so she's bending over backwards to be sweet. You add that to the fact that Harrison was here yesterday morning . . . and what you told me about the bed.' Pen frowned at her sister. 'It makes me think that maybe you've been right about her all along. She wouldn't be sleeping with Harrison if she loved Dad.'

'She never loved Dad,' Melanie said. 'She just wanted his money.'

'But that doesn't mean she tried to kill him,' Bodie pointed out.

Melanie stabbed him with her eyes.

He grimaced. 'Woops.'

'What are you talking about?' Pen asked. 'Tried to kill *Dad*?'

Bodie tried to look sorry for his slip of the tongue. With a shrug, he said, 'Maybe you'd better tell her, Melanie.'

'*Neat* play.'

'It just came out.'

'I wish somebody would tell me what the hell's going on,' Pen demanded. 'My God, I think I have a right to know. He's my father, too.'

Leaning back against the refrigerator door, Melanie folded her arms across her chest. She sighed, gave Bodie another fierce glance, then met Pen's eyes. 'Joyce and Harrison fixed it up so Dad would get hit by the car.'

Pen's eyes went wide. Her mouth dropped open. She shook her head. 'That's insane,' she muttered.

'I *told* you she wouldn't listen.'

'Go on,' Bodie urged. 'Tell her the rest.'

'What's the point?'

Bodie looked at Pen. 'Harrison was driving the car that ran your father down. Melanie saw him. It was that vision she had last night in the hospital room.'

'I saw him behind the windshield,' Melanie said. 'It was as if I were looking with Dad's eyes.'

'You can't make an accusation like that based on nothing more than . . . your imagination.'

'It wasn't my imagination.'

'Maybe it was telepathy,' Bodie suggested. 'Maybe your father communicated it to her.'

'Don't tell me *you* believe it, too?'

'I don't know. I guess maybe I do.'

'You're both bananas.'

Bodie wondered if, perhaps, Pen was playing it a bit *too* skeptical.

'Joyce made the dinner reservations,' Melanie said, a certain eagerness sneaking into her voice. 'She knew Dad always parked behind the bank, knew he'd have to cross the street. Harrison parked and waited till Dad started across.'

'It could've happened that way,' Bodie said.

'It *did*.'

'You'd need proof,' Pen told her. 'You can't base this whole thing on some kind of psychic experience.'

'Let's *get* proof,' Bodie suggested.

'I already know,' Melanie said.

'Your visions aren't always right,' Pen pointed out. 'Remember Dad's honeymoon?'

'That was a fluke.'

'Maybe this is a fluke.'

'It's not.'

'Then let's get some proof we can take to the police,' Bodie said.

Melanie sighed.

'We'd need to take a look at Harrison's car,' Pen said. 'If he hit Dad, the car might've sustained some damage. And there'd be . . . traces. Even if he tried to wash it off . . .'

'Joyce claimed it was a sports car,' Bodie said. 'Harrison drives a Mercedes.'

'Joyce could've lied,' Melanie said.

'Harrison owns a Porsche,' said Pen. 'He has a Mercedes and a Porsche.'

'You *would* know that.' Melanie smirked at Bodie. 'They were lovers, you know.'

'We were *not* lovers.'

'Uh-huh, sure.'

'We went out a few times, that's all.'

'Do you know where he lives?' Bodie asked.

'Of course she does.'

Bodie wished he hadn't found out about Pen and Harrison. Thoughts of them together . . . 'Let's drive out to his place,' he said quickly, 'and see if we can get a look at his Porsche.'

Melanie shrugged. 'I guess it can't hurt.'

'Why don't we have breakfast first?' Bodie suggested. 'I'm starving.'

'You and your stomach.'

'Harrison's house is only a few miles from here,' Pen said. 'Why don't we eat afterwards?'

'Two against one,' he said. 'It ain't fair.'

Bodie drove west on San Vicente. Melanie sat in the van's passenger seat. Pen, crouched behind them, held onto the seatbacks, her left hand inches from Bodie's shoulder. Her face was in the gap, and he saw it each time he looked to the right. Her shampoo, or perfume, had a fresh clean scent.

Bodie's stomach didn't feel right – maybe simple hunger, maybe being so close to Pen, or maybe a reaction to finding out about her and Harrison. Lovers? She'd denied it. But she had admitted going with him. Bodie didn't like that. The guy was movie-star handsome, cool and smooth.

Drives a fucking Porsche.

An asshole.

Even if they hadn't been lovers, Pen must've liked him. They must've kissed. He must've had his hands on her.

159

Such thoughts didn't improve the condition of Bodie's stomach.

Whatever went on between them, he told himself, it's over now. Pen doesn't seem to like him. Maybe he dumped her. I hope she's the one who did the dumping.

'Make a left at the light,' she said.

Bodie steered into the turn pocket and waited for the green arrow.

'You know,' Melanie said, 'he probably didn't use his own car.'

'He's arrogant enough,' said Pen. 'Maybe he did.'

'Arrogant doesn't mean stupid.'

'It's still worth checking,' Bodie told them, and made the turn.

'You'll want to hang a right on the third street down.'

He nodded.

'Either rented a car or stole one.'

'Not necessarily,' Pen said. 'Renting would leave a trail.'

'He could've paid cash.'

'You have to show ID. Maybe he's got a fake ID, but that's tricky to pull off. The driver's license has your photo.'

'It's not *that* tricky,' Melanie argued.

'Besides, the rental person could identify him.'

'Not if he wore a disguise.'

'I don't think he'd do anything that elaborate – and risky. As you said, he's not stupid. He would know that the simpler he made it, the less chance of tripping up.'

Bodie turned right. The residential street was shaded by trees. The houses, mostly two stories, looked old but well kept. A peaceful neighborhood, its occupants probably well-off if not filthy rich.

'Two blocks,' Pen told him. 'Then make a left.'

'He must've stolen it, then,' Melanie said.

'That's not so simple, either. It's not as easy as they make it look on TV. Especially if we're talking about a sports car. You can't just jump in and hotwire the thing in five seconds and take off. You've got to bypass the steering wheel lock – and most of these newer cars have alarm systems.'

'Sports cars get stolen all the time,' Melanie told her.

'Mostly by pros, guys with the equipment to pull the ignition . . .'

'You sound like a pro yourself,' Bodie said.

'I've written about this kind of stuff. I had to do some research.'

'I just can't believe he would use his own car,' Melanie said.

'There must be a thousand Porsches in LA. At least. He slaps some stolen plates on his Porsche before he goes after Dad, and he's home free as long as he doesn't take it in for repairs. He's got the Mercedes. He can leave the Porsche in his garage for a few weeks, then maybe get it repaired out of state. Turn here, Bodie, then take the first left.'

He slowed, steered around the corner, saw the intersection a short distance ahead, and flicked the arm of his turn signal.

'It'll be the third house on the right,' Pen said.

'What'll we do,' Bodie asked, 'drop in and ask to see his Porsche?'

'Just go by, for starters. Don't even slow down.'

Even as he made the turn, he spotted Harrison's gray Mercedes parked in the driveway of the third house.

'Damn it,' Melanie muttered.

'Too bad he's not at mass with Joyce,' Bodie said.

Harrison's home, unlike those of his neighbors, was a single-story ranch house. It looked more modern than the others. Red brick, a red tile roof, white trim. In front of the Mercedes stood a wrought-iron gate.

Pen's head blocked Bodie's view as she strained forward between the seats to look out Melanie's window. When she settled back, they were beyond the house.

'The Porsche must be in his garage,' she said.

'So what'll we do?' Bodie asked.

'We can't do anything while he's there.'

'Why don't we get some breakfast?'

'All right.'

He stopped at the corner, waited for a Mustang to go by, then drove through the intersection and saw, parked at the curb, a black Lincoln Continental. His heart gave a kick.

'My God,' Melanie gasped.

Bodie hit the brakes.

Pen leaned forward again. 'It's Dad's, all right.'

'Are you sure?'

'That pipe holder on the dash? I gave it to him for Christmas a few years ago.'

Bodie shook his head. 'Guess who's not at mass.'

'That miserable bitch,' Pen muttered. 'She really *is* making it with . . . oh, man. Oh, that dirty . . .'

'*I* knew it all along.' Melanie sounded proud of herself.

'God, if Dad ever found out he'd die. How could she *do* something like this!' Pen dropped backward out of sight. 'I want to go home,' she said in a small voice.

Bodie started his van moving again.

'*Not* to her home.' She sniffed. 'I never want to see her again.'

Melanie grinned.

'Your apartment?' Bodie asked.

'Please.'

'What about the caller?'

'Who cares?'

163

CHAPTER FOURTEEN

Bodie insisted on escorting Pen up to her apartment. Melanie stayed with them. This time, no note had been left under the door.

'Are you sure you'll be all right here?' Bodie asked.

'I just need to be alone.'

'I don't know why you're so upset all of a sudden,' Melanie said. 'I thought you already believed they were screwing around. All that happened is that we confirmed it.'

'Yeah, we confirmed it. I'll see you guys later, okay? Could you do me a real favor and bring my stuff over sometime? I really don't want to go back there unless I have to.'

'Sure, we'll do that,' Bodie said. 'Maybe you should reconnect one of your phones in case we need to get in touch about something.'

She nodded.

Then they were gone.

Pen sat on her sofa, propped her elbows on her knees, and rested her chin on her hands. She stared at the wall.

Hell no, she hadn't believed that Joyce was making it

with Harrison. She'd suspected it, of course, but she hadn't *believed*. It was too damned outrageous.

Probably in Harrison's bed right now, this instant, fucking. And Dad in the hospital, barely alive.

And yeah they did it yesterday, too. Right from the hospital to Dad's home and fucked in Dad's bed.

What kind of scum is she?

The kind of scum, maybe, who *would* try to kill Dad. Why not? A piece of shit like that doesn't have any conscience.

How about Harrison?

Yeah, how about him.

Dad trusted him, treated him like a son, thought I'd lost my mind when I refused to see the guy any more, probably had our wedding all planned in his head and was looking forward to the grandchildren. I damn near wept at the pitiful look on his face. 'You two are so perfect for each other.' Right, Dad, but he's a shallow egocentric sadistic sleaze. Only I couldn't hurt you by telling on him. Big mistake.

Hey, Dad, this apple of your eye Harrison raped me. What do you think about that? He wasn't any too gentle about it, either. Want to see the bruises, the teeth-marks?

Trembling, Pen leaned back against the cushions of the sofa. She hugged a corduroy-covered pillow to her chest.

She'd been a fool to let him take her to his home that night.

But they'd had dinner at Scandia where he'd been charming and amusing and they had shared two bottles of cabernet sauvignon after the margaritas. She was feeling no pain by the time they left.

'What're we doing here?' she asked when she found his car stopped in the driveway of his house.

'*The Maltese Falcon*. Starts in five minutes. You want to watch it, don't you?'

'We're gonna watch TV?'

'Have some coffee, sober up, drive you home after.'

Her mind whispered a warning, but she ignored it. They went inside. She sat on the couch. Harrison took off his jacket and necktie, and turned on the television. He went into the kitchen to make coffee. When he returned, he sat beside her. He held her hand, but that was all right.

He went away during the first commercial and came back with mugs of coffee.

'I bet you didn't know I was a private eye. A regular Sam Spade.'

'*You* were a private eye?'

'Bet you didn't know that.'

'Bet I don't believe it.'

He went away. Pen drank some coffee. He came back with a shoe box and sat beside her, the box on his lap. He lifted out a holstered revolver. 'My snub-nose .38,' he said.

Here we are, drunk, and he's got a gun in his hand. 'Let's see,' she said. He handed it to her. She removed it from the holster and turned the barrel toward her face.

'Hey, watch out.'

The bullet heads were visible inside the cylinder holes. 'Christ, it's loaded.'

'Of course.'

She put it on the coffee table at their knees. 'Ever shoot someone?'

167

'No, but I had to draw it a couple times. The firm I worked for did some security work.'

'Must've been exciting.'

'At first. It got boring fast. What *was* exciting was the repos.'

He took a leather wallet from the box and handed it to her. She opened it. Inside was a silver badge engraved, 'Special Agent'. The card holder showed his ID indicating that he was an agent of Robert Abrams Private Investigations, Inc. 'Amazing,' Pen said. 'You really were a private eye.'

'For two years while I was in law school. I needed the money and I figured it'd be good experience. Get a load of these babies.' He lifted a pair of handcuffs out of the box.

'Ever use these?'

'Sure. I made a couple of arrests. Show you how it's done?'

'I don't know.'

'Hey, you wanta be a writer, don't you? You gotta know this stuff. Here, stand up.'

'What are you gonna do?'

'You're a suspect. I just got the drop on you.' He stood, aiming his index finger at her, stuffing the cuffs into his pocket. 'On your feet.'

Laughing, Pen stood.

'Over to the wall.'

She bumped the lamp table, grabbed the base of the shaking lamp until it stopped wobbling, then stepped to the wall. 'This is just an excuse to frisk me,' she said.

'Hands against the wall.'

She raised them overhead, pressed them to the paneling.

Harrison poked her side. 'Don't try any funny stuff.'

'That what you said really?'

'I think I said, "Move and yer dead meat." '

'That's even worse.'

One of his feet hooked around Pen's right ankle and jerked her foot backward. He did the same to her other foot. Without the wall's support, she would've fallen on her face.

'Now I've got you immobilized,' Harrison said. 'You need both hands to hold you up.'

'True.'

He stuck his finger against her back and began to pat her down using his left hand.

Here it comes, she thought. 'Don't get carried away, huh?'

'Gotta make sure you ain't packin'.'

He ran his hand down her sides and her legs. He stayed away from her breasts and groin and rump. Pen was impressed. Maybe I've got him wrong, she thought. Maybe he's okay, after all.

'Okay, you're clean,' he said. He snapped a cuff around her right wrist and pulled her arm down behind her back. He brought her left arm down, pulling her away from the wall, and snapped the other cuff around her wrist. 'Any questions?'

'Got a key for these?' Pen asked and turned around. And saw the look on his face.

'Now the prisoner is in my control.'

'Harrison.'

'You're under arrest.'

'Let me go.'

'Uh-uh.'

She backed against the wall. 'Don't.'

He reached behind her neck to untie the cords of her gown.

'I'll scream.'

'Then I'll stuff something in your mouth, and that'll make it a little tough for you to breathe. Just relax.' The cords loosened. He drew them down, uncovering her breasts. His eyes were glassy, his face deep red. He pulled at the gown until it slipped to Pen's feet. He licked his lips. He squeezed her breasts.

'I'll have you arrested,' she said, her voice shaking. 'You'll get disbarred.'

'Bullshit. It's common knowledge you've been going with me. You came over here after an expensive dinner. Who's gonna believe you were forced into anything?' His hands slid down her body. He pushed his fingers under the elastic of her pantyhose.

'Bastard!' She kneed him, but missed the target, caught him instead in the thigh.

He cried out, staggered backward, then lunged at her, a shoulder driving her hard against the wall. A fist smashed her belly. Breath blasting out, she sagged.

Then she was on the floor, dazed and fighting for air as he yanked the pantyhose down her legs. 'It's time, baby,' he muttered. 'It's time.' He pulled her panties off. 'Time to pay the piper, babe. Can't string a guy along forever.' He tugged his belt open. 'A guy can just take so much. What does it take, huh? I'm not good enough for you? Maybe you're a dyke, huh? Is that it?' He flung his slacks aside.

'Bastard,' she gasped.

'That's me, that's me.' He tugged down his under-pants and stepped out of them. 'And what are you? Fuckin' iceberg. What's it take to get in your pants, huh? Act of fuckin' Congress?' He made a sharp laugh. 'Handcuffs, that's what it takes.' He kicked her legs apart, dropped to his knees between them and tore off his shirt.

'Don't.'

'Time to pay the piper, babe. I'm gonna fuck your brains out. And know what? You're gonna like it. Yeah. When's the last time you got your brains fucked out?'

'No!'

What did he say?

Fuck your brains out.

Did he really say that? That's what the guy on the phone said.

Pen felt tears trickling from the corners of her eyes.

She was slumped backward on the sofa, teeth clenched, pillow squeezed to her chest, legs pressed together so tightly that they ached. She sat up. She wiped her tears on the shoulder of her blouse. Her right ear felt wet inside. It had caught a tear. She wrapped a fingertip with her shirttail and swabbed out the ear.

Christ, the rape.

Harrison had been very apologetic about it. Later that night. The next morning on the telephone. He'd even sent a dozen long-stemmed red roses. Pen knew he wasn't remorseful, just afraid she might tell on him.

I was drunk, I didn't know what I was doing.

You knew, all right.

I'm gonna fuck your brains out.

Could Harrison be the one who phoned Friday night? The voice hadn't sounded like his. Maybe he disguised it.

171

But why would he call me? He and Joyce . . .

It wasn't him, Pen told herself.

Are you sure?

She went into the bathroom. She blew her nose. In the mirror, her eyes were red, the lids pink and swollen. They narrowed suddenly.

She hurried into her office. The tape cassette was still in the answering machine where Melanie and Bodie had left it. She rewound and played it.

Listening to the voice, she saw Harrison kneeling over her, naked. Her stomach clenched. Her heart pounded. Her legs felt weak. She was on the floor, Harrison thrusting into her, biting her, her arms cuffed behind her back fiery with pain, the foul words filling her head.

Then came Joyce's voice. She switched off the answering machine and sank onto the desk chair.

The voice hadn't sounded at all like Harrison.

The man who'd made those filthy calls, who'd left the note under her door, wasn't Harrison.

But he had Harrison's soul.

'Fuck you, buddy,' she muttered, 'and the horse you rode in on.'

Bodie finished reading the Traffic Collision Report and passed it to Melanie. The detective on the other side of the desk was busy at his computer terminal. He was a touch typist, and fast. Hardly fits the stereotype of the two-fingered cop, Bodie thought. But then, this is Beverly Hills. He supposed that Beverly Hills cops weren't quite typical.

When Melanie finished reading, she set the report on the detective's desk. He swiveled his chair and faced them. 'Did you find what you were looking for?' he asked in a pleasant voice.

He looked younger than Bodie.

'There was only the one witness?' Bodie asked.

'The spouse? She's the only one we know about at this time.'

'What happens now?' Bodie asked.

'We've put out a notice to all the auto body shops in LA and Orange Counties. They're instructed to let us know if a sports car is brought in with front end damage. Also, we're checking auto theft reports. If a driver gets involved in a hit-and-run, usually the first thing he'll do is report his vehicle stolen.'

'That makes sense,' Bodie said.

'We've had better than two dozen reports of stolen autos since the time of the accident, and we're looking into them. I think there's a good chance that one of them will turn out to be the vehicle that struck Mr Conway.'

'I hope so,' Bodie told him. He looked at Melanie.

'I guess that's all,' Melanie said, and stood up. 'Thank you for helping us.'

'That's what I'm here for. If I can be of any further assistance, don't hesitate to call or come by.' He handed his business card to Melanie. She looked at it and nodded.

'Why didn't you tell him?' Bodie asked as they crossed the parking lot.

'I never intended to.'

'They might have focused their investigation on Harrison.'

'What would I say, that I know the bastard did it because I'm psychic?'

'At least you could've told about him and Joyce having an affair.'

'So could you.'

'I didn't think it was my place to bring up something like that. I mean, it's your family. If you wanted it out, you had the opportunity.' He opened the van door for Melanie, went around to the driver's side, and climbed in.

'Let's go back to Harrison's place,' she said. 'Maybe they're gone by now.'

Pen hesitated at the door and wiped her sweaty hands on her shorts. Calm down, she told herself. There's no reason to be nervous. You're not going in for a physical or to have a cavity filled. Nothing bad will happen. What do you think, they're going to grill you?

She opened the door and stepped inside.

There were several other customers, but she felt conspicuous, an alien who had no right to be here. A trickle of sweat dribbled down her side. She pressed her arm against it, blotting it with her blouse.

Some of her tension eased when she spotted a book rack over near the counter. Books. Familiar territory. She stepped to the rack and saw *The Shooter's Bible*. Her copy at home was probably five years old, its information outdated. She lifted one of the heavy volumes off the rack, flipped through its pages, then tucked it under her arm to buy.

I'm not so out of place, after all, she thought. I probably know more about firearms than a lot of the people who come in here.

I know that revolvers don't have safety switches. A silencer is fine on an automatic, but stupid on a revolver because noise escapes around the cylinder. You don't get shot by a shell – that's the part of the cartridge that stays in the chamber. And it doesn't get ejected if you're talking revolvers. An automatic, all you've got to do is hold the trigger down but with a semi-auto you've got to pull the trigger for each shot. A .357 magnum will take .38 caliber ammo.

Hell, I'm not totally ignorant.

Feeling more confident, she turned away from the book rack and walked up an aisle. She could see rifles and shotguns standing upright in wall racks behind the counter at the far end of the store.

She stopped in front of the glass display case. The clerk at the far end was ringing up boxes of ammunition for a man in a safari jacket.

Inside the case were handguns, telescopic rifle sights, handcuffs, knives . . .

Handcuffs.

She stared.

They had cut off her circulation so her hands went numb. Their edges had left deep grooves in her wrists and red marks that turned to bruises just above her buttocks. She had felt them under her, digging in as Harrison rammed.

'Could I show you a pair of those bracelets?'

Pen looked up, surprised to find the clerk in front of her. 'Uh, no. No thank you.' She lifted *The Shooter's Bible* onto the counter. 'I'd like to get this. A gun, too.'

He nodded. His head, on top of a long neck, looked too small for his body. His tightly curled blond hair was cut short and his mustache was nearly invisible. He blinked at her through wire-rimmed glasses. 'Would this be for personal defense, or perhaps . . . ?'

175

'Personal defense,' Pen said.

His small head bobbed some more. 'That narrows it down. You'll want something lightweight but with some stopping power.' His head tipped down and swiveled as he searched the case. 'We have a mean little Walther PPK, a seven-shot semi-auto. You'd probably want either the .32 or the .380.' Crouching, he reached down to slide open the back of the case.

'No,' Pen said. 'Actually, I was thinking in terms of a shotgun.'

His pale eyebrows lifted.

'A 12-gauge shotgun.'

He stood up straight. There seemed to be admiration in his eyes. 'You *do* want stopping power.'

'That's what it's all about.'

He turned away. He lifted a shotgun down from the wall rack. 'This is your Marlin 12-gauge pump-action, walnut stock and fore-end, all steel action and parts. A five-shot magazine with your standard shells, or four if you use the magnum shells.'

'Magnum?'

'They're three inches long, not two and three-quarters like your standard shells. High velocity buckshot loads.'

'I see.'

'Here, try this on for size.' He passed the shotgun to Pen. It was heavy. It felt dangerous. She liked it. But she didn't know what to do now that she was holding it. After peering down its sight ramp, she handed it back to the man.

'The perfect weapon for home defense,' he told her. Then, speaking softly as if sharing a secret, he said, 'You're in your home at night, somebody breaks in – nobody in the world is going to mess with you, you've

176

got one of these babies. Not even a guy with a handgun. He just has to know you've got it and he's gone. I mean *gone*.' A grin spread over the young man's face. 'Odds are, you won't even have to fire a shot. You shut your bedroom door. You hear him coming. You wait till he's just outside the door, then you . . . ' His arm jerked, snapping the pump-action back and forth with a snick and clatter of steel: 'He hears that and he knows what you've got. He's out of there. Best deterrent in the world – just the *sound* of it cocking.'

'Sounds good to me,' Pen said. 'How much is it?'

'Two-twenty-five, and I'll throw in a box of those magnums.'

'I'll take it.'

'Great.'

'How many shells to a box?'

'Five.'

'Give me an extra four boxes, then.'

'You'll want a cleaning kit.'

She nodded.

Driving home, Pen felt pleased with herself. She had really done it – really bought herself a shotgun.

She wished she'd had it Friday night. Things would've been different. No cord stretched across her doorway, for starters. No header into the wall, damn near splitting open her skull.

Wouldn't have panicked.

Wouldn't have stabbed Bodie.

It had cost a bundle, but it was worth every dime.

Besides, she told herself, just moving to a new apartment would've cost more than the shotgun.

And it would've been running away.

You don't run, now. You don't run ever.

You've got a 12-gauge pumpgun with magnum high-velocity buckshot loads.

You hold your ground.

CHAPTER FIFTEEN

They drove past Harrison's house. His Mercedes was still parked in the driveway. Joyce's Lincoln Continental was still at the curb on the next block.

'Why don't we go on back to your Dad's place?' Bodie suggested. 'We can pick up Pen's things and take them over to her.'

'Okay,' Melanie said.

Bodie didn't like it that Pen would be staying at her apartment. He would miss her. No more chances to be in the spa with her. No more sneaking into her room after Melanie was asleep.

Maybe they could talk her into returning.

Maybe *I* could. No help could be expected from Melanie on that. Remind Pen about the caller, the note left under her door, frighten her into coming back. If I push too hard, though, Melanie won't like it – might suspect I have something more on my mind than Pen's safety.

At least I'll have a chance to see her again when we take the suitcase over.

Maybe she's already changed her mind. She's had some time to cool off. With a little luck, maybe the caller struck again.

Bodie turned onto San Vicente and thought about calling her, himself. Use Joyce's phone. He'd have to get away from Melanie long enough . . .

What if Pen recognized his voice?

I want to come in your mouth.

I want to spread your legs and stick my cock up your . . .

I can't talk to her that way. Not a chance.

I could just call her up and say nothing. That'd spook her.

A rotten trick, but it might really be dangerous for her to stay alone in that apartment. The guy just might pay a visit.

Bodie wondered if she had reconnected her phones.

'Have you decided what to do about school?' Melanie asked.

He shook his head.

'You don't have to stay here, you know. All this . . . it's not your problem.'

'Trying to get rid of me?' he asked, and grinned at her.

'I just don't want you to feel that you *have* to stick around. You've got those classes to teach, and . . . There's no telling how long Dad might last.'

'He might surprise you and recover.'

'Yeah, sure,' she muttered.

'I'll stay a few days. Besides, I want to help you get to the bottom of this business with Joyce and Harrison.'

'That won't take long,' Melanie said.

'You've got a plan in mind?'

She shrugged.

'We could always beat Joyce with a rubber hose until she spills the beans,' he suggested.

'Good idea.'

He turned and drove slowly up the narrow lane to the house.

Inside, he said, 'Do you think we could eat before I keel over?'

'Sure.'

Melanie found hot dogs in the refrigerator, buns in the freezer. She put them in the microwave. While they heated, she filled two glasses with Pepsi and found an open bag of potato chips. Bodie ate some chips while he waited. They were a little stale, chewy and with a strange under-taste that reminded him of drinking water from a garden hose.

Melanie put the steaming buns and hot dogs on plates. Bodie lathered his buns with mustard. They sat at the kitchen table to eat.

'I guess you should pack up Pen's things when we're done.'

Melanie chewed.

'Want me to help?'

'You'd like that,' she said.

Indeed I would, he thought. 'I can wait down here.'

And call Pen?

And breathe.

It'd be for her own good.

But when they finished eating, it was Melanie who went to the telephone. She dialed 411.

'Who are you calling?'

'Directory assistance.'

'I *know* that.'

'Santa Monica,' she said into the receiver. 'Harrison Donner. On Twenty-first Street.'

Bodie's back stiffened.

Melanie pressed down on the cut-off button, let it up, and began to dial.

'What the hell are you doing?'

'You'll see.'

'That's what I'm afraid of.'

'Hello. Harrison? This is Melanie Conway . . . Just fine. Dad's come out of it . . . Yeah. I'm calling from the hospital. He's just come out of his coma . . . Yeah, isn't it great? Anyway, the thing is, he says he has to talk to you . . . No, I don't know what it's about but I guess it's pretty important. Could you come right over? . . . Great. See you in a few minutes.' She hung up.

Bodie stared at her.

'Let's get going,' she said.

'What . . . ?'

'We're gonna take a look at his Porsche,' she said.

'Good Christ, Mel.'

Pen sat on the sofa with the shotgun box heavy across her lap. She opened it and lifted out the weapon. The wood and steel were glossy in the light from the window at her back. There was a faint, pleasant odor of oil.

Though she'd never fired a shotgun, a boyfriend had taken her out to the hills near Valencia one Saturday and they'd had a fine time plinking cans with revolvers and his rifle. The rifle was a .30 caliber lever-action. She remembered the way it crashed her shoulder when she fired it. And the godawful noise.

The shotgun would probably be similar.

She raised it, pressed it firmly to her shoulder, and sighted along the narrow strip of steel that ran the length of the barrel to a bead on its muzzle.

Paul's rifle had had a telescopic sight. With that, she'd

hit the cans more often than not.

With this – if she ever actually needed to use it – her target wouldn't be more than twenty feet away. She couldn't possibly miss.

She worked the pump. It made a sliding snick-clack. Her finger curled around the trigger, but she didn't squeeze it.

The thing's not loaded, she told herself. It shouldn't be. But if it is, you'll blast your wall open.

She set the shotgun across her knees and spent the next few minutes studying its instruction booklet. Then she checked the chamber. Empty. She pulled the trigger. Click. Then she opened a box of cartridges and fed four of them into the magazine.

Leaving the weapon uncocked, she pressed a switch to activate the safety. She worked the switch back and forth a few times until she felt familiar with it.

All set, she thought.

She had already decided on the best place to keep it. She carried the shotgun into her bedroom, knelt beside her bed, and pushed it beneath the draping side of her coverlet.

Then she lay down on the bed.

Someone's here!

She threw herself off the mattress, snatched out the shotgun, swept its barrel high to clear the bed, and swung it toward the door.

'Pow,' she whispered.

She shook her head. She felt a little silly, like a kid playing soldier, but she returned the shotgun to its place. This time, she took off her shoes and got beneath the covers. She tried the maneuver again. The covers slowed her down, but not by much.

She practiced three more times, then stripped off the sheets and pillow cases and piled them on the floor.

Sunday. Laundry day.

You're home now, you're not running away, you might as well do your regular chores as if nothing has changed.

Bodie drove past Harrison's house. The Mercedes was no longer in the driveway.

'It worked,' Melanie said.

'Sure it worked. But what's he going to think when he gets to the hospital and finds out you lied?'

'It'll sure make him wonder, won't it?' Melanie didn't sound bothered.

'He'll wonder, all right.'

On the next block, Bodie found an empty stretch of curb where the Continental had been. He pulled over and parked.

'What time is it now?' Melanie asked as they met on the sidewalk.

Bodie checked his wristwatch. 'Twelve-forty.'

'Good.'

'It's kind of tight, if you ask me.' He hurried to stay with her.

'No problem. I phoned at twelve-thirty. Say it took five minutes for them to clear out. Should take them fifteen minutes to reach the hospital, at least five to find out they were tricked, and fifteen to get back here. And that's assuming they're real fast about it. So we should be all right till ten after one.'

'Right. So we check his garage and get away clean as a whistle. Only what the hell are you going to say when Harrison wants to know about your call?'

184

'That'll depend on what his Porsche looks like, won't it?'

'It damn well better be smashed up.'

The driveway gates beneath the porte cochere were seven feet high and locked. Bodie looked at the gate's mechanism. 'It opens by remote,' he said.

Melanie didn't hesitate. She hurried onto the porch, walked across it and boosted herself onto its low brick wall. Then she swung her legs over and dropped onto the driveway behind the gate.

With a groan of despair, Bodie did the same. He followed Melanie toward the garage.

This really bites, he thought. It's crazy.

The driveway was bordered by a high fence, but the neighbor's house was two stories. He could see its upstairs windows.

If someone happened to be looking down . . .

He imagined a police car swinging into the driveway. Oh man, oh man.

Behind Harrison's house, the narrow driveway flared out in front of the two-car garage.

Melanie tugged at the handle, trying to lift the garage door.

'That'll be on remote, too,' Bodie told her.

'You try.'

It's no use, he thought. But he pulled hard on the handle. The door didn't budge.

The door had no windows.

A walkway led around the corner of the garage. It led to a side door with glass panels.

Melanie cupped her hands against one of the windows and peered inside. 'There it is,' she said.

'How does it look?'

'Dark.' She tried the knob, shook her head, then turned toward Bodie.

'Let's give it up,' he said.

'Do you want to kick the door open?'

'Are you kidding? Christ, we're already trespassing. Do you want to end up in *jail*?'

She glanced sideways. Then her arm shot back. Bodie flinched, stunned and disbelieving, as her elbow rammed one of the lower windows. The glass blasted inward, shards clinking and shattering as they hit the garage floor.

'Mel!'

'I'm not giving up,' she said. Reaching through the broken window, she opened the door. 'You can wait here if you're scared.'

'Let's make it quick and get out of here.'

Inside, the garage was cool and dark. Bodie quickly shut the door.

Melanie flipped a switch. An overhead bulb came on. The Porsche, on the far side of the garage, gleamed fire-engine red.

Bodie glanced around as they walked toward it. Along the near wall were wash basins, a clothes washer and drier, shelves stacked with cardboard boxes. Closer to the garage door were rakes, a power lawn mower, shovels, bags of fertilizer. The stale, dank odor of the garage was mixed with the smells of fertilizer and gasoline.

Bodie shivered. It was the cool, closed-in air. It was *being* here.

God, this is insane.

Melanie stopped in front of the Porsche. Her eyes roamed its windshield and hood.

They looked fine to Bodie. He moved to her side as she crouched to inspect the headlights, grill and bumper.

'Not a scratch,' Bodie said.

'It just means he probably didn't use this car. He still could've stolen or rented one.'

'That'll be pretty tricky to prove.'

'God *damn* it!'

'Come on, let's get out of here.'

She followed Bodie to the door. After opening it, he twisted his hand on the inside knob to smear the fingerprints. Then he pulled it shut and did the same to the outside knob.

Melanie, well ahead of him, walked quickly to the back door of the house. She opened it and stood peering inside as Bodie ran to her.

'No!' he snapped. He grabbed her shoulder.

'What time is it?'

'Mel, no. We can't.'

'Come on, what time is it?'

He checked. 'Ten till one.'

'We've got at least fifteen minutes.'

'What do you want to do in there?' he asked. His voice was shaky, his heart thumping wildly.

'Just take a quick look around.'

'God, Mel.'

'There might be evidence. *I'm* going in.'

'No!'

'Let go of me.'

He dropped his hand from her shoulder.

He entered the kitchen behind Melanie. He felt sick. Breaking into the garage was bad enough. *This* was utter madness.

He realized he wanted badly to urinate.

If we're caught in here . . .

Why the hell didn't Harrison lock his back door?

Maybe someone's here!

Don't even think that.

The house was silent.

What if he's got a silent alarm?

'What if he's got a silent alarm?' Bodie whispered. 'It might be tied in directly to the police or a security patrol.'

Melanie ignored him.

'Two minutes,' he said. 'You've got two minutes, then we're out of here even if I have to drag you.'

They passed a bathroom. He could sure use it. He didn't dare.

He followed Melanie into a bedroom.

The covers and top sheet hung off the foot of the king-size bed. The pillows were mashed. Near the center of the blue satin bottom sheet was a wet place.

Melanie, leaning over, swiped at it with her forefinger. She rubbed her fingertip with the ball of her thumb, then sniffed it.

Bodie struggled not to gag.

She turned to him. A corner of her mouth twitched. 'Guess we know what *they've* been doing.'

Bodie grabbed her wrist. 'We're getting out of here *now.*'

'Okay, okay, don't pull.'

Letting go, he rushed ahead of her – out the bedroom, down a corridor to the living room, across the living room to the foyer. He opened the front door. Melanie stepped out. He twisted his hand on the knob, remembered that Melanie had left prints on the back door, and wondered if he should race through the house to wipe them off.

A patrol car might be racing toward the house right now.

He stepped outside and pulled the door shut by its edge.

They walked slowly over the flagstones to the sidewalk.

When they reached the end of the block, Bodie realized they were safe. He filled his lungs. His heart was still hammering. He still had to urinate, but the need wasn't as strong as before.

They climbed into the van. He pulled away. 'Thank God that's over,' he said.

'We didn't accomplish much.'

'We found out Harrison's car isn't smashed up. And I presume your sniff-test eliminated the possibility that their relationship was purely Platonic.'

'I wish I could be there when they get back from the hospital.'

'They'd no doubt have some very interesting comments about you.'

'That's right.'

'You should've thought about that before you made the call.'

'I did. My message wasn't just to get rid of them. It was to worry them, stir things up.'

'I'm sure you succeeded. And when Harrison finds the busted garage window, he'll really get stirred up. He'll know exactly who did it. And why.'

'That's right,' she said calmly.

'Maybe we'd better move in with Pen.'

'Oh, you'd like that.'

'What I *wouldn't* like is facing Harrison after what we did. He'll know what we were up to.'

'I don't care what he thinks.'

'Do you care what he might do?'

'He won't bring in the cops, if that's what you're afraid of.'

'If he's innocent . . .'

'He isn't innocent.'

'If he's *not* innocent, that's even worse.'

When they entered the house, Bodie hurried ahead of Melanie. 'My teeth are floating,' he said.

'Hey, I left my purse in the van.'

He tossed the keys to her and rushed into the bathroom. He swung the door shut, unzipped, aimed at the toilet and released the tight hold he'd been keeping for so long. He sighed. He counted the seconds until he was done. Sixty-three. No record. His record was ninety-eight seconds one night last year after walking back to his apartment from a beer drinking session at Sparkey's.

He zipped up, flushed the toilet, and washed his hands.

Melanie should wash *her* hands, he thought. She actually touched that stuff. And sniffed it.

The girl is definitely mad.

He dried his hands and left the bathroom.

Melanie didn't seem to be back yet. He went to the kitchen. The thoughts of Sparkey's had whetted his thirst. He found several bottles of Corona beer in the refrigerator. Taking one out, he felt a small tug of guilt.

It's not as if I'm stealing the thing, he told himself. Joyce said we should make ourselves at home.

He searched a drawer, found a bottle opener, and pried off the cap.

She might not be quite so generous, however, if she knew what we've been doing.

Hell, it isn't her beer, anyway. It's Whit's. He's the breadwinner around here, the beer-winner. He certainly wouldn't begrudge me a brew. Look what I've gone through on his behalf.

Bodie took a drink. It was cold and very good. He sat at the table and drank some more.

Poor sod, he thought. They certainly screwed you over, Whit. Your law partner and your dear wife. You'll have some nasty surprises if you ever come to.

But did they run you down? Ah, there's the question.

Nice to make them pay, if they did.

And how do we go about that? Harrison, the slime, was smart enough not to use his own car. So where do we go from here?

I guess we don't *have* to go anywhere from here. Melanie has already hurled the crapola into the fan. We only have to sit back and watch where it flies.

Perchance to duck.

Taking her one long time to fetch her purse.

Bodie suddenly knew why.

He set down his beer bottle and sighed.

'Melanie,' he muttered. 'Oh, for Christsake.'

He walked out to the street. His van was gone, all right.

CHAPTER SIXTEEN

Pen carried her laundry basket down the stairs and past the pool in the courtyard. The apartment building was silent and she saw no one. A typical Sunday afternoon. The tenants were either gone, or hidden away in their rooms.

She entered the short passageway between the courtyard and alley. The utility room's door stood ajar. It was supposed to be kept locked to prevent vandalism and unauthorized use of the machines. Alicia, from the corner apartment, had told her once about walking in on a shopping cart lady doing her wash – a filthy woman who screeched and jibbered like a lunatic when Alicia confronted her.

Pen set down her basket and swung the door wide. She peered into the gloom. Seeing no one, she reached around the corner and turned on the overhead light. The room looked deserted. The two washers and two driers were silent. She picked up her basket and entered.

The washing machines were top loaders. She opened each and looked inside. They were empty.

My lucky day, she thought.

She had separated her laundry before coming down. Bending over her basket, she lifted out a bundle of white fabrics. A sock fell to the floor on its way to the machine. She squatted to pick it up.

'Beautiful ass.'

She flinched. Her head snapped around so fast she hurt her neck.

In the doorway stood Manny Hammond from 202. He'd played football at USC and usually wore a jersey to remind everyone of his glory days. This afternoon, he wasn't wearing the jersey – just a pair of faded red gym shorts and thongs. The shorts were extremely tight.

'You startled me,' Pen said. She picked up the sock and dropped it into the machine.

'You gotta loosen up.'

'I'll keep that in mind.'

Damn it, where'd he come from?

'Aren't you missing a game on TV?' she asked.

'Why would I watch a game when I can watch you?' He leaned against the doorframe, crossed his ankles, and folded his arms across his massive chest.

With a sigh, Pen crouched to pick up her bleach and detergent. She could feel his gaze. She straightened up. Her hand trembled as she filled the measuring cup.

'Gotcha rattled, huh?'

'You didn't have to sneak up on me like that,' she said, keeping her eyes away from him as she dumped the detergent, then the bleach, into the washer. She closed the lid. She turned on the machine and heard water rush in.

'Why don't you toss in the rest?' he suggested, grinning. 'That stuff you got on looks like it could use a good wash.'

'Some other time.'

'No time like the present. Come on, honey, it's laundry day. Get *everything* good and clean.'

She glared at him, heat spreading over her face. 'Why don't you take a hike, Manny?'

He grinned. 'Bet you say that to all the guys.'

'Just the jerks.' Embarrassed and angry, she picked up her basket and tumbled its contents into the other washer.

'You aren't a dyke, are you?'

'Shut the hell up.'

'I mean, 'cause it'd be a shame, a piece like you. A real loss to mankind.'

She didn't bother with the measuring cup. She shook the detergent into the machine and set the basket aside.

'Yeah, I guess you are a dyke.'

She slammed the lid down and whirled around. 'I'm not a lesbian and you're a piece of shit.'

He looked amused. 'That's no way to talk. Glad to hear you're not a dyke, though. So what is it, you just frigid?'

Seething, Pen turned away. She started the washer and picked up her empty basket. With a shaking hand, she set the detergent and bleach inside it. She held the basket with its edge against her belly and faced Manny.

'Not leaving already, are you?' He stepped into the middle of the doorway.

'Please move,' she said.

'When was the last time you had a good fucking?'

'Get out of my way.'

'That's gotta be your problem, you know. And I'm just the guy to help you with that.' He lowered a hand and patted the front of his shorts. It was obvious from the bulge that he had an erection. 'I'm well equipped to handle that problem for you, honey. Wanta see?' Grinning, he drew the shorts down a fraction.

'Stop it.'

'Tell you what. Why don't you toss these in with your stuff? *All* your stuff. Know what I mean? And I'll show you what it's like to . . .'

'Move,' Pen said and walked toward him, the basket braced in front of her.

'Hey, now. This is your big chance.'

'Move!' she yelled in his face.

He flinched and stepped aside.

Pen walked past him, half expecting to be grabbed.

He muttered, 'Cunt.' But he kept his hands to himself.

She hurried through the doorway, out of the shadowed area and into the sunlight. She was trembling and she had a hard time catching her breath. At the foot of the stairs, she looked back.

Manny, standing near the corner of the pool, raised his middle finger and rotated it.

Pen hurried up the stairs, along the balcony to her apartment, and unlocked the door. Inside, she leaned against the door. Her chest hurt. She panted for air.

The filthy bastard.

When was the last time you had a good fucking?

I wanted to talk to you about my big hard cock and your hot juicy cunt.

Her legs folded. She slid down the door and stared over the tops of her upraised knees.

Manny?

The voice wasn't quite the same, but he could've disguised it when he made the calls.

Manny.

Over in 202. With a clear view of her front door and windows. Knowing who she saw and when. Knowing when she was here and when she was gone and when she went to bed.

Knowing when she was alone.

Manny.

Melanie must have made it.

She would've been back around one-twenty, no later than one-thirty, if she'd reached Harrison's house, found his Mercedes in the driveway, and given up.

So she must've beaten him back to the house, snuck in the back door, and hidden herself. In the closet, or maybe under the bed.

Bodie looked at his wristwatch. Two minutes had passed since the last time. It was now five till two.

If Melanie had turned back, she would've been here half an hour ago.

He stared at the empty beer bottle as he turned it slowly in his fingers.

And what, perchance, do *I* do about this curious turn of events?

For starters, have another beer.

Bodie got up and took another Corona from the refrigerator. He opened it. This one, he took outside. He stretched out on the lounger. The mild breeze kept the sun from feeling too hot. Closing his eyes, he pictured the way Pen had looked this morning when she was on the same lounger.

He took a drink.

What was she doing right now? Had she gone out to find a new apartment? Was she wondering why they hadn't shown up yet with her things?

Hey, I'm stranded here. I'd bring the stuff to you if I could. I'd rather, by far, be there than here.

As soon as Melanie gets back.

That could be a while.

She's stuck there until she has a chance to sneak out. They might, of course, catch her.

I could walk over there. Wouldn't take more than half an hour.

Or phone Pen. She has a car. We drive over to Harrison's and then what? Knock on the door and ask for Melanie? Real cute.

But the thought of phoning Pen made his heart quicken. He could tell her about Melanie. They could discuss the situation. Maybe she would even come over. They'd be alone in the house. Oh, come off it, he told himself.

I'd better call her.

He set his beer bottle on the table and went into the house. He dialed Directory Assistance, gave Pen's city and name to the live operator and heard a computer voice give the number. He wrote it on a wall pad, and dialed.

He let the phone ring ten times, then hung up.

He went outside again and sat in the sun. He drank some beer and put the bottle down. He shut his eyes.

So much for having a visitor.

He could call a cab and go over to Pen's place. There's a thought.

Hi. Just dropped by to see how you're doing. Where's Melanie? Oh, she's hiding in Harrison's house, gathering clues.

★ ★ ★

Pen, finding herself incapable of reading after her return from the laundry room, had turned on the television and sat gazing at its screen, her mind preoccupied with swirling, disjointed thoughts about her encounter with Manny, the calls, her father, the shotgun, whether she should move to a new apartment after all, Joyce and Harrison betraying her father and possibly trying to murder him, Melanie's 'vision', Bodie in her bedroom last night, Melanie's jealousy.

Then had come the blare of her timer's alarm, and the need to go down again to the laundry room.

The shotgun was out of the question, so she'd taken a steak knife along, wrapped in a towel beneath her arm.

Transferring her damp laundry from the washing machines to a drier, she had expected Manny to sneak in, maybe even assault her this time, but he never showed up.

Now she was waiting again. In a few minutes, the drying cycle would finish and she would have to return once more. The towel with the knife inside lay on the table in front of her. She wouldn't go down there without it.

Maybe Manny was all talk. He hadn't *tried* anything.

Maybe I should forget the knife.

That was a hard-on in his shorts, and he wanted to stick it in me. He made that pretty damn obvious. If I'd shown the slightest interest, he would've had me on the floor and . . .

Manny isn't the caller.

Manny didn't slip the note under the door.

Manny confronts you in the laundry room, half naked, and tries to bully you into putting out. He's not the type to make anonymous telephone calls.

Pen slumped back on the sofa, frowning at the television screen.

There had been, she realized, a certain comfort in believing it was Manny. He was real and known, an enemy to protect herself against. Not a faceless presence, not a stranger out there somewhere, wanting her. Better Manny with his smirk and his pecs and his bulging gym shorts than . . .

She jerked rigid at the sudden jangle of a bell.

I want to come . . .

Not the phone, the timer.

She stood up, patted the pocket of her shorts to make sure she had her keys, then picked up the towel with the knife inside. She clamped the towel under her arm, lifted the laundry basket, and left her apartment.

Manny's curtains were open. She didn't see him at any of the windows, but that proved nothing; he could be standing back a few feet, concealed in the dimness of a room, watching her undetected.

She hurried along the balcony and down the stairs. Walking past the pool, she heard faint music from one of the apartments. A sign of life. She found that reassuring.

She had left the laundry room locked, and it was locked when she reached it.

Manny, of course, would have a key of his own.

Setting the basket down, Pen dug into her pocket and took out the keys. She unlocked the door, swung it open, and peered inside.

Nobody there.

She flicked the light on. Then she toed her basket through the doorway and shut herself inside.

The drier still rumbled.

She had set it for an hour.

It should've stopped five minutes ago.

Picking up her basket, she stepped over to the machine. The timer dial showed that it still had three or four minutes to run.

I must've set my kitchen timer wrong, Pen told herself.

Either that, or someone had been in here and fooled with the dial on the drier.

I am so damn paranoid. I've gotta cut it out.

Bending over, she curled her fingers around the handle of the drier's door. Suddenly, she was afraid to open it.

Anything might be inside.

How about a dead, mangled cat? A note tied to its tail: 'How about a little pussy?'

You're losing your grip, Pen old pal.

She forced herself to open the door. The machine went silent and her breath snagged as the corner of a sheet flopped out.

Crouching, she looked into the dark drum. Nothing seemed to be in there except her laundry.

She reached inside and clutched warm fabric with both hands.

Tiny, needle-sharp teeth didn't nip her fingers.

Of course not.

There's nothing wrong except in my mind.

She lifted out a bundle of laundry and dropped it into the basket.

Shit, she thought as she reached in again. Plenty is wrong. The whole damn world is caving in.

But nobody left me a gift.

You hope.

Quickly, she finished unloading the machine.

She pressed the towel-wrapped knife into the soft pile of her laundry, lifted her basket, and hurried from the room.

Half the pool was in shadow, but she walked in sunlight and shook her head.

A dead cat in the drier.

Hungry rats?

God Almighty, things are bad enough without me *inventing* nasty little surprises.

She reached the bottom of the stairs.

Almost safe.

Climbing them, she imagined Manny staring out his window at her.

He's the least of my worries, she told herself. He's a creep, but he isn't the caller. I can handle him.

She was tempted to look around as she walked along the balcony, but if he was watching she really didn't want to know. She unlocked her door, entered, and nudged it shut with her rump.

Safe.

The door was locked behind her. The phones were disconnected. The shotgun was under the bed.

No one can touch me now.

Pen took a few long, slow breaths, trying to calm herself, then carried the basket into her bedroom and upended it on the mattress.

She began to sort her laundry: sheets and pillow cases in one pile, another pile for clothes that would need to be ironed, a third for undergarments. When the sorting was done, she carried her brassieres two at a time to her dresser and stacked them neatly in a drawer. Then she folded her panties. Except for the tattered white pair she'd worn to bed Friday night, the panties were new and skimpy and brightly colored – red, blue, pink, lavender.

Her black panties weren't there.

She knew she had worn them.

So where are they?

She searched the two remaining piles, thinking the black panties may have been caught in a blouse or sheet. They weren't there. She checked the basket, the floor beside the bed. Then she looked once more through the laundry, more carefully this time, lifting each article and shaking it, expecting the panties to flutter out.

They didn't.

'Goddamn it,' she whispered.

Her chest felt tight.

She must have left the panties inside the washer or drier. They were small and dark, easily missed when removing the rest of her clothes from the machines. Normally, she ran her hands around the metal to make certain nothing was left behind. But she hadn't done that today. Too preoccupied. Too careless. Too eager to get back to the safety of her room.

Good move.

She didn't want to go back down. She wanted to stay right here, locked in with the phones unplugged, maybe have a glass of wine and take a long, hot bath.

Better get the panties before someone else does.

She hurried out and was halfway down the stairs when she realized she had forgotten her knife.

She quickly patted the pocket of her shorts and didn't feel the bulge of her keys. Her heart galloped. She slapped her other front pocket. She *never* kept them in that pocket, but that's exactly where they were.

Thank God.

Really great if you'd locked yourself out.

Striding alongside the pool, she pulled the key case from her pocket and had the proper key out, ready in her hand, by the time she reached the laundry room.

Inside, she bent over the washing machine to peer inside, felt between the wings of its agitator and ran her fingers under the top in case the panties were clinging there. She crouched in front of the drier and swept a hand around the inside drum. She even checked the washing machine she had used for her white laundry. Then she searched the floor.

The panties were definitely gone.

Someone had come in and taken them.

Manny? What if it *wasn't* Manny?

Tight and cold inside, Pen hurried back to her apartment. She leaned against the door, shaking.

Calm down.

Calm down, *hell*. Someone took my panties – wanted them and stole them and *has* them.

Watched me come and go from the laundry room.

I've got to get out of here.

CHAPTER SEVENTEEN

After waking up, Bodie wandered over to the gazebo. He slipped his fingers through the cool water of the spa, and remembered last night in the swirling heat, Pen so beautiful, Melanie topless and flirting and later bottomless as well, so urgently striving to keep Bodie's attention from her sister.

Where is she now? Crouched in Harrison's closet? Hiding beneath his bed? Maybe caught.

He supposed he should do something about it, but what?

Stepping around the wooden platform, he found the controls. Turn a knob, flick a switch, he could probably get the water hot.

Go ahead.

He did.

The machinery hummed and the clear surface stirred a bit. Lowering an arm into the water, he felt along the side until a warm current pushed at his wrist.

He returned to the house. Upstairs, he found the bikini trunks he'd worn last night and put them on. With a towel draping his bare shoulders, he went down to the kitchen. He took a beer from the refrigerator, opened it, and walked out to the spa. He climbed in.

The water made him shiver, but he sat in front of the lead-in pipe. The water from there blew warm against his back.

He was sitting where Pen had sat last night.

Closing his eyes, he pictured the way she had looked – her face shimmering in the red glow, her blond hair the color of a harvest moon, a few damp locks clinging to her forehead, the shiny satin of her wet shoulders, the way the water rippled over the tops of her breasts.

The water felt warmer, now.

'Hi.'

Bodie's eyes flew open. For a moment, he couldn't believe that Pen was standing there. But she was, oh yes. 'Hello,' he said.

'I didn't think anyone was here.'

'Just me.'

'Where's everyone else?'

'Joyce is still . . . out.'

Pen nodded, an angry look flaring for a moment in her eyes.

'Melanie's sort of abandoned me here.'

She climbed up, left her sandals on the platform, and sat on the edge with her legs hanging in the water. 'It could be hotter.'

He shrugged. His heart was thudding.

'I freaked out a little bit, staying over there alone.'

'I called you earlier.'

Her eyebrows lifted.

'I guess you weren't home.'

'I haven't plugged in my phones. Not yet. Who knows, maybe never.'

'That bad, huh?'

'I know it's silly.'

'I don't think so.'

'Thanks. What did you call about?'

'Why don't you put on your suit and come in?'

'Is that why you called?'

'I called about Melanie.'

Pen nodded for him to go on.

'We went back to Harrison's. First, we went to the police station, but we didn't find out much. Then we went to Harrison's. He and Joyce were still there so we came back to the house and Melanie phoned him – said your father had come out of his coma and wanted to see him.'

'Are you serious?'

'It worked. We sped back there and he was gone, so we broke into his garage for a peek at the Porsche.'

'What do you mean, you broke in?'

'Melanie smashed a window.'

'Jesus H. Christ, and you *let* her do all this stuff?' Pen didn't sound angry at him, just perplexed.

'Well, not exactly. I didn't know what she was up to. When she phoned Harrison with that wild story, I had no idea what she was going to say till it was out of her mouth. Even then, I couldn't believe my ears. The same with breaking the garage window – she just *did* it. I was ready to call it quits, and the next thing I know she's driving her elbow through the glass.'

'You were supposed to stop her from doing crazy stuff. That was the whole idea behind investigating Harrison.'

'Well, part of the idea was to look for evidence.'

'Did you find any?'

'The Porsche looked fine. If he's the one who hit your father, he must've used a different car.'

She nodded. 'It figures. He's too smart to use his own car for something like that.' Leaning back, she braced herself up with stiff arms. She rolled her head around as if trying to work kinks out of her neck muscles. Her untucked plaid blouse had slipped upward, showing a triangle of skin between the last button and the waist of her shorts. At the top of the opening was her navel. A little more belly was exposed as she raised one hand to rub the back of her neck.

'Headache?' Bodie asked.

'Not yet. Just a stiff neck. I've been a little tense.'

'The hot water would do it good.'

'You're determined to get me in there.' She smiled slightly as she said it.

Bodie smiled back. 'Nah.'

'All we'd need is for Melanie to come back and find me in there with you.'

'Not much worse than if she'd found me in your bedroom last night.'

'True. But I don't think we should press our luck. Where *is* she, anyway?'

'I'm not exactly sure.'

'Where do you *think* she is?'

'In Harrison's house, spying on the suspects.'

'*What?*'

'I don't know for sure.'

Pen sat up straight. Frowning, she leaned forward a bit as if to hear him better. Her hands settled on her thighs. 'She's *in* his house?'

'That's my guess. When we were there before, the back door was unlocked.'

'So she went in, of course.'

'We both did.'

'Good God.'

Bodie shrugged. 'I figured, what the hell, we'd already broken into the guy's garage.'

'So did you find anything in the house?'

He ran a few euphemisms through his mind. Semen by any other name . . . 'There was some indication that they had, indeed, been making the beast with two backs.'

Pen blushed. She said, 'You're so literary.'

'A regular Robert B. Parker.'

'Nothing . . . more incriminating?'

'We didn't linger. I dragged Melanie out of there as fast as I could.'

'But you think she's there now?'

'She wasn't exactly eager to leave. We no sooner got back here than she took off in my van. That was around one o'clock. She's been gone ever since.'

'That was almost *three* hours ago!'

'I know, I know. And I'm just sitting here.' Reaching back, he picked up his bottle of beer and took a drink. 'Want some?'

'Bodie!'

'Have *you* got any ideas?'

She reached out a hand. Bodie stood. She glanced down his body and quickly away as he waded forward a step and gave her the bottle. She drank from it, head tilted back and eyes sliding shut for a moment. She handed the bottle back to him. 'Thanks.' She rubbed her hand on her bare thigh. It left a moist smear.

Bodie sat down, the hot water climbing to his shoulders. He raised the bottle to his mouth, felt it against his lips. Seconds ago, Pen's lips had been here.

'That stupid damn idiot,' she muttered. She shook her

209

head. 'Sorry. I shouldn't be . . . What were you planning to do, just wait around and hope she comes back?'

'Something like that. If she is in Harrison's house, she's hiding somewhere. So she might not be able to just take off when she wants to. Basically, she's stuck there until she can find a chance to sneak out. Even when the chance *comes*, she might not take it. I mean, the girl has to be pretty desperate or she wouldn't have gone in there in the first place. She probably figures this is her last, best chance to get the goods on those two.'

Pen was nodding. She understood and agreed. 'On the other hand, maybe she's been caught.'

'I know.'

'What if they *are* the ones who . . . did this to Dad?'

'Then Melanie's in plenty of trouble.'

'Or worse.'

'But if they haven't caught her and we go charging to the rescue . . .'

'We can't just *wait*.'

'We don't want to blow it for Melanie, though. She'll never forgive us if we rush in and pull her out before she's had a chance to hear something really incriminating.'

'I can live without her forgiveness. I've been getting along without it this long.' Pen's eyes took on a frantic look. 'He's got a *gun*, Bodie. Harrison has a gun.'

'All the more reason not to charge in on him.'

'I bought a shotgun today.'

'Oh, great. We can have a shoot-out.'

'He might *kill* her. I know him. He's capable of . . . almost anything.'

'Okay. We'll do something. I don't know what, but . . .'

210

'We have to.'

Bodie took a drink of beer and stood up. Pen continued to sit on the edge, right beside the steps. Turning around, he reached over the side and turned off the heat.

'Maybe we can come up with a plan,' she said, still sitting there.

Bodie waded toward the steps.

'I don't know what,' she said.

'We'll think of something.' His throat felt tight. He stared straight ahead so he wouldn't have to see where she was looking as he climbed the first step and felt the water level slide down to his thighs. The bikini trunks hugged him.

Pen stood up. Bodie, pulling the towel off his shoulders, offered it to her. 'Want to dry your legs?' he asked.

'Thanks.' She took it and bent over, her hair swaying at the sides of her face as she ran the towel down her legs. She gave it back to him. She stepped into her sandals.

'Would you hold this for me?' he asked.

She took the beer bottle. As he dried himself, she moved past him and stepped down from the platform.

Looking up at him, she said, 'We need a way to trick them out of the house.'

'Like phoning to say your father wants to see them?'

'Oh, sure. Right.' Her glance flicked downward and quickly aside. She squinted as if peering at something in the bushes. 'I don't know,' she said, and took a sip of beer.

Bodie, done with drying, wrapped the towel around his waist and climbed down the stairs.

Pen stepped backward. She followed him toward the

211

house. 'You know,' she said, 'Melanie might not even *be* at Harrison's house. She could've gone anywhere. I mean, she didn't come out and tell you where she was going?'

'No, she didn't.'

'Before we do anything else, we should drive by and see if your van's in the neighborhood.'

'I'd like to take a quick shower first.'

'Go on ahead.'

He pulled open the sliding glass door, stepped aside to let Pen pass, and entered the kitchen behind her. The seat of her white shorts was soiled a little. He let his gaze glide down the backs of her legs. 'I'll hurry,' he said.

Pen stayed in the kitchen and Bodie went upstairs. He tried not to think about the fact that he was alone in the house with her, but he could think of little else. His insides felt quivery.

Nothing's going to happen, he told himself. Don't get excited. You wouldn't dare, and she wouldn't go for it. Neither of you wants to stab Melanie in the back.

But he left the bathroom door unlocked. He peeled the swimsuit down his legs and wrung it out over the sink.

Pen's white bikini was hanging over the top runner of the shower door. It would get wet if he left it there. He pulled it down. Saw her wearing it in the hot spa. Saw her taking it off here in the bathroom. Tempted to caress the garment, he quickly draped it over a towel rod.

He showered. He imagined Pen sneaking in and sliding back the frosted door. She was naked. *Mind if I join you?*

Don't torment yourself, he thought. She won't.

She didn't.

When he was done, he walked down the hallway to the bedroom with a towel wrapped around his waist. Quickly, he dressed and went downstairs. He found Pen on the living room sofa, leaning back with her legs stretched out. Her purse was beside her, its strap over her shoulder. 'Ready to go?' she asked.

'I guess so.'

They went out to her car. Bodie, in the passenger seat, watched her climb in and start the engine. She turned the car around. On San Vicente, she lowered the visor to shield her eyes from the late afternoon sun. Below the visor's shadow, soft down on her cheek and over her lip shone golden in the sunlight.

She looked at him.

'Just thinking,' he said.

'Oh?'

He hadn't been thinking about anything, just admiring Pen's face. 'What if Melanie's not there?' he asked.

'I guess that would be quite a relief.'

'If she's not there, where is she?'

Pen shook her head slightly. 'More to the point, what'll we do if she *is* there?'

'Who knows?'

'I wish she'd just stayed in Phoenix.'

The words hurt Bodie.

'I don't mean you,' Pen said as if she knew.

'I brought her out.'

'You were just being gallant. I bet you're sorry now, though, aren't you? Got yourself right in the middle of a real mess.'

'It has its compensations.'

Pen kept her eyes on the road.

I shouldn't have said that, Bodie thought. Lord!

'Yeah,' Pen said. 'I heard Melanie compensating you last night. Thin walls.'

For a moment, Bodie didn't understand. Then he realized she had heard them in bed.

That wasn't what I meant by compensation, Bodie thought.

It's what she *thinks* I meant.

Good thing.

My God, she heard us screwing.

'I guess we should've turned the radio higher,' he said.

'She probably wanted me to hear,' Pen said. 'The way she was acting last night, it wouldn't surprise me.'

'Wanted you to hear?'

'So I'd know she had something I didn't.'

Me?

She's talking about me, here.

'Trying to make you jealous?' he heard himself ask. His voice sounded distant.

'It wouldn't surprise me,' she said.

'*Were* you?' He couldn't believe he had asked that.

'Jealous?' She glanced at him. 'What do you think?'

He swallowed. 'I wouldn't . . . hazard a guess.'

'And I won't hazard an answer. If I say yes I was jealous, I'm as much as asking you to put moves on me, and I couldn't do that to Melanie. If I say no, you're insulted.'

'Good point.'

'Let's just stay friends.'

'Good idea.'

'Better keep an eye out for your van.'

He realized that she had just turned onto Harrison's street.

The Mercedes was parked in his driveway. Joyce's Continental was at the curb in front of his house.

'Interesting,' Pen said. 'She didn't bother parking up the road this time.'

'Their secret love's no big secret any more.'

'Mel's call saw to that.' Pen turned the corner. 'I wonder what they had to say about *that*.'

'Whatever it was, Melanie probably heard some of it.'

'If she's there.'

They found Bodie's van parked on the opposite side of the block.

Pen pulled in behind it. Bodie got out. He peered through its windows and returned to the car. 'She's not inside.'

'She really is in Harrison's place.'

'Looks that way.'

'Any bright ideas?' Pen asked.

'Leave her there.'

'Brilliant.'

'I'm serious. She got herself in there, and I suspect she's perfectly capable of extricating herself when the time is right.'

'What if she's not? What if they already have her? What if they came back from the hospital and *said* things, talked about running down Dad, and then caught Melanie?'

'Then the situation takes a quantum leap into Shitsville. But I'd prefer to believe that hasn't happened. For all we know right now, those two had nothing to do with the hit-and-run. They aren't going to . . . get violent with Melanie . . . just because she knows they're having an affair.'

Pen looked at him. Her eyes were somber. 'We can't

just leave her there,' she said in a whisper.

'I know.'

'But you said . . .'

'Just trying to talk us out of doing something stupid.'

'Like what?'

'I'll go in and get her. Alone. You stay in the car and get the cops if we don't come out in five minutes.'

'That's your plan?' Pen asked.

'Great, huh? Simple and direct.'

'He's got a gun.'

'He won't shoot anyone. Not with you waiting.'

'I don't like it.'

'What's your plan?'

'Why don't *I* go in and you wait in the car?'

'I can think of one excellent reason.'

'What?'

'Because I won't let you.'

CHAPTER EIGHTEEN

Pen steered her car into the driveway and parked behind Harrison's Mercedes. She kept the engine running.

Bodie took off his wristwatch. Handing it to Pen, he said, 'Five minutes.'

'I'm frightened.'

'Not me.'

'Yeah, I can tell.'

'It's been nice knowing you.'

'Very funny.'

Bodie climbed from the car. He felt as if his breath had been knocked out. His legs seemed ready to collapse, but he forced them to move, one after the other, until he reached the front door.

He pressed the doorbell. Chimes rang inside the house.

He struggled to breathe.

He wondered whether Pen had started the five-minute countdown when he left the car, or planned to wait until he was inside.

He reached up to ring the bell again, and the door opened.

Harrison arched a single eyebrow. He wore a blue warm-up suit with white stripes down the sleeves and legs, and he didn't hold a gun. 'What have we here?' he asked.

'Sorry to bother you,' Bodie said, trying without success to keep his voice from shaking.

Harrison leaned sideways and looked past him. 'One accounted for. Where's the other sister, trapped in a telephone booth?'

'Could I come in and talk to you?'

He stepped back to let Bodie enter. 'I take it you've been selected to represent the grievance committee.'

'Something like that.'

He shut the door behind Bodie. 'What's on your mind, punching me out?'

'No, thanks.'

'Then what?'

'We know about you and Joyce.'

Harrison smirked. 'That's rather obvious at this point. You're way off base, however, if you think I had anything to do with running down Whit.'

Bodie's stomach dropped. 'I don't know what you're . . .'

'Oh, you weren't in on the cute little telephone call or breaking into my garage?'

Bodie's eyes caught movement off to the side. Turning his head, he saw Joyce lean against the entryway from the hall. She wore a bathrobe that was too large for her. The sleeves were rolled above her wrists. 'When I get back to my house tonight,' she said, 'I want all three of you gone. I never want to see any of you again.'

'Fine,' Bodie said.

'Who's going to pay for the garage window?' Harrison asked.

'Melanie,' Bodie said, and wondered if his voice was loud enough to carry to her hiding place.

'I knew it,' Joyce said.

'That crazy little bitch.'

'Listen, mister . . .'

'No, you listen. We don't appreciate being the targets of this lunatic vendetta, and the courts have remedies . . .'

'MELANIE!'

'What the fuck are . . . ?'

'MELANIE, GET OUT HERE!!!'

Joyce clenched her robe tight and stood there rigid, a look of alarm on her face.

'Is she *here*?' Harrison raged. 'Goddamn it, if that little bitch is in my house . . . !'

Bodie stepped past him.

Harrison clamped his shoulder. Whirling, Bodie knocked the hand away. 'We'll be out of here in a . . .'

Joyce shrieked. Harrison's glower changed to shock. Bodie spun around in time to see Joyce slam against the floor with Melanie on her back. Straddling her rump, Melanie tore at her hair, jerked her head up and smacked a fist into her cheek.

Bodie, rammed aside by Harrison, fell against a chair. He shoved himself up. As he raced across the room, he saw Harrison grab Melanie by the neck of her sweatshirt and try to hoist her off Joyce. The loose, sleeveless sweatshirt flew up her body, covered her face, caught her arms for an instant, then released her. Harrison staggered off balance, waving the empty shirt at the ceiling. He landed on his rump.

Melanie, naked to the waist, punched the back of Joyce's neck.

Harrison was getting up.

Bodie, ignoring him, grabbed Melanie's arm and dragged her off Joyce.

'Leave go!' Melanie yelled.

'Come on!'

She stumbled along on her knees, pulled by Bodie.

'Everybody calm down!' he shouted. 'We're getting out of here. We're going.'

'Crazy bitch!' Joyce shrieked.

Harrison moved in.

'Leave her *alone*!' Bodie warned.

Harrison kicked. The toe of his running shoe smashed Melanie in the ribs just below her armpit. Her hand jerked from Bodie's grip. She tumbled, her face striking the edge of a table. Bodie snatched her sweatshirt. Harrison, hanging onto it, lunged against him. Hooking an arm around Harrison's head, he twisted and flung the man over his hip. As Harrison hit the floor, Bodie dropped and drove a knee into his belly. Harrison's breath blasted out. 'I told you to *leave her alone*!' He tore the sweatshirt from Harrison's grip.

Melanie was on her knees, hanging onto the table with one hand while she pressed the other hand to her cheek. Blood spilled out between her fingers. Her side had a red scuff from the kick.

Crouching, Bodie gave her the sweatshirt. He glimpsed a small gash over her cheekbone before she pressed the sweatshirt against it. 'Come on,' he said gently. 'Let's get going.' Hands beneath her armpits, he lifted her. She was very heavy for a moment. Then her legs were supporting her weight. He steered her toward the door.

'I'm gonna . . . get the cops on you!' Harrison yelled.

Bodie looked around. The man was curled on his side, hugging his stomach. 'Go ahead, asshole. But you'd better have a good alibi for Friday night.'

'Fuckin' lunatics! Both of you!'

Joyce, on her knees, clutched her robe shut with both hands and stared through strings of hanging hair. She said nothing.

Melanie got the door open.

Bodie, with an arm around her back, helped her down the porch stairs. It was still daylight and the sweatshirt was pressed to her face, but her breasts were hidden beneath her arms.

Pen, looking stunned, rushed around her car and opened the rear door. 'My God, what happened?'

'Let's get out of here.'

Melanie ducked into the back seat. Bodie followed her. Pen ran to the other side and flung herself behind the steering wheel. She shot her car out of the driveway and sped forward. 'Where to?'

'My van.'

'Should we take her to emergency? What happened to her?'

'A small cut below the eye. She fell against a table.'

'I'm okay,' Melanie muttered.

'We'd better take her to emergency,' Pen said.

'*I'm all right.*'

'I have a first aid kit in my van.' Bodie pulled her down so that her head rested on his lap. 'Let me take a look.' He lifted the sweatshirt away from her cheek. The cut was half an inch below her left eye. Blood filled the wound and began leaking out. He dabbed it away.

'What went on in there?' Pen asked. 'Was there a fight?'

'A wee scuffle.'

'You sure nailed Harrison,' Melanie said, smiling up at him.

'Why don't you put this on?'

Sitting up, she slipped her arms through the sleeve holes. She drew the sweatshirt down over her head, then lifted the bottom of it and held the cloth against her wound. Her left breast stuck out like someone peering from under a stage curtain. It had a smear of blood beside the nipple.

'Did you find out anything?' Pen asked.

'They know we suspect them,' Bodie said.

'What about you, Mel? Where were you all afternoon?'

'In the bedroom. Under the bed.'

'What did you hear?'

'They did it, all right.'

'Hit Dad?'

'Yeah.'

'What did they say?'

'Not now. I don't . . . feel too good.'

'She caught a kick in the ribs, too.'

Pen stopped behind the van. Melanie gave the keys to Bodie, and he opened the rear doors. He was glad to see that she had lowered her sweatshirt before leaving the car.

All three climbed into the van. As Bodie shut the doors, Melanie lay down on the sleeping bag. She raised the blood-spotted sweatshirt to her cheek.

Bodie took out his first aid kit. He spread disinfectant

cream on her cut, then applied a bandage.

Pen, crouching at his side, asked, 'Now what should we do? Go to the police?'

'I don't think so,' Bodie said. 'Melanie was in the house illegally. And she's the one who started the fight. I imagine we could both wind up charged with all kinds of shit.'

'Great,' Pen muttered.

'As it is, Harrison threatened to call the cops on us. I'm not sure he has the guts to go through with it, though.'

She looked down at Melanie. 'Did you actually hear him admit to hitting Dad with the car?'

'Yes.'

'What about Joyce?'

'She was in on it. They did it together, just like I thought.'

CHAPTER NINETEEN

Pen finished packing and waited in the living room. Bodie came down a few minutes later, carrying luggage. Melanie was behind him. She had washed the blood from her face and changed into a clean white blouse.

'Can we stay with you?' Melanie asked.

'Of course,' Pen said. She looked at Bodie. 'Are you sure you shouldn't drive back tonight?'

'Well . . .'

'I'm not eager to get rid of you, but if Harrison presses charges you'd be better off out of state.'

'He won't press charges,' Melanie said. 'He knows we'd tell everything.'

'It probably would be better,' Bodie admitted, 'to get a good night's sleep before starting out. We'll leave first thing in the morning.'

'Fine.'

Not fine, Pen thought. She didn't want them to leave at all. But she'd known they couldn't stay long. Starting tomorrow, they would both be missing school and Bodie had classes to teach. Also, it was best that they go back as soon as possible before Melanie got a chance to make more trouble.

She was surprised, however, by Melanie's apparent willingness to return in the morning.

We'd better watch her, she thought.

'I'll stop by a fast-food place,' Bodie said, 'and get us all some supper.'

'There's a Jack-in-the-Box . . .'

He nodded. 'I saw it. What would you like?'

'Tacos would be fine. They've got great tacos.'

Outside, Pen hesitated in front of the door. 'I wonder if we should leave the house keys.'

'Screw that,' Melanie said. 'It's still Dad's house. Joyce doesn't have any right to be kicking us out.'

'I suppose not.'

Melanie went with Bodie to his van. Pen climbed into her car and followed them out to San Vicente.

Driving back to her apartment, she wondered if Melanie would change her mind about leaving in the morning. It hardly seemed possible that she would abandon her hopes of nailing Joyce and Harrison, especially now that she'd apparently heard them admit their guilt.

She must have a plan. Maybe she intends to sneak out, tonight. And do what? God only knows. She'd been crazy enough to hide in Harrison's house – and attack Joyce.

We'd just better make damn sure she doesn't get away from us. Even if it means staying awake all night.

When Pen parked in front of her apartment building, she considered waiting in her car for them to show up. The stop for food should only take them five minutes.

Don't be a chicken, she told herself. If you're not going to move out – and that was the whole point of buying the shotgun – you'd better get used to the place again.

He took my panties. He was here this afternoon. Maybe he's a tenant like Manny.

But not Manny. Someone else.

I can't go on living here, she realized.

Nor could she move out of her car seat.

It'll be all right with Bodie here.

Tomorrow, I'll find a new place. I'll stay in a motel for as long as . . .

Tomorrow, Bodie will be gone.

He has to go. He has to get Melanie away from all this.

I wouldn't mind getting away from all this, myself.

I can't go anywhere, though. Not while Dad's the way he is.

Should call the hospital. Maybe go over there tonight.

What if Joyce is there?

We have to do something about those two. They can't get away with it.

I could go to the police tomorrow and tell them everything. If they focus their investigation on Harrison, they might turn something up. I'll do that. Unless they show up here, first, to arrest Melanie and Bodie.

At least we got her out of Harrison's house in one piece.

Bodie was right, we should've left her there. She probably would've managed to sneak out on her own with nobody the wiser.

Or maybe not.

They might've caught her. God only knows what Harrison would've done.

It was the right move.

What's *their* next move? They know the three of us are onto them. What'll they do about it? Maybe nothing.

Harrison's an attorney, he knows we haven't got any evidence.

Maybe it's too much that we suspect them.

So what's he going to do, kill the three of us?

That would bring down an awful lot of heat. He wouldn't risk it unless he was feeling mighty desperate.

Melanie and Bodie will be gone tomorrow. Once he finds that out, it'll relieve the pressure. And once I've gone to the cops, I'll have done my share of the damage. He won't have any motive, then, to shut me up.

We just need to get through the night.

In her mind, Pen saw Harrison kick open the apartment door and rush in, his .38 blasting. A slug smashed Melanie in the chest, slamming her down. She and Bodie ran, but a bullet caught him in the back. She made it to her bedroom, whipped the shotgun around and cut Harrison in half when he lunged through the doorway. She hurried into the living room. Melanie was dead, but Bodie still breathed. You'll be all right, she told him. You'll be fine.

Real nice, she thought. I kill off my sister and let Bodie survive.

Pen knew *she* wasn't psychic. That was Melanie's department. But she recognized the value of daydreams. What she had imagined was a possible scenario. Unlikely, but possible.

Just in case, she would brace the door with a chair and keep her shotgun within reach.

Harrison, she told herself, would have to be insane to barge in shooting.

But he does have the gun.

And those handcuffs.

A former private eye. How come he didn't have to give

back the badge and ID when he stopped working for that agency? Maybe he claimed he lost them. A couple of items like that could be very useful, especially if a guy is into rape.

Not as useful as the handcuffs.

Don't start thinking about that, she warned herself. Get off it quick.

But something he'd said that night . . . something about the job. What was it? Ever shoot someone? No, but he'd drawn his gun a couple of times. Said it was a boring job.

Except for the repos.

Holy shit!

She flinched as someone rapped on her window. Melanie looked in at her. Pen climbed out of the car.

'Been here long?' Bodie asked. He had sacks of food in his hands.

Pen shook her head. 'Just a few minutes.' Should she tell them about Harrison, that he'd had experience stealing cars and might even own the tools for it?

Might just set off Melanie.

A midnight search for the tools?

Let's not rock the boat. Save it for the police.

She took out her suitcase and led the way through the front gate. Heading for the stairs, she swept her eyes across all the apartments surrounding the pool. Did *he* live in one of them? Pen knew only a few of the tenants. He might be one she didn't know.

But he knows me.

He has my panties.

He'd like to fuck my brains out and . . .

Stop it!

She hurried up the stairs, telling herself to stay calm.

The creep wouldn't try anything tonight, not with Bodie here.

And this is my last night here, you filthy scum. Tough luck.

She opened her apartment door and looked down at the carpet. No message had been slipped under the door during her absence.

While she and Melanie set the kitchen table, Bodie went down to get the rest of the luggage.

'Are you really going to leave tomorrow?' Pen asked.

'I guess so. I'll come back if Dad . . . changes.'

'Do you want to go over to the hospital tonight?'

'What's the point? He's just . . . it's like he's dead. I can't stand to see him that way.' Melanie sank into a chair and held her head. 'I just want to forget everything. I want to sleep.'

'How do you feel?'

'I've got an awful headache.'

'I'll get you some aspirin.' Pen went into the bathroom and opened the medicine cabinet. As she reached for the Excedrin, she saw a bottle of sleeping pills. They were Quaaludes, 150 mg, a drug she had been prescribed by her doctor when she complained of insomnia during a bad period following the rape. The expiration date had passed. But the pills shouldn't cause any harm. Even if they weren't quite as strong as they had once been, a couple of them should certainly knock out Melanie for the night. And put a stop to any plan she might have for sneaking out, later on.

Pen's hands trembled as she shook two of the tablets onto her palm.

It's a dirty trick, she thought.

They'll wipe her out. Bodie and I won't have to spend

the night standing guard over her.

She put away the bottle. With the two pills in her hand, she left the bathroom.

Bodie was sitting down at the table when she entered the kitchen. She took a tumbler from the cupboard and filled it with water. 'I got Mel some aspirin,' she said.

Bodie nodded.

She set the glass in front of Melanie and dropped the pills into her palm. 'It's a new brand,' she said. 'They're extra-strength. They may make you a little drowsy, but . . .'

'Fine,' Melanie said. She cupped them to her mouth and drank half the water.

'You don't have blurred vision or nausea, do you?' Bodie asked her.

'No. Just a headache.'

'Better lie down after you eat,' Bodie said.

'Yeah.'

Pen got a bottle of beer for Bodie and poured wine for herself and Melanie to drink with the meal. Sitting down, she took her tacos from their paper envelopes and put them on her plate. Bodie and Melanie unwrapped their bacon cheeseburgers. Bodie had bought an order of nachos for each of them – tortilla chips smothered with melted cheese and green chilis.

'All we're missing is a mariachi band,' Bodie said.

'I should've whipped up some margaritas,' said Pen. It was just as well that she hadn't, she realized; she wouldn't have dared give Melanie the sleeping pills. Some wine on top of the pills might not cause a problem. Tequilla and triple sec, though . . .

'Why don't you tell Pen what happened this afternoon?' Bodie suggested.

Melanie raised a shoulder. 'Not much to tell,' she said, and took a bite of her burger.

'Apparently,' Bodie said, 'they had quite a lot to say about the three of us. None of it very flattering.'

'Harrison *really* tore into you,' Melanie said, looking rather gleefully at Pen. 'He used names on you that'd make that caller of yours blush.'

'Sweet of him,' Pen muttered, and bit into a taco.

'Yeah. He thinks you were the brains behind my phone call and breaking into his garage. Said you're out to get him.'

'Did he happen to say why?'

'Told Joyce it was because he dumped you.'

'Is that so.'

'Said he'd fix your wagon.'

'My wagon isn't broken.'

'Said he'd like to ream your ass,' Melanie added.

Bodie set down his beer. 'I should've laid waste to that prick when I had the chance.'

'What did he say about the accident?' Pen asked.

'They know we know. First thing Harrison did when they got back was check the garage. He had it figured out even before he found the broken window that the call was a trick to get rid of him so we could check out his car. When he came back in, he said to Joyce, "I knew it. Those fucks are onto us." Then he told her not to worry, we'd never be able to prove anything.'

'He was probably right about that,' Bodie said.

'Joyce is afraid Dad saw Harrison driving. She thought maybe they should inject air into his veins.'

Pen stiffened. 'At the hospital?'

'Yeah. But Harrison told her they'd be idiots to do anything that risky since Dad probably wouldn't ever come to, anyway. He said they should wait and see. Even if Dad *does* revive, there's only a slight chance he'll have any memory of the accident.'

Bodie nodded. 'It's very unlikely that he would remember. I fell off a roof when I was a kid, and I *still* can't remember falling.'

'What were you doing on a roof?' Pen asked.

'I don't know. I ate lunch about an hour before it happened, but the rest of it's a blank until I woke up in an ambulance.'

'That's how Peter Hurkos became psychic,' Melanie said. 'Fell off a ladder or a roof or something.'

'Well, it didn't make me psychic. Thank God. One around here is . . .'

'One too many?' Melanie supplied, and raised an eyebrow.

Bodie looked annoyed for a moment, then just somber. 'I was going to say, "One is enough." '

'I bet.'

'Cut it out,' Pen told her.

Melanie fixed Pen with a knowing gaze. 'I'm sure *you* can't wait to get rid of me.'

'Hey, look, we're on your side.'

'Then how come you're both so eager to get me back to Phoenix?'

'It's for your own good,' Bodie told her.

'Oh, sure.'

'Look what you did today,' Pen said, trying to keep her voice calm. 'You broke God knows how many laws . . .'

'Lot of good *the law* is.'

'Christ, you went ape, you actually assaulted Joyce.'

'She tried to kill our father!'

233

'Maybe so.'

'No maybes.'

'On top of that, you put yourself in real danger. Bodie, too. You both could've ended up killed because of that dumb stunt you pulled.'

'And you were safe in the car.'

'Hey,' Bodie said, 'somebody had to stay out to get help in case the shit hit the fan. Pen wanted to go in instead of me.'

'Sure, stick up for her.'

'*Damn it!*' Bodie slammed his bottle down on the table. Pen flinched. Melanie jumped, then burst into tears and rushed from the kitchen.

Bodie watched her go. He looked at Pen, shook his head, and muttered, 'Sorry.'

'She was asking for it.'

'I know, but . . .' With a sigh, he pushed back his chair and stood up. 'I'd better apologize to her, or something.'

Bodie found her in Pen's room, lying on the bed with a pillow hugged over her eyes. He sat beside her.

'Leave me alone,' she mumbled.

'Hey, I'm sorry I lost my temper. Why don't you come on back and finish eating?'

'I'm not hungry.'

'Don't you want to grow up to be big and strong?'

'Ha ha ha.'

'Come on, Mel.'

'I just want to sleep. I'm tired and I've got a headache.'

'You'll feel better if you come out and finish your hamburger.'

'No, I won't.'

Bodie put his hand on her belly. Her skin was warm through the blouse. 'I don't like seeing you upset.'

She sniffed. 'You're both against me.'

'No we're not. Maybe we were a little quick to snap at you, but it's been pretty tense. We didn't know what was happening to you while you were in that house.'

'I was fine.'

'We didn't know that. We were really worried, and the only reason we worried is because we love you. Nobody's *against* you. Well, maybe Joyce and Harrison.'

Her mouth trembled into a smile. She pushed the pillow away from her face and drew it down beneath her head. With fingertips, she brushed the tears from her face. She took a deep breath and let it out slowly. 'I didn't mean to cause you so much trouble.'

'It's all right. Hey, it was kind of exciting.'

'Did Pen really want to go in and get me herself?'

'Yeah. I had to threaten her bodily harm to keep her in the car.'

'I shouldn't have talked to her like that.'

'I'm sure she understands. The past couple of days have been tough on all of us.'

'Would you close the curtains for me?'

Bodie got up. He found the draw cord and pulled, shutting out the late afternoon light.

'I'll come out as soon as I feel better.'

'I'll stay.'

'No, go ahead and finish eating.'

'Are you sure?'

'Yeah. Just don't eat up the rest of my burger. I'll be out a little later.'

Bodie bent over the bed. He kissed her gently on the lips. 'Sleep tight,' he whispered.

Leaving the room, he started to pull the door shut. Then he realized that Melanie might get the wrong idea, so he left it wide open.

He returned to the kitchen. Pen, still at the table, looked over her shoulder as he approached. 'How is she?'

'Fine. She wants to take a nap.'

'That's probably a good idea.'

'She warned me not to polish off her dinner.'

'I guess she is feeling better.'

Bodie sat down across the table from Pen. He felt relieved to have Melanie out of the way, and guilty about the feeling. His bacon cheeseburger was no longer warm. It still tasted good. He washed down a mouthful with beer.

'She doesn't seem very happy about going back tomorrow,' Pen said.

'I'm not overjoyed by the prospect, myself.'

'I'd think you might be glad to get out of this.'

'I don't like the idea of leaving you holding the bag. Melanie made a real mess of things, and you'll be left with the consequences.'

'I'll be okay. I wasn't involved in the hairy stuff. With you and Melanie gone, Harrison might figure he's won. He'll probably pretend the whole thing never happened. He's good at that.'

'What do you mean?'

Pen shook her head. 'He won't try anything with me.'

'I hope you're right. But Melanie said he thinks you were behind all this today.'

'Let him think what he wants.' Pen lifted a chip to her mouth. Some cheese clung to her upper lip. She chewed, then licked it off. 'Maybe you shouldn't tell Melanie – at least not before you're gone – but I plan to visit the police tomorrow and tell them everything.'

Bodie frowned. 'Do you think that's a good idea?'

'It's self-preservation, for one thing. Once I've talked to the police and accused those two, I don't think they'd dare to come after me. It wouldn't look good if anything happened to me after that. Besides, I plan to make believers out of the cops. Maybe they'll turn up some evidence.'

'Better them than us.'

'That's for sure,' Pen agreed.

'I don't know where we'd go from here, anyway.'

'Melanie might have a few ideas about that.' She glanced around as if to make sure that her sister wasn't sneaking through the kitchen, then said, 'I suspect she might have one last move up her sleeve. It's a long time from now till morning.'

'Yeah,' Bodie said. 'Yeah, I see what you mean. She takes a nap now, and sneaks out tonight after you and I are asleep. I wouldn't put it past her. We'll have to make sure she doesn't get the chance.'

CHAPTER TWENTY

When they finished eating, Pen and Bodie cleaned off the table. Pen wrapped the remains of Melanie's burger and put it in the refrigerator. She took out a can of coffee and began to prepare a pot.

'Good idea,' Bodie said. 'It's going to be a long night.'

'We could sleep in shifts,' Pen said.

'I didn't bring one.'

She laughed. 'You can borrow one of mine.'

'A tempting offer,' Bodie said. He excused himself and headed for the hallway.

While he was gone, apparently to use the toilet, Pen finished making the coffee. Then she carried a kitchen chair to the front door and tipped it backward, bracing its back under the knob. Just like Friday night, she thought, and remembered her terror the next morning when she saw an arm reaching in, trying to dislodge the chair. It had been Bodie, though, and she'd stabbed him.

'I don't think that will keep Mel in,' Bodie said as he entered the living room.

She smiled at him. 'Oh, darn.'

'What's it for?'

'Just in case.'

'You afraid Harrison might try something?'

'I doubt it. But you never know.'

'You're about the most cautious person I've ever met.'

'A streak of paranoia,' she said. 'I think it runs in the family.'

Bodie sat near an end of the sofa. 'A broken clock has the right time twice a day, and even paranoids have enemies.'

'Sometimes imaginary enemies. Look how I stabbed you yesterday.'

'A mere nick.'

'Fortunately. But it shows what can happen if you lose control.'

'Hell, I was trying to force my way in. You didn't know who I was. I'd say the attack was justified.'

'Justified, maybe, but a mistake. The coffee's probably ready.'

She went into the kitchen, filled two mugs, and brought them out. She gave one to Bodie. 'Did you look in on Melanie?'

'She's zonked out.'

'Good. I need to get something.' Pen set her mug on the table and went to her bedroom. The closed curtains kept out the dim evening light. Melanie was a vague shape on the bed. Pen crept close to her. She heard the girl's long, slow breaths.

Zonked, all right.

With those Quaaludes in her, she wouldn't be waking up for a very, very long time.

Pen thought of her father in a coma.

I did this to Melanie.

She'll come out of it, Dad won't.

Yes, he will. He has to.

Crouching, Pen slipped the shotgun out from under the bed. She carried it back into the living room. Bodie's eyes widened. 'What, me worry?' Pen asked.

'Lordy lordy, I'd sure hate to get on your bad side.'

'Damn right. I'm one bad dude.'

'Can I see it?'

'Sure. It's loaded, by the way.'

'Wouldn't do much good otherwise.'

She handed it to him, then picked up her coffee mug and sat at the other end of the sofa. She turned sideways to face him, bringing her knees up against the back cushion.

'A beaut,' Bodie said. He shouldered the weapon, aimed it across the room, lowered it onto his lap and stroked its walnut stock. 'Real nice.'

'I just bought it this morning.'

'Twelve-gauge?'

Pen nodded. 'With special magnum cartridges.'

'Wicked. I guess Harrison better not mess with *you*.'

'I didn't have him in mind,' she said, and took a drink of coffee as Bodie turned to look at her.

'The caller?'

'Yeah.'

'I'd almost forgotten about him. All this other stuff going on.'

'I wish I could forget about him,' she said, and drank more coffee. 'I'd better put that shotgun someplace.' She set her mug on the table.

Bodie leaned sideways and passed the weapon to her. She stood up. 'I want to keep it handy in case.'

'You don't want Melanie to spot it,' Bodie advised.

'You must be a mind reader.' She propped the shotgun against the wall between the front door and the end of the sofa, hidden behind the curtains. Then she pulled the draw cord. The curtains skidded shut. 'A symptom of paranoia,' she said. 'You don't want people looking in.'

'An uncle of mine was killed that way,' Bodie told her. 'He was in his living room one night with the lights on and the drapes open. Someone out on the street plinked him.'

'My God, really?'

'It was just one of those random things. I guess he made an irresistible target.'

Pen shook her head. 'The things that happen in this world.'

'Can't be too careful.'

'My motto.' She turned on a lamp. 'More coffee?'

'Sure.'

She took the mugs into the kitchen, filled them and returned. She gave a mug to Bodie, then sat at her end of the sofa. 'It's all a little frightening,' she said.

' "We are here as on a darkling plain swept with confused alarms of struggle and flight . . ." '

' "Where ignorant armies clash by night," ' Pen said.

Bodie grinned. 'Hey, how about letting me read one of your stories?'

Pen's stomach did a little flip. 'Okay,' she said. 'If you're sure . . .'

'Sure.'

Nervously, she took another drink of coffee. Then she got up and went to the bookcase. She pulled down a copy of *Ellery Queen's Mystery Magazine* and handed it to Bodie. 'Remember, William Faulkner I ain't.'

'They paid you for this, right?'

'Yep.'

'Then, Faulkner or not, it's quite an accomplishment.'

'Thanks,' she muttered. 'Page 93.'

He opened the magazine and began to read.

My story, Pen thought. She was pleased, but embarrassed. She didn't know what to do with herself while he read it, so she crouched over her suitcase and took out the paperback she had started reading Friday night in the tub.

She sat on the sofa and opened it.

Bodie turned a page.

She wondered if he liked the story so far.

It was pretty shallow, really.

She tried to read the paperback, but her gaze kept straying from the page to Bodie at the other end of the sofa. His face looked solemn. He brushed a hank of light brown hair off his forehead, but it flopped down again.

Pen forgot about the book on her lap and forgot to worry about Bodie's reaction to her short story. She stared at him – his hair glossy in the lamplight, his shirt rumpled in front from the way he was slouched, one foot propped on the other knee, the old running shoe half off and dangling from his toes, a disk of pink skin showing through a hole in the heel of his sock.

She wanted to scoot over the sofa to his side.

Ah, but you won't, she told herself.

Melanie's out for the count.

Don't even consider it.

Bodie, eyes still on the story, shook his head and muttered, 'Oh, my God.' He closed the magazine. He looked at Pen and shook his head some more. He grinned. 'Man, I was worried sick about her and all the time *she's* the one hunting *them*.'

'Does that mean you liked it?'

'You reversed everything. The final line of the story, you turned it all upside-down. Yeah, I think it's terrific. Nice writing, too. I felt as if I were inside her, feeling everything she felt, going through it all. Really nice. If you turned this in to me as a student, I'd give it an A minus.'

Pen, delighted, forced herself to scowl. 'Why the minus?'

'To keep you from getting cocky.'

She laughed. 'Thanks, anyway.'

'Do you have some more I could read?'

'That's the only published one.'

'I don't care.'

'Let's quit while I'm ahead.'

'Come on,' he said. 'We've got all night.'

And only tonight, Pen thought. I don't want to spend it all watching him read my stories. 'Well, maybe one more.'

She drank the rest of her coffee, then went into her office and turned on the light. She felt shaky and excited.

She needed badly to use the bathroom – all that coffee. But she sat at her desk and slid open the deep bottom drawer. Each of the manila folders was labeled with a story title. She flipped through them with trembling fingers.

Better pick one fast, she thought, before I burst.

She pulled out the folder for 'The McDougal Stone' and opened it on her lap. On top of the paper-clipped manuscript were three rejection slips.

Maybe he can tell me what's wrong with it.

Hell, I thought it was good.

She took out the manuscript and put the folder away.

As she stood up, her eyes met the answering machine. The voice filled her head, tearing apart her good feelings, turning her insides cold and tight. She looked quickly at the window. Its curtains were shut.

He can't see me.

Maybe he saw the light come on. If he lives in the building . . .

But he can't call and he knows I'm not alone. Nothing to worry about. Not tonight.

He has my panties.

She rushed out of the office and some of her fear eased when she entered the living room and saw Bodie in the lamplight, looking so calm and comfortable – and happy.

'This one's been rejected a few times,' she said, handing the story to him.

'Must really stink.'

She laughed. 'Back in a minute,' she said, and hurried to the bathroom. Bodie had left the toilet seat down. Very considerate. She quickly opened her white shorts and pulled them down her legs. She hooked her thumbs under the sides of her panties, tugged them down, and sat.

And stared at the skimpy lace panties drawn taut between her ankles.

Bodie heard the toilet flush. Expecting Pen to return in a few seconds, he watched the dark entrance to the hallway. And waited.

Apparently, she wasn't coming back right away.

He read more of the story, and almost finished it before he heard a door open. Pen's footsteps were slow and quiet in the hallway. Then she stepped into the living room.

She raised a hand in a hesitant greeting. A smile faltered on her face. Her nose was a little red and her eyes were red and puffy. 'More coffee?' she asked in a chipper voice.

'No thanks. Are you all right?'

Nodding, she sat at her end of the sofa. 'Finished the story yet?'

'No. What's wrong? You've been crying.'

'It's ridiculous.'

'It can't be ridiculous if it upset you that much.' Leaning forward, he dropped the manuscript onto the coffee table. He turned toward Pen. She was bent forward, elbows on knees, her head drooping. Bodie, frowning, scooted closer and put his hand on her back. She didn't flinch or tell him to stop. He rubbed her gently between the shoulder blades, aware of her warm smoothness through the blouse.

'Ever get the feeling that you've lost your grip?'

'Slipped a few cogs?'

She nodded. The hair hanging over her face shimmered in the lamplight.

'Yeah,' Bodie said. 'Sometimes. What happened?'

'It's that guy who called Friday night. Even with everything else, I haven't been able to get him off my mind.'

'That's understandable.'

'My God, he had me so rattled that I stabbed you. I mean, I blew everything out of proportion. I put that stupid trip-cord across my doorway and damn near cracked my head open, then I stabbed you, for Christsake.'

'I'm not complaining.'

'I was so messed up, I actually believed he would come here and try to rape me. I was certain of it.'

'There was a real danger that he might,' Bodie said. 'I was worried, too.'

'Then he left that message under my door. I was petrified. But I thought, I'm not going to let him run my life. I won't let him scare me away. So I went out this morning and bought the shotgun. I'll fix him, right? Just let him come. The shotgun's a magic wand – wave it and I'm safe. Only thing is, I got back here and I was alone and I was *still* scared, damn it. But I wasn't going to let him get to me, right? So I go down to the laundry room and some creep puts moves on me and I'm so messed up I think *he's* the caller. I actually take a knife with me when I go back down. I probably would've stabbed *him* if he'd shown up again. That would've been real cute. Stab two innocent guys in two days. Maybe I could go down in the *Guinness Book of World Records*.'

'You shouldn't be so hard on yourself,' Bodie whispered.

'Oh, you haven't heard the good one yet. Talk about paranoia. When I went to put away my laundry, something wasn't there. A pair of underpants. Neat, huh? My obscene caller snuck into the laundry room and stole my panties. That really freaked me out. He not only knows where I live, but he is *here* and spying on me, maybe even a tenant in the building, and he's got my goddamn panties. Only here's the thing.' Pen's voice quavered. She turned her head toward Bodie. Strands of hair hung across her face and her eyes were shiny. 'Here's the real corker.' Her chin trembled. 'I was wearing them the whole time. I had 'em *on*. Nobody stole them. I've been wearing them all day. I've got them on right now.' She made a choking sound that may have been an attempted laugh but came out as a sob. 'How's that for nuts, huh?'

'Oh, Pen,' he whispered. He stroked her hair.

Then she was turning, putting her arms around him, weeping with her face against his chest.

'It's all right,' he said. 'It's all right.' He sank against the cushion, holding her gently. He stroked her hair, her back. She felt big in his arms, broader across the back than Melanie. A breast was pressing against him. He told himself to ignore it. Just holding her gave him a good, warm, comfortable feeling and he didn't want the extra guilt of growing aroused but he couldn't help it.

'I have to tell you something,' he said, and eased her away.

She nodded and sniffed, her face close to his, her hands on his sides.

'This is all my fault,' Bodie said.

Pen shook as she took a deep breath.

'Partly my fault, anyway.'

She had a confused look in her eyes.

'That caller of yours . . . he never came here. He made the telephone calls, but he didn't come here. Remember how it took me so long to pick up the pizza last night? I didn't get lost. I stopped by a drugstore and bought a birthday card. I used its envelope. I'm the one who left that message under your door.'

'No, you didn't. You're just trying to make me feel better.'

'I'm sorry. It was a dumb trick.'

'No, you . . .'

'I really did it.'

'Why?'

'So you wouldn't stay here last night. I heard that guy's voice on the tape. I was afraid . . . afraid he *might* come over. I didn't want you to be here alone. And I knew you were frightened about staying and it was just Melanie forcing you into it.'

Pen stared into his eyes.

'A dumb trick,' he said again. 'I should have known it would make things worse for you. Hell, I *did* know. I just didn't care. I wanted you over at the house no matter what.'

'Because you were worried about me?'

'Yeah.'

Leave it at that, he warned himself.

I've gone this far. I have to finish.

'And also . . . because it wasn't fair. You'd asked us to stay with you and I knew we should – it was the right thing to do because you asked first and you really needed us here and I thought we should stay with you but Melanie went and told Joyce we'd stay at her house. She only did it to spite you.'

'She did it to keep you away from me,' Pen said.

'I know. I didn't *want* me away from you.'

'Oh, Bodie.'

'Well . . .'

'I guess it's not much of a surprise,' Pen said.

'Happens all the time,' he said. 'Melanie shows up with a boyfriend and he falls all over you. I know I'm a jerk. We'll be gone in the morning, and that'll be the end of it.'

She curled a warm hand behind his neck. 'The end of it,' she whispered. 'I know. Tonight's our . . . Those tablets I gave Melanie before we ate? They weren't aspirin. They were sleeping pills. Strong ones. She won't be getting up tonight.'

'My God.'

'I was afraid she might try to sneak out later,' Pen said. 'That's why I did it. Not for this. Not so we could be alone.'

Bodie shook his head.

'It's no worse than you writing that note, is it?'

'Better,' he heard himself say. 'A lot better. We're quite a tricky pair, you and me.'

'I'm not proud of drugging her, but . . . I'm going to miss you so much, Bodie.' She lifted her face to him and they kissed.

We shouldn't, he thought.

Pen's mouth was warm and moist.

He felt giddy. He felt like a high school kid somehow miraculously being kissed by the one girl he'd been longing for, the girl admired only from a distance and daydreamed about. It seemed unreal.

He put his arms around her. She sank against him, pressing him into the cushion.

Oh, this is real.

Her weight on him was real. Her breasts pushing against his chest were real. And her mouth, open against his, and her tongue, and her breath going into him.

Pen's mouth eased away. His lips were wet. She stared at him, her eyes moving a fraction from side to side. He felt as if he could see into them, but not deeply enough. He wanted to look into her mind, to be inside with her thoughts and feelings.

'What are we gonna do?' she whispered.

'About what?'

'Us.' Her eyes, so close to his, kept moving just a bit, looking from his left eye to his right and back again.

'What do you want to do?' he asked.

'It's not that simple.'

'Why not?'

'I can't hurt her, Bodie. I won't.'

'She's asleep. You said . . .'

'What about after tonight?'

Bodie's heart sped up.

'We'll work something out,' he said. His voice sounded as desperate as he felt.

'How?'

'I don't know.'

'Neither do I,' Pen said. She leaned forward against him, her forehead resting in the curve of his neck. He stroked her back.

'I can't lose you. All my life I've been hoping that someday . . .'

'Pen and Bodie sitting in a tree, k-i-s-s-i-n-g.'

Pen lurched in his arms.

Beyond the doorway, barely visible in the darkness of the hall, stood Melanie.

CHAPTER TWENTY-ONE

Melanie dug a hand into a pocket of her corduroy pants. The hand came out with two pills in its palm. 'I knew they weren't aspirin,' she said, her voice flat. She stared at Pen with blank eyes. 'You gave me sleeping pills. So you could have the night with Bodie. So you could seduce him.'

'Oh, man,' Bodie muttered.

'That's not the reason,' Pen said. 'I was afraid you'd sneak out and go after Harrison.'

'Slut,' Melanie said calmly.

'Mel!' Bodie snapped.

Her head turned slowly toward him. 'What?' she asked.

'Don't talk that way. She's on your side. We both are.'

'You want me out of the way.'

'Don't be crazy.'

A placid, humorless smile curled Melanie's lips.

My God, Pen thought, what have we done to her?

Bodie turned to Pen. 'We'd better leave,' he said. 'I don't think we should wait for morning. I'll take her back now.'

'Yeah.'

'We can't leave,' Melanie said. 'You haven't fucked

her yet. You have to fuck her. Everyone has to fuck her.' The mild way she said it, smiling, made goose-bumps crawl up Pen's back.

Bodie stood up. He stepped around the coffee table, passed in front of Melanie, and picked up the two suitcases he had left near the wall after bringing them up from the van. Melanie, standing motionless, followed him with an empty gaze.

Pen got to her feet. She removed the chair from under the knob and opened the door.

Bodie looked at her with such agony that she wanted to throw her arms around him. 'It'll be all right,' he said.

'I don't think so.'

'She'll get over this once we're away.'

Will she? Pen thought. I won't, and neither will you.

'Come on, Melanie,' he said gently.

She walked toward him, her dead eyes staying on Pen. 'First came love,' she chanted in a low voice, 'then came marriage, then came Penny with a baby carriage.'

'Bye,' Bodie said.

She nodded.

Then they were out the door. Stepping onto the balcony, Pen watched her sister follow Bodie to the stairs and down. When they were out of sight, she heard the courtyard gate squeak open and shut. She folded her arms over her breasts for warmth against the night chill. She pressed her bare legs together. She clamped her teeth shut so they wouldn't click.

Then came the faint sound of Bodie's van starting up.

That's it, she thought. They're going.

'Hey babe, I'll warm you up,' Manny called out his door.

She didn't feel annoyed or threatened. She felt

nothing about him. He didn't matter.

Stepping inside her apartment, she closed the door. She slipped the guard chain into place and looked at the chair she had used earlier to brace the door shut.

Why bother?

She wasn't afraid. She thought vaguely that she should be pleased she was no longer afraid, but she just didn't care.

She plugged her kitchen telephone back into the wall.

Let the bastard call, she thought. He can't hurt me. Sticks and stones can break my bones, but words . . .

Pen and Bodie sitting in a tree, k-i-s-s-i-n-g.

Words can never hurt me.

How could everything have gone so wrong?

They're gone. I'll never see Bodie again. Melanie hates my guts. She thinks I . . . she's right.

Bodie. Oh, God, Bodie.

She wandered into her bedroom and turned on the light. She wanted to lie down, to sleep, to forget.

Not even nine o'clock.

Nine. They'd missed visiting hours at the hospital.

She had hardly even given her father a thought, today.

I'll go see him tomorrow, she promised herself.

In the bathroom, she brushed her teeth and washed her face. She returned to her bedroom. She took off her clothes, her panties last.

Sitting on the edge of the bed, she held the panties in her hands.

Nobody took them. All in my head.

We have nothing to fear but ourselves.

She dropped them to the floor, turned off the lamp, and crawled between the sheets of her bed. The sheets were cool at first on her naked body, then warm.

She thought about Bodie driving through the night, Melanie silent in the passenger seat. Was he trying to apologize? Would Melanie listen? Or was she too far gone, lost in a private world of pain?

Don't feel too sorry for her, Pen thought. Bodie and I, we've got our own world of pain, and all because we didn't want to hurt her.

But we did.

We hurt her good. Ourselves, too.

Goddamn it.

Why didn't she take the pills!

Maybe it's best this way. If she'd stayed asleep, Bodie and I . . . we would've ended up making love.

Probably.

No probably.

Don't think about it. Just don't think.

She drew the extra pillow down and hugged it tightly to her breasts.

She remembered the feel of kissing him.

The needle on Bodie's gas gauge showed that he was down to a quarter of a tank. He was driving south on Robertson Boulevard. If he remembered correctly, he was only a couple of miles from the on-ramp to the Santa Monica Freeway. Once on the freeway, stopping for gas would be a lot of trouble.

As he waited at a traffic light, he saw a self-service station on the other side of the intersection.

The light turned green. He rolled through the intersection and swung into the station. He stopped beside the pumps. He took his key from the ignition. Twisting around, he peered into the dark rear of the van and said, 'I'll be back in a minute.'

Melanie didn't answer.

What if she's not back there?

She has to be. Bodie knew he would've heard the rear doors open if she had tried to sneak out.

But he wondered.

Turning on the light, he saw Melanie stretched out flat on the sleeping bag, her hands folded on her belly. 'Are you all right?' he asked.

She said nothing. She didn't move.

'Don't worry about it,' he said. 'Okay? Nothing happened between me and Pen. There's no point brooding over it.'

She didn't respond.

Bodie climbed from the van. He put the keys in his pants pocket and took out his wallet as he walked toward the office cubicle. Along the way, he glanced back a few times.

He didn't really expect Melanie to bolt, but she'd been full of surprises lately.

He slipped his credit card into the trough beneath the glass partition. The swarthy, grinning man on the other side picked it up. Bodie told him the number of the pump he planned to use, then headed for the van.

Even though he'd tried to keep an eye on it, he cautioned himself to make sure, before driving off, that Melanie was still inside.

She's not going anywhere, he thought. She's in shock or something.

He pushed the pump nozzle into his tank and held the lever down.

She'll probably be fine tomorrow. Just pissed as hell

and full of accusations. She'll probably dump *me*, and save me the trouble.

When the flow clicked off, Bodie shoved the nozzle into place on the side of the pump. He screwed his gas cap on tightly and started for the office.

It's less than a month till the end of the semester. One way or another, we'll be finished by then and I'll come back to Pen.

Bodie scooped up his credit card and signed the slip. He tore off the customer receipt and dropped the rest into the trough. The man thanked him.

He headed back for the van.

He climbed in, turned on the light and checked the rear. Melanie was still lying there. She looked as if she hadn't moved a muscle the whole time he was filling the tank.

He turned off the overhead lights, dug out his keys, and started the engine.

Maybe I'll luck out, he thought, and she'll stay this way the whole trip.

He drove onto a sidestreet, stopped at the corner, then made a right onto Robertson. On the track again, he wondered whether to make a right or a left when he reached the freeway.

Just wait for the signs.

Whichever way goes east – you know you don't want to end up at the ocean.

Maybe by summer there will be a vacancy in Pen's apartment building.

He stopped for a traffic light.

The real question is, can I wait for the semester to end? I have to. Gotta finish the MA.

He heard a quiet sound of movement behind him.

At least Melanie's not paralyzed.

I could always drive over on weekends. Once I've settled the situation with Melan . . .

Pain blasted through Bodie's head.

Pen jerked awake, gasping and shaking, her heart thundering.

A bell was ringing.

Someone at the door!

It blared again.

The telephone?

She hurled herself off the bed and rushed across her room, afraid the caller might hang up before she could reach the phone – afraid he might not.

Who?

She hoped it was Bodie. It could be anyone.

The obscene caller. Harrison or Joyce. The hospital.

My God, don't let it be bad news!

Maybe a wrong number, a salesman.

The phone rang again.

The hallway was faintly lighted from the living room lamp she hadn't bothered to turn off.

She slapped a hand against the kitchen doorframe to stop herself, reached around the corner and snatched up the phone. 'Hello?'

'This is *you*, isn't it?'

She knew the voice. Her skin seemed to shrink. She felt it tighten and prickle.

'Not a recording, this time?'

'No.'

'Do you know who I am?'

'What do you want?' she asked, her voice trembling.

'I want to talk. I've missed you. Have you been away?'

Hang up, she thought. Sure. If I do, he'll just call again.

Or come over. He knows I'm here.

Pen remembered the shotgun. She'd left it in the living room, propped against the wall near the door, hidden behind the curtains.

Let him come over. Give him a big surprise.

'Or were you just afraid to pick up the phone? You're not scared of me, honey, are you?'

'Why should I be scared?' she asked, trying to steady her voice.

He laughed. It was a quiet, dry laugh that made a cold place in her stomach.

'I've been hoping you'd call again,' she told him.

'Really?'

'Those things you said . . . I've listened to the tape so many times. I love it.'

'Makes you hot?'

'It sure does. I'm getting hot right now.'

'What are you wearing?' he asked.

Not a stitch. Pen wished she'd grabbed her robe on the way to the phone.

He can't see me.

'Jeans. And a sweater.'

'A brassiere?' he hissed.

She almost said yes. She wanted to be wearing one. She wanted to be dressed in tight, heavy clothes. She had never felt so exposed and vulnerable.

Don't back out now, she told herself.

Shivering, she said, 'No.'

'Ah, fabulous. A sweater and no brassiere. I can see it. Yes. Oh, my cock is getting big and hot. Do you know what I'd like to do? I'd like to lift your sweater and suck your tits.'

'Would you like me to take it off?' she asked.

'Oh, yes.'

What the hell am I doing? she wondered. Am I mad? 'There,' she said, 'it's off.'

He sighed. 'Are your nipples hard?'

She looked down. They were hard. But not because of desire. 'They sure are,' she said.

'I'd like to rub my cock on them. Would you like that?

'I sure would.'

'Oh, I know it, I know it. Wouldn't you like to take off your pants?'

'Sure. Just a second.'

'And your underpants, too. I want you naked.'

She heard his raspy breathing. As she listened, she leaned against the doorframe. She rubbed her cold legs together. Looking down, she saw that her thighs were spickled with goosebumps.

'Okay,' she said. 'I'm naked. Are you?'

'Of course. And oh, my cock is *huge*. He wants you.'

'He?'

'Spike.'

Almost funny, she thought. The creep's got a name for his penis. A dog's name, Spike. But also a term for a very large nail.

'I bet Spike's big and powerful,' she said. 'I wish I could feel him.' She heard the words. This isn't me. This is a character in one of my stories, talking to a madman.

'What would you do with him?'

'I'd pet him. He likes to be petted, I bet.'

'Oh, yes.'

'Then I'd suck on him.'

'Oh, honey!'

'I'd suck on Spike till he throbbed in my mouth and I'd swallow every delicious drop and then I'd lick him clean.'

I'm as mad as he is.

Method in my madness, tra-la, tra-la.

'Would you like that?' she asked in a husky voice.

'Oh, yes, yes. Then what?'

'Wouldn't *you* like to know?'

'Tell me.'

'Why don't you come over and find out?'

'Tell me first.'

'I'd rub you all over with honey. And then you'd rub me all over with more, so we're all slick and sticky. Then we'd lick it off each other and when it's all gone, I'd spread my legs and . . .'

'Yes yes!'

'Oh God I'm hot! Let's not talk about it.'

'Please.'

'I want you to fuck me. I want Spike in my cunt. You want that, don't you?'

'YES!'

'Come over.'

'What?'

'Now.'

There was silence except for his harsh breathing.

'Or are you just one of those guys who likes to talk about it? All words and no action?'

He laughed, that same dry chuckle like rustling paper. 'You'll find out. I'll *ream* you, honey. I'll fuck your brains out!'

'So get over here and do it. No more talk.'

More breathing.

God, am I really going to blow his head off?

You damn betcha.

Magnum loads.

I can't do it.

Oh, no? Oh, no?

'Come on, lover,' she whispered. 'I'm *hot*! I want you! I've gotta have you! Get over here!'

'Yeah. Yeah. Okay. Just tell me where you live.'

What?

'You *know* where I live.'

'I will once you tell me.'

'My address is right in the phone book.'

'So what's your name, you sweet stuff?'

'You don't know my *name*?'

'Fuck, no. I just dialed some numbers. Wrote 'em down so I could call you back, but . . .'

Pen slammed down the phone. With a tug at its plastic base, she removed it from the wall jack.

For a long time, she stood leaning against the doorframe, gasping, arms folded across her breasts, legs tight together. She trembled badly. She knew that she should be feeling relief, even triumph.

Instead, she felt sick.

Knowing such a man was out there, even though she would get her number changed and he would be out of her life forever.

Knowing what she had said to him.

The foulness.

And knowing, worst of all, that she had actually tried to lure him to her.

To kill him with the shotgun.

She felt soiled.

Pushing herself away from the wall, she walked on

shaky legs down the hallway toward the bathroom.

Bodie woke up and groaned at the pain in his head. He felt as if his lids were all that held his eyes inside his sockets, that if he opened them, his eyes might burst out from the pressure behind them.

He also felt ready to throw up.

Must've really tied one on last night. He couldn't remember getting smashed, but . . .

What the hell was he lying on? Not a bed.

He rubbed the surface.

Grass. Dewy grass.

He opened his eyes. The pain and nausea swelled. He thrust himself to his hands and knees and vomited. The spasms wracked him, driving white-hot nails into the base of his skull. When he had finished, he knelt above the mess and clutched his head. The hand above his right ear pressed against an enormous lump.

Not a hangover. I've been . . .

He'd been driving, taking Melanie back to Phoenix.

A crash? He must've crashed and been thrown clear of the van. Melanie!

He turned his head, groaning at the new surge of pain. The van was nowhere in sight. Neither was a road. Bodie was on his knees behind a hedge. To his right was a field with playground equipment near the far corner. Turning some more, he saw a building – a school?

Where the hell am I? What am I doing here?

Bodie pushed himself carefully to his feet and stood motionless, waiting for a wave of dizziness to pass. He dragged a handkerchief from his pocket, blew his nose, and dropped the handkerchief to the grass. Then he walked slowly through an opening in the bushes.

He found himself on a sidewalk. In front of him was a narrow street, homes on the other side. Cars were parked along the street, but not his van. To his left, about a block away, was a busy road with cars passing through its intersection. He walked toward it and tried to remember.

I was at Pen's apartment. With her on the sofa. We kissed. Oh, we did kiss. It had been so . . . and then Melanie came in. She was supposed to be asleep but she hadn't taken the pills. Should've taken the damn pills. Acting very weird. Time to get her out of there, take her back to Phoenix. She was in the back of the van, wouldn't talk. I stopped for gas. Then what?

He could remember signing his credit card slip, but nothing after that.

But we didn't crash. If we crashed, where's the van?

He gingerly fingered the bump on the side of his head.

Melanie . . . could she have hit me with something? Must've. Knocked me out. While I was *driving*? Maybe I was stopped at a light. She could've knocked me out, shoved me over to the passenger seat and got behind the wheel.

Wasn't ready to go back to Phoenix.

Found the school yard, unloaded me, and dragged me behind the bushes.

Strong enough to do that?

They say crazy people . . .

Crazy.

She's gone after someone.

Unfinished business.

Pen?

Bodie's head throbbed.

She's gone after Pen.

No, maybe not, maybe it's Harrison and Joyce. That's okay. Who gives a shit?

But what if it's Pen? What'll Melanie do to her?

Bodie stopped at the corner of the busy street. It was Robertson Boulevard, just as he'd suspected, and he could see the freeway overpass in the distance.

He had to warn Pen.

He raised his left hand to check his wristwatch.

The watch was gone.

No way to know how long he'd been unconscious in the field.

If it was only a few minutes, he might still have time to warn her.

He spotted pay phones across the road.

He slapped the rear pocket of his pants. His wallet was gone. He shoved a hand into his front pocket. No change.

No way to phone Pen. No way to warn her.

He started to run.

Bolts of pain shot through his head but he didn't slow down.

I won't make it in time, he thought. *It might already be too late.*

What'll Melanie do to her?

All my fault.

Oh shit oh shit oh shit!

The pain!

I've got to save her!

Ahead of Bodie, a man came out of a burger joint with a bag of food, crossed the sidewalk, and stepped in front of a parked Cadillac.

'Hey,' Bodie called, rushing toward him. 'Mister! Can you give me a ride? Please? It's really urgent.'

'Are you nuts?'

'Somebody's gonna get killed. All I need is a ride. It won't take long. Please!'

The man chuckled, shook his head, and reached into his pocket for the keys. 'Does this look like a taxi, pal?'

'I'm not kidding, mister. It's an *emergency*!'

'Fuck off.' He turned toward the door of his car.

Bodie grabbed his jacket, spun him around, and smashed a fist into his belly. He was fat and soft. His breath whooshed out. He doubled over and Bodie chopped the back of his neck. The man's knees hit the pavement. Bodie yanked him forward by the back of his jacket, and he flopped.

'I'm sorry, mister. I'll make sure you get it back.'

He tore the keys from the man's limp fingers, unlocked the driver's door, and jumped in. As he started the car, the man's face appeared in front of the bumper.

Bodie shot the car backwards. The man crawled toward it, yelling.

The road was clear.

Bodie whipped the car around in a U-turn and floored the gas pedal.

God Almighty, he thought, what have I done?

Assault and battery, grand theft. *Jesus*!

Just don't let the cops stop me.

Though he ached to keep the accelerator floored, he lowered his speed to forty-five.

He checked the rearview mirror.

No cars on his tail.

No one had seen him rip off the guy's Caddy and come after him. Lucky lucky.

A red traffic light.

Damn!

267

He didn't dare run it.

He pounded his fist on the steering wheel while he waited for the green.

'Come on, come on!'

It changed. He rammed the car forward.

I stole this thing.

I beat that guy up and took his car.

Oh, we got us a crime wave, folks.

Top o' the world, Ma!

God Almighty.

Yesterday a mild-mannered student, today a felon.

He felt a tickle in his throat. A giggle? It might come out a scream.

Almost there.

Let her be all right. Please, God, let her be all right.

Bodie swung onto Pen's street.

Almost there. Let her be all right.

Dead on the floor, her body torn by knife wounds, blank eyes staring at the ceiling . . .

No, no, no!

He was on her block, darting his eyes from side to side, looking for his van. He jerked the car to a stop in front of her building. Still no sign of the van, but Melanie might've parked it around a corner.

He leaped from the car, dashed across the street, threw open the iron gate and ran to the stairs. He charged up the stairs three at a time and raced along the balcony to her door. Light shone through the curtains of the picture window. He pounded on the door. 'Pen!' he called. 'Pen, it's Bodie!'

Seconds passed.

He pounded again.

The door was opened.

By Pen, wearing a blue velour bathrobe.

She looked all right. She looked wonderful. She had a worried look in her eyes.

'Is Melanie here?' Bodie asked.

Pen shook her head.

Bodie stepped inside. He swung the door shut, put his arms around Pen, and hugged her hard.

CHAPTER TWENTY-TWO

It felt so good to see him, to have him back, to hold him. She squeezed him tightly. She didn't want to know why he was here, what had gone wrong. She wanted only to go on holding him.

He was panting for air, and she could feel the beat of his heart against her chest.

'Are you okay?' she whispered after a while.

'I am now. Except for a splitting headache.'

'I'll get you some aspirin.'

'I'll go with you.'

He followed her. 'What happened?' she asked.

'I don't know for sure. I guess Melanie brained me.'

Pen looked back at him, frowning. 'She *hit* you?'

'I woke up in a school playground over near the freeway. The van was gone. I was afraid she'd come here.'

'I haven't seen her.'

In the bathroom, Pen opened the medicine cabinet. She took out the bottle of aspirin and swung the mirrored door shut.

Bodie, behind her, slipped his arms around her waist. Pen watched him in the mirror. His face, above her

271

right shoulder, looked pale and hurt.

'I was so afraid she might have done something to you,' he said.

'Oh, Bodie.'

One of his hands slipped inside her robe. The hand was cool against her skin. It moved slowly upward and held her breast. Sighing, she leaned back against him. She hooked a thumb under the cloth belt of her robe and pulled. The belt fell open. Bodie parted the front of her robe. She saw him gazing at her in the mirror. His face, still pale, no longer looked tight with pain. His hands drifted lightly over her breasts, palms brushing her rigid nipples. He held her breasts. He squeezed them and Pen squirmed, moaning. As his hands curled beneath them, the sides of his thumbs rubbed across her nipples, making her breath catch.

His hands roamed downward, caressing her belly, sliding over her hips and down her thighs. Then they began moving gently upward. Pen closed her eyes. The hands slipped away, returning to her hips.

The aspirin bottle fell from Pen's fingers. She took Bodie's right hand and guided it between her legs. He moaned when he touched her there. Pen's legs went weak. His hand pressed her, and she writhed against it.

I'm sorry, Melanie, she thought. I'm sorry, I don't care, we tried.

She eased Bodie's hand away and turned around. The robe fell from her shoulders. Bodie's hands moved down her back, cupped her buttocks.

With trembling fingers, she began to unbutton his shirt.

'What about Melanie?' he whispered.

'I don't care any more. She hurt you. She doesn't deserve you.'

'She must've gone over to Harrison's.'

'No.' Pen didn't want to think about Melanie.

'I don't like the idea of chasing after her, but I can't just let her . . .'

'Let her what?'

'I don't know. I have to go after her, though.'

Pen leaned against Bodie's chest. He held her gently. 'I'll go with you,' she said.

His hands slid up her back as she crouched to pick up her robe. They caressed her shoulders. She stood, turned away, and lifted the plastic aspirin bottle out of the sink where it had fallen. 'You'd better take some,' she said. She gave him the bottle, then waited at his side while he cupped water from the faucet and swallowed four of the tablets.

She walked ahead of him to the bedroom. He stood in the doorway, watching as she hung her robe on the closet door.

'Were you asleep?' he asked.

'Earlier I was. Then I got a call. From *him.*'

'Oh, no.'

She opened a dresser drawer and lifted out a pair of blue panties. 'We talked,' she said, stepping into them. Balancing on one foot, then the other, she pulled on a pair of white socks. She looked at Bodie. He was gazing at her, his mouth open a little. 'It turns out the guy won't be coming over. He doesn't know where I live, or even who I am. I'll get a new phone number and that'll be the end of him.'

'How'd he get your number?'

'Just dialed it at random.'

'My God.'

'All that worry for nothing. There was never any way he could've . . . paid me a visit.'

'That's great.'

'Yeah,' Pen muttered. She squatted and opened the bottom drawer. She took out a pair of faded blue sweatpants and put them on. She tossed the matching sweatshirt onto her bed. Still naked from the waist up and feeling Bodie's gaze, she went to the closet. She took out her running shoes and carried them to the bed. There, she sat down. She put them on and tied the laces. Picking up her sweatshirt, she walked toward him.

'Trying to rub it in?' he asked.

'It's *your* idea to go after her. See what you're missing?'

He smiled slightly, staring into Pen's eyes as he touched her breasts. 'Things have a funny way of working out.'

'Real funny,' Pen said, arching her back as he caressed her.

'If she hadn't whacked me, we'd be on our way to Phoenix.'

'She'd be safe.'

'I wouldn't . . . be here with you.'

Her breath went ragged as he pressed her nipples. 'Oh God, Bodie.'

'Worth a bump on the head.'

'We'd . . . better go.'

His hands lowered and held her sides. She pulled the sweatshirt down over her head.

'I wish we *could* just forget about her,' he said.

'We can't.'

'I know.'

'Do you really think she went to Harrison's?'

Bodie nodded.

'What'll we do, go over there again?'

'I guess so.'

They walked down the hallway to the living room. Pen picked up her purse and slung its strap over her shoulder. At the end of the sofa, she swept the curtain aside and lifted her shotgun.

'Are you kidding?'

'Just in case.'

'If we need that, we're really in deep shit.'

'I know he's got a .38.'

'Here, let me take it.'

'I can handle it.'

'If it comes to shooting, I'd better do it.'

'What are you, some kind of a sexist?'

'Right on, babe.' He held out his hands for the shotgun.

Pen shook her head. 'We can't just walk around with this.' She slipped the barrel inside her baggy sweatpants. It was cold against the side of her leg. She raised her sweatshirt and pulled it down over the stock.

'Can you walk with it there?'

'I can try.' Holding it against her side, she stepped onto the balcony. Bodie shut the door. He went ahead of her, glancing back occasionally as she limped to the stairs and made her way slowly down them. She kept her right leg stiff.

At the bottom, he took hold of her left arm.

He opened the gate for her.

She hobbled along beside him.

When they reached her car, she eased the shotgun down her leg until its muzzle rested on the pavement.

Clamping her arm to the stock, she took her keys out of her purse and opened the door. She looked around. Saw no one. Lifted her sweatshirt over the stock. Pulled the shotgun out of her pants and quickly swung it into the car.

'I'll be in the Cadillac,' Bodie said, and nodded toward the street.

Pen saw the big car parked on the other side. 'Where'd you get . . . ?'

'Tell you later. Follow me. Just a couple of blocks, then I'll ditch it and we'll be on our way.'

Pen climbed into her car. When the headlights of the Cadillac came on, she backed onto the road. She followed the Caddy down the block, away from Pico.

Where on earth did he get that thing? she wondered. He must have stolen it. No other possibility. He'd been stranded . . . worried about me. Actually stole a car in order to get to me.

He could wind up in prison.

Though frightened for him, Pen felt grateful. He'd put himself on the line for her, risked his freedom, his future.

'Get out of there,' she whispered.

He kept driving.

'Come on, come on.' She checked her rearview, half expecting to see a police cruiser, but the street behind her was clear. 'Damn it, Bodie! Come on!'

He turned right.

Pen followed. And let out a long breath when he pulled over to a curb. But he didn't get out.

'What're you *doing*?' she blurted. Driving slowly past the car, she glanced inside and saw him leaning across

276

the seats. A light shone from the open glove compartment.

Just beyond the Cadillac, she stopped. She killed her headlights to darken her license plates – in case someone should notice Bodie abandoning the stolen car and getting into hers.

'Hurry, would you?' she muttered.

Finally, he climbed out. Pen leaned across the passenger seat, shouldering over the shotgun, and unlatched the door. She grabbed the barrel in time to keep the gun from falling out as he opened the door. Straightening up, she pulled it with her. The interior light was on, but just for a moment. Then the door bumped shut and darkness came back.

Pen drove away with her headlights off. 'I thought you were going to stay in there all night,' she said.

'I had to find the registration. I'll try to call the owner when I get the chance, tell him where to find his car.' Then he told Pen how he had stolen it.

Pen listened, stunned.

'I didn't even think about it,' he said. 'All of a sudden, I was just doing it. The funny thing is, I don't even feel very guilty. I'm just glad I wasn't caught.'

Pen turned the corner and put on her headlights. 'Me, too.'

'I've never done anything like that before.' He sounded apologetic.

Pen reached over and squeezed his hand. 'If you think I'm going to hold it against you . . . I feel badly that you hurt the man, but . . . hey, the gallant knight can't come to the rescue if he ain't got a charger.'

'Only thing is,' he muttered, 'the damsel wasn't in distress.'

'You didn't know that.'

'It's the thought that counts, right?'

She glanced at him. Her throat felt tight. 'The thought counts plenty. You better believe it.'

Bodie's fingers tightened around her hand.

Pen stopped for a traffic light at Pico. 'I guess I'll go surface streets,' she said. 'Either way, it'll take a while to reach Harrison's.'

'Take the slowest route.'

'You don't mean that.'

'I know.'

The light changed. Driving through the intersection, she looked up the road and saw the hospital in the distance. She thought of her father lying in bed, kept alive by tubes. 'I didn't even go and see him today,' she said.

'We'll go tomorrow.'

We. The word made her feel good. 'You're not going back to Phoenix tonight?'

'It's a little late for that. Besides, things have changed. Things *have* changed, haven't they?'

'A lot,' Pen assured him.

'You're not going to let Melanie . . . ?'

'She smashed you on the head. She might've killed you, doing a thing like that. She lost whatever claim she had.'

'I don't think she'll see it that way.'

'Tough.' Pen made a left onto Olympic, and picked up speed.

'What's the hurry?' Bodie asked.

'You got me,' Pen said, but she didn't slow down.

'Melanie's had about an hour to do whatever she wanted to do.'

'What do you think she *is* doing?'

'Who knows? I was absolutely certain she planned to murder you. I was wrong about that, thank God. Who knows? I just hope it's all over before we get there.'

'I don't want anything to happen to her.'

'I don't either, but . . .'

'It'll be our fault. We pushed her over the edge, Bodie. Whatever happens, we're responsible. You and me.'

'Don't forget she spent the afternoon in Harrison's closet. That was before she caught us together.'

'Did you see the look on her face when she found us on the sofa?'

'I'm not saying she wasn't upset. But the fact that she didn't take the pills *proves* she planned to sneak out.'

'She thought I wanted to put her out so you and I could be alone.' Pen sped up to make it through a yellow light. 'Maybe she was right. I didn't consciously do it for that reason, but . . . maybe it was in the back of my mind.'

'Whatever our guilt may be,' Bodie said, 'we're doing our penance now. We could be back in your apartment. Instead, we're racing to the rescue.'

'Or to pick up the pieces.'

Harrison's Mercedes stood in the driveway of his house. Joyce's Continental was no longer parked in front.

'Playing it smart,' Pen said as she drove slowly past the front of the house. 'For all they know, we've been to the police. Wouldn't look too good if Joyce spent the night with him.'

'So she went home,' Bodie said.

'And where's Melanie?'

Bodie shrugged. He had been checking both sides of

the street for his van, but so far hadn't spotted it. 'Keep going,' he said. 'Maybe she left it in back.'

Pen turned, then turned again. She drove past Harrison's block, then made another right, returned to his street and stopped at the corner. 'What do you think?'

'Don't ask me,' Bodie said. 'I've been wrong twice already.'

'She must've gone to Dad's.'

'The house? That'd be my guess, too. This is looking better and better. I figured we'd have a run-in with Harrison. Of course, he might've gone there with Joyce. In her car.'

'I doubt it,' Pen said. 'They probably split up.'

'Should we check his place?'

Shaking her head, Pen made a left turn on Harrison's street, heading away. 'We're looking for Melanie,' she said.

She waited for a break in the traffic on 26th Street, then turned left.

'I just hope . . .'

'What?' she asked.

'Melanie might've already been to Harrison's. They might've . . . gotten her. That could be why the van wasn't there. Maybe Harrison drove her away in it. Joyce would've followed in her car to pick him up after they . . . disposed of her.'

Pen glanced at him. In the dim gray light from the streetlamps, her eyes were wide, her lips twisted.

'It's just a possibility,' he said, wishing he'd kept the theory to himself.

'If he's hurt Melanie . . .'

'We'll probably find her at your dad's house.'

Pen stopped for a red light at San Vicente. Leaning

forward, she pressed her forehead against the top of the steering wheel.

Bodie reached over. He rubbed her back through the soft sweatshirt. 'It'll be all right,' he said.

'Will it? Dad's in a coma. Melanie . . . God knows.' She turned her head. Her face was a mask of agony. 'It's all my fault.'

'It's Harrison's,' Bodie said.

A car horn beeped behind them.

The light had gone green, and the car ahead of them was moving into the intersection. Pen turned right onto San Vicente.

'I could have stopped it all,' she said. 'If I hadn't kept my mouth shut. I didn't want to hurt Dad. It would've been such a blow to him. He thought Harrison was such a terrific guy. But if I'd told . . . maybe the bastard would be in prison right now, though I doubt it. Would've been tough convincing a jury I wasn't asking for it. But it might've changed everything. I should've told, damn it.'

Bodie, breathless, stared at her. He felt as if he'd been kicked in the stomach. 'Asking for it?'

'Harrison raped me.'

'No.'

'I should've told.'

'Were you . . . hurt?'

She faced Bodie. She nodded. Tears were glistening in her eyes. They looked silver in the streetlights. 'I was battered up some,' she murmured.

'Did you fight him?'

'As much as I could,' she said, her voice shaking. 'He had me handcuffed.'

Bodie groaned.

'He worked on me . . . for a long time.' With the back of her wrist, she wiped tears off her cheek. 'I haven't been with a man since then.' Sniffing, she looked at Bodie. 'You'll be the first – if you still want me, now that you know . . .'

'Oh, Pen.' He put a hand on her thigh and squeezed it gently through her sweatpants. Heat seemed to flow up his arm. 'I've never wanted anyone the way I want you.'

'It doesn't bother you that . . . ?'

'I'd like to kill the bastard,' Bodie muttered.

'I never told anyone,' she said. 'I just pretended it never happened, and Harrison acted as if it really *hadn't* happened, and after a while it was almost as if . . .'

'A way to live with it,' Bodie said.

'I should've told. Maybe none of this would've happened.' She rubbed a sleeve across her face.

Bodie stroked her leg as she slowed the car and turned left onto the narrow road leading to her father's house. He wished he could pull her into his arms and hold her tight and make all the pain go away – her pain and his own.

Harrison had raped her. Handcuffed her, beaten her up, fucked her.

The scum.

The piece of shit.

'Bodie, you're hurting me.'

'I'm sorry.' He unclamped his fingers from Pen's thigh and wrapped them around the steel of the shotgun's barrel.

Then he looked along the roadside for his van. They drove slowly past a Ferrari, a Porsche, a Jaguar.

Pen stopped her car in front of the garage. 'She's not

here. It must be like you said and they took her away in the van.'

'Drive on a little further.'

Pen steered around a bend in the road and there was Bodie's van, snug against a leafy hedge. Bodie felt his bowels tighten.

Pen shifted to reverse, twisted herself sideways, hooked an arm over the seatback, and looked out the rear window. She backed up slowly.

Bodie gazed at her.

It seemed important, somehow, to see what she looked like right now and to keep it for a memory and never lose it.

The dim silhouette of her face. The pale white of her eye and the silver trail of a tear leading down from its corner. The flow of soft hair. The way her lower lip was caught between her teeth. The curve of her jawline. The hollow of her throat. The way her breasts pushed out her sweatshirt, forming soft mounds, the right higher than the left because her right arm was raised onto the seatback.

His gaze followed Pen's left arm to the steering wheel. The sleeve was drawn up above her slim wrist. Her hand, moving the wheel slightly from side to side, seemed small and fragile. He looked at the way her sweatpants were gathered over her lap, and how they draped her thighs. Then he looked again at her face.

So beautiful. All of her. And she's mine now.

I'll never let anything bad happen to her again, he thought, and felt a terrible hollow ache of loss because he knew it was an empty promise. The future would hurt them both, kill them both sooner or later no matter what.

Pen stopped the car broadside in front of the garage door. She set the brake, shut off the headlights, and turned to Bodie.

He lifted the shotgun out of the way. He put his arms around her and drew her gently against him. They kissed. He slipped his hands beneath the sweatshirt, moved them up the velvety skin of her back.

'I wish we didn't have to go in there,' she whispered.

'We don't have to.'

Pen kissed him lightly, then eased herself away. She took the key from the ignition. She opened her door.

Bodie climbed out, taking the shotgun with him.

CHAPTER TWENTY-THREE

Pen stopped at the front door and searched through her keys with trembling fingers. 'I wish we knew whether Joyce is here,' she said.

'The garage have any windows?'

'No.'

She found the house key and opened the door. She started to enter, but Bodie put a hand on her shoulder. He stepped inside. Pen followed.

And heard Melanie's voice.

'. . . here alone, or I'll kill her . . . I don't think you want to do that. I've got a paper here that the cops would find very interesting.'

Pen silently shut the door and followed Bodie across the foyer.

'You'll see when you get here. You'd better make it quick. I'll kill her if you're not here in ten minutes.'

She hung up as they stepped into the den.

'Melanie?'

She turned around. 'The lovebirds,' she said, staring at them through strands of black hair. She stroked the hair away from her face, her fingertips drawing stripes of blood across her forehead. Her white blouse was untucked, its front smeared with blood as if she had used it repeatedly to wipe her hands.

'Oh, Mel,' Pen muttered, 'what have you done?'

With a smirk, she raised a sheet of paper.

Bodie took it from her and studied it.

'You guys would've let them get away with killing Dad.'

'They didn't kill him,' Pen said.

Melanie's lips quivered. 'You just wanted to take Bodie away from me. That was all you cared about. You didn't care what they did to Dad.'

'Of course I care,' Pen said, realizing that Melanie now seemed more coherent than she'd been when Bodie took her away from the apartment. More coherent, but no less crazy.

The girl's lips peeled up, a dog snarl that changed into a sick grin. 'You cared about spreading your legs.'

Bodie handed the paper to Pen. Its edges had bloody fingerprints. She read the shaky handwriting:

This is my confession. I, Joyce Conway, conspired with Harrison Donner to murder my husband, Whit Conway. We were lovers behind his back. We wanted him dead so as to get his insurance and inheratence.

'That was Harrison you told to come over?' Bodie asked.

'Who else.'

'He'll probably show up with a goddamn SWAT team.'

'I don't think so.'

I let Harrison in on where and when we planned to have dinner and he waited in his car. When Whit

286

started to cross the street, he hit him with the car.
It was a stolen car, as he didn't want to use his own.

Joyce's signature was scribbled at the bottom in the
same handwriting as the confession.

'Where is she?' Bodie asked.

'Want to see her?' Melanie looked at her wristwatch.
It was Bodie's. 'I guess we have a few minutes.' She took
the paper from Pen and stepped past them. As they
followed her to the stairway, she glanced back. 'We'll
have to hide before Harrison shows up. The element of
surprise, you know.'

At the bottom of the stairs, Bodie looked at Pen. His
face was gray. He took her hand. His fingers felt like ice.

They rushed up the stairs behind Melanie. She led the
way along the corridor.

Pen knew they would find carnage. She felt light-
headed and numb. The lights seemed too dim. When she
blinked, an electric-blue aura surrounded Melanie. Pen
was nauseous. Just like Friday night, she thought, the
mystery writers' meeting, the coroner's shock-show.

Post-mortem lividity, bite marks on the corpse's but-
tock, the gray penis of the dead man, fly eggs in the
nostril.

I've gotta get out of here.

Fresh air.

Bodie stopped her at the door of the master bedroom.
'Wait here,' he said.

Pen leaned against the doorframe, her back to the
room. Bodie let go of her hand. He stepped past her.
Sliding down, Pen hung her head and stared between
her knees at the carpet.

I shouldn't, she thought. Shouldn't let him face it

alone. It'll help him if I'm there.

She forced herself to stand.

She heard nothing from inside the room.

Turning to the doorway, she saw Bodie and Melanie standing side by side. Their backs were toward her. Their bodies blocked her view of whatever they were looking at. Whatever? Joyce.

Pen walked slowly closer.

She smelled blood, and gagged. Quickly, she lifted the front of her sweatshirt. She pressed the soft fabric to her nose and mouth. It had a fresh scent that masked the coppery odor of the blood. She stopped gagging. She blinked the tears from her eyes and stepped to Bodie's side.

Joyce, on a straight-backed chair, gazed at her from a crimson face. She blinked away the blood that dribbled into her eyes from her cut forehead. She was gasping through her nose. A strip of cloth, probably a robe belt, was tied across her mouth.

'I had to do a little number on her,' Melanie said.

Bodie tipped the shotgun toward Pen. It was resting on the floor, barrel up. Keeping the sweatshirt over her mouth, she gripped the barrel with her other hand and held the weapon upright while Bodie stepped behind the chair.

Joyce's feet were tied to the chair legs. Her nightgown clung to her with blood, but Pen couldn't see any other wounds. All the blood, she thought, had come from the cuts on Joyce's forehead.

If that was all, she ought to recover.

Could've been worse, Pen thought. A lot worse.

She looked at Melanie. Melanie was staring at the shotgun. No, she realized. Not at the shotgun.

288

At me with my sweatshirt pulled up.

A chill squirmed up her back. She tugged the sweatshirt down. Melanie's gaze lifted to her face.

Pen could hardly believe the hatred in her sister's eyes.

The gaze shifted away from her as Bodie slipped the cloth from Joyce's mouth. 'What're you doing?' she demanded.

'For Godsake,' Bodie muttered. He crouched to untie Joyce's hands.

'Leave her alone.'

Pen realized that Joyce's mouth was stuffed with something. Stepping closer, she shifted the shotgun barrel to her other hand and bent over the woman.

'Don't do that,' Melanie warned.

'Shut up,' Pen said, and dug fingers into Joyce's mouth. She pulled out a sodden rag. A nylon stocking.

Joyce gasped for breath.

'You want her to warn Harrison?'

'Are you all right?' Pen asked.

'Muh . . . my face.'

'Are you hurt anywhere else?'

'Has a nasty bump on the back of her head,' Bodie said.

Pen patted the wadded stocking gently against Joyce's forehead. Lifting the nylon away, she looked at the wounds. The letters AM had been carved into her brow. Holding the cloth to the cuts, she scowled over her shoulder at Melanie. 'What the hell *is* this!'

'You two are such fucking literary types, figure it out.'

'I can't get her hands undone,' Bodie said.

'Why did you *do* it?' Pen blurted. 'God Almighty, Mel . . .'

' "A" for adultery, "M" for murder.'

'*Why did you do it!*'

'To get her confession, of course.'

'You idiot! That confession's no good. It's worthless. You *tortured* it out of her.'

'She wouldn't write it. I had to make her.'

'Lying,' Joyce murmured. 'She did this . . . after. Just . . . to hurt me.'

'The confession's no good,' Pen repeated.

'Too bad,' Melanie said. Lunging sideways, she rammed Pen.

'Hey!' Bodie yelled.

Pen's feet tangled. She struck the floor shoulder first and cried out as the shotgun barrel hammered her fingers against the carpet.

Bodie sprang up from his crouch behind Joyce. He shouted, 'NO!' and flung his hands forward to shove Melanie away.

Too late.

The knife (where did *that* come from?) slashed Joyce's throat and a spray of blood whipped across the front of Melanie's blouse as Bodie's hands smashed her shoulders and sent her stumbling away.

She landed on her back.

Pen, getting up, watched Bodie run through the flying blood. He bent over Melanie. 'Give me that!' he yelled. He reached for the knife and drew his hand back fast as Melanie slashed at it. 'Give me that! God! God!'

Melanie squirmed and twisted on the floor, kicking at his shins and slashing at him. Bodie kept yelling and trying to snatch her knife hand.

Pen picked up the shotgun. 'Get out of the way!' she snapped at Bodie.

He looked at her.

Melanie's right leg kicked up, her shoe smashing him in the groin. His eyes bulged. Clutching himself, he doubled over. His knees pounded the floor.

Melanie rolled away from him.

Pen aimed the shotgun at her as she scrambled to her feet. 'Stop!'

Melanie walked slowly toward Pen, hunched over, the knife in her right hand, her eyes almost hidden behind hanging ropes of hair. 'Gonna blow me away, sister? Go ahead. Well, do it. It's you or me.'

Pen backed away from her.

'I'm gonna cut you up. I'm gonna cut up that gorgeous face for you. I'm gonna cut off your precious tits. Then we'll see, won't we? Think Bodie's gonna want you then? Do you? Huh?'

The wall stopped Pen's retreat. She flicked the safety off. 'Just stop.'

'No, no, no, not me.'

Pen pulled the trigger. The shotgun jerked in her hands. Its roar blasted her ears. A circle of ceiling beyond Melanie's head exploded away. White dust and chunks of plaster fell.

Melanie grinned. Taking one more step, she gripped the muzzle with her left hand and pressed it to her chest. 'Go ahead, sister. Try again.'

'Mel . . . for godsake!'

Glancing past Melanie's shoulder, she saw Bodie on his hands and knees, trying to get up.

The barrel flew upward, thrust high by Melanie. In disbelief, Pen saw her sister duck beneath it and drive the knife at her chest. She lurched sideways. A hot streak burned across the skin under her left breast. She rammed out with an elbow. It caught Melanie in the armpit, knocking her out of the way. But she still held the shotgun. She wrenched it from Pen and hurled it to the floor.

Pen shoved herself off the wall. She tried to dodge past Melanie, hoping to regain the gun, but Melanie rushed ahead to block her way. And slashed. Pen dropped back as the blade whipped across her belly. It snagged and ripped her loose sweatshirt, but missed her skin. Whirling around, she ran for the bedroom door.

Melanie's feet pounded the carpet close behind her. They stayed behind her as she raced along the corridor.

'You've had it!' Melanie yelled. 'You've had it!'

At the top of the stairs, Pen grabbed the newel post and swung herself around it.

She was three steps down when she was hit. She cried out, more in alarm than pain, as the blade went in. The impact threw her forward. Her feet left the stairs and she flew headlong toward the bottom.

Bodie staggered across the bedroom, each step wracking him with pain as if pliers were squeezing his testicles. He bent over, groaning, and picked up the shotgun. His ears still rang from the blast.

Lurching through the doorway, he swung to the left. The corridor was empty. He heard footsteps on the stairs, but saw no one. The wall blocked his view for a few yards. Then it ended, and he threw himself against the railing of the balcony over the living room.

Melanie, knife raised overhead like a madwoman, was charging down the stairs. Pen was at the bottom, scrambling away on her knees and one hand. Her right forearm, bent at an odd angle, looked broken. The back of her sweatshirt had a slick oval of blood.

'Mel!' Bodie yelled.

She didn't stop. She was halfway down the stairs.

Pen, now on her feet, stumbled toward the foyer, her broken arm flapping.

Bodie jacked a shell into the shotgun chamber.

Melanie, hearing the noise, looked over her shoulder.

'Stop!' he cried out.

He peered down the sighting ramp. The bead at the muzzle's end wavered back and forth across Melanie's neck. He noticed her choker. A memory flashed through his mind of the time in bed when she was naked except for one of those chokers and he started to take it off and she clutched her ears to hold her head on.

His finger eased its pressure on the trigger.

'Just stay put!' he ordered. 'Don't move! Drop the knife!'

Her head turned away.

Bodie shifted his eyes to the right. Pen was at the front door, pulling it open.

Melanie looked back at him, then at the door again.

'Don't!' he shouted.

She raced down the stairs.

Bodie tracked her with the shotgun, knowing that a hit would probably kill her, hating to kill her, wondering if Pen had enough headstart, then swinging the muzzle well ahead of Melanie and firing. The shotgun leapt and kicked his shoulder as the blast slapped his eardrums. The front door, left ajar by Pen, crashed shut as the pellets punched through its bottom.

He ran for the stairway, grimacing each time a foot landed and sent a new shockwave of pain from his testicles.

293

Melanie reached the front door at the same moment as he started down the stairs.

Running had hurt, but pounding his way down the steps was glaring white agony.

Melanie threw open the door and dashed out.

Bodie worked the pump-action. The spent shell tumbled away.

He leaped down the final three stairs, crying out as his feet struck the floor and pain exploded through his body. He hobbled across the foyer and out the front door.

Melanie, her white blouse a pale bobbing target, was halfway across the dark yard. The dim, running shape of Pen was not far ahead of her.

When Pen reached the closed gate, Melanie would get her.

No question.

'Stop!' Bodie shrieked, shouldering the gun.

What if some of the pellets go past her and get Pen?

He aimed at the center of Melanie's back. His finger tightened on the trigger.

Pen was one stride from the gate.

The gate crashed open, smashing her, hurling her aside.

A man charged into the yard, hunched over as if he had just thrown a body-block against the gate. He straightened up abruptly as Melanie, not changing course to fall upon Pen, flew at him.

Harrison.

Harrison had raped Pen.

Bodie held fire.

The man put out both hands to stop Melanie. He yelled, 'Hey!' Then she hit him, driving the knife into his chest as the force of her impact carried him backward to the walkway. Melanie dropped on top of him.

Even from the porch, Bodie heard the thunk of his head striking the concrete.

He ran toward the sprawled shapes.

Harrison, on the bottom, didn't move.

Melanie, on top of him, moved a lot.

Her arm did.

Punching the knife into his body, yanking it out, stabbing him again and again until Bodie stopped her with a quick stroke of the shotgun butt.

He dragged the shotgun beside him as he staggered over to Pen. Letting it fall to the grass, he knelt down next to her. She lay on her back, panting, clutching the wound beneath her breast.

'How bad are you?'

As if it didn't matter, she shook her head. 'What happened?' she gasped.

'Mel . . . I think she killed Harrison. I knocked her out.'

Groaning, Pen struggled to sit up. Bodie pressed her shoulders gently to the ground. 'I think your arm's broken.'

'Tell me about it.'

'Just rest. I'll call the police.'

'No. Help me up.'

'Pen . . .'

'Please.'

He pulled her by the shoulders. When she was sitting, she hooked her left arm around his neck. He clutched her sides, just beneath the armpits, and lifted her. She was very heavy at first, then weightless as her legs took over. 'Okay,' she muttered. Bodie held onto her arm, but found that she needed no support as she led him back to the motionless bodies. 'Would you get her off him?'

Crouching, Bodie pulled gently at Melanie until she rolled away from Harrison. As one of her hands flopped to the ground, she moaned. Her eyes stayed shut.

Pen sank to her knees beside Harrison and stared at him.

Bodie, stepping around Melanie, squatted near his head. The man's eyes were closed, his mouth hanging open. The knife hilt protruded from his chest.

Pen put a hand to his throat.

'She must've stabbed him five or six times,' Bodie said.

'I can't find a pulse.'

'I could've stopped her. I was ready to shoot her, but when she went for him instead of you . . . The man raped you. And he ran down your father.'

'Where's his gun?' Pen asked.

'I didn't see one.'

Leaning over the body, Pen pulled a revolver from the pocket of his jacket. 'I figured he had to have it. I don't know if this'll help much, but . . .' She swung the revolver toward the front of the house and fired twice.

Straddling the body, she put the gun into Harrison's hand and slipped his forefinger through the trigger guard. She pressed his fingertip against the trigger. With the bottom edge of her sweatshirt, she wiped her prints off the rest of the gun.

'What about Joyce?' Bodie asked.

'I don't know.'

'There's no way to make *that* look like self-defense.'

'If we could get rid of the body . . .'

Bodie heard a siren, its distant alarm blaring through

the night. 'Too late for anything like that,' he said.

Melanie, sprawled on the grass beside her victim, looked as if she were sleeping.

'Can you think of a story?' Bodie asked Pen.

'Nothing to cover all this. The truth, I guess. It'll have to do.'

'Except for the revolver.'

The siren swelled to a high scream.

Pen stood up.

Bodie, rising, put a hand low on her back. Together, they stepped through the open gate. Pen leaned her head against his shoulder. 'I wish we could go back in time,' she said, 'and change it all.'

'I guess Harrison and Joyce got what they had coming,' Bodie said.

'But Melanie.'

'Yeah.'

'What did we do to her?'

He put his arms around Pen and gently drew her against him. Holding her, he turned slowly until he could see the open gate beyond her head. Melanie was on her hands and knees. Her face lifted. It was a dim patch in the darkness with black pits for eyes.

Staring at us, Bodie knew.

Hating us.

He felt a shiver climb his back.

Would she go for the shotgun?

The siren was a deafening shriek.

She went for the knife.

She tugged it out of Harrison's chest.

Bodie tensed for the attack.

Melanie pushed the knife slowly into Harrison's throat. Clutching it with both hands, she worked its blade back and forth. Her long black hair swayed in front of her face as she rocked above him, putting her weight into the cutting.

'What's wrong?' Pen asked.

'Nothing.' Bodie stroked her head. 'Everything's fine.'

CHAPTER TWENTY-FOUR

'No funny business,' Pen said. She was in bed, naked except for her white shorts, a white bandage beneath her left breast, and a white cast on her arm. The discarded sling lay rumpled on the sheet beside her. 'I am, after all, an invalid.'

'You look valid.' Bodie cupped her breasts and gently thumbed the nipples. Pen squirmed.

'You can validate me later,' she said. 'This is serious business.'

'Of course.'

Bodie's hands went away. Pen raised her head off the pillow. With an open hand, she lifted and flattened her breast and peered over it to see what he was doing. 'Be gentle,' she warned, smiling.

Bodie picked at a corner of the tape with his finger-nail. 'Difficult to concentrate,' he said, 'when beholding such a vision of loveliness.'

'Yep. No doubt.'

He pulled the tape slowly, watching the adhesive lift her skin and peel away from it.

'Owooo.'

'Maybe one quick yank.'

'Don't you dare.'

'We should really change this bandage more often than the one on your back. Such scenic surroundings.'

The bandage came off, revealing a four-inch laceration cross-hatched with stitches.

'Yuck,' Pen said.

'Coming along nicely.'

'Easy for you to say. I'm the one looks like the bride of Frankenstein.'

'You look terrific. It gives you character.'

'Sure.'

Bodie unrolled a pad of cotton and gauze, snipped off a section slightly longer than the wound, and taped it into place.

'Good job.' She released her breast and lowered her head to the pillow.

Her fingers had left faint red prints on her creamy skin. Bodie watched them fade.

I'm gonna cut off your tits!

'What's wrong?' Pen asked.

'Melanie. She keeps coming back.'

'Yeah.'

'I wonder how she's doing.'

'I don't know,' Pen muttered. 'At least she probably won't have to stand trial. That would've been tough, nothing going for her except Joyce's confession.'

Bodie put a hand on Pen's belly. He lightly stroked the smooth skin. 'Do you suppose they're treating her okay?'

'It isn't the Hilton. Later on, maybe we can get her moved to a better facility.'

'At least she nailed those two.'

'I wonder if it was worth it.'

The telephone rang. 'I'll get it,' Bodie said. He patted her belly, then stood and hurried toward the kitchen. Suddenly scared. Pen had changed her number. Only the police, the people at Melanie's psychiatric ward, and the hospital had the new one. The call had to mean trouble. He picked up the phone. 'Hello?'

'Is this Penelope Conway's residence?' asked the male voice.

'Yes, it is.'

'May I speak to Miss Conway?'

'Who may I say is calling?'

'This is Dr Herman Gray of the Beverlywood Medical Center. I'm calling about Miss Conway's father.'

Bodie's stomach clenched. 'Just a moment, please.' He let the phone's handset dangle by its cord, and hurried back to the bedroom. Pen was sitting up.

When she saw Bodie, the color left her face.

'It's Dr Gray,' he said.

She clamped her lower lip between her teeth.

Bodie followed her to the kitchen. He stood behind her while she picked up the phone. He put a hand on her bare back. He stared at the bandage over her right shoulder blade.

'This is Pen Conway,' she said.

She listened.

'Oh my God,' she said, and began to cry.

'What the *hell* happened to you?'

'What the hell happened to *you*?' Pen retorted. Then she fell to her knees beside the bed and, weeping, kissed her father.

When her mouth left his, he said, 'Hey, you're getting me wet, babe. Turn off the fountain.'

'God, Dad.' She kissed him again.

His hand came out from beneath the sheets and stroked her hair. 'Sure is good to see you again,' he said. 'Good to see anything, for that matter.'

'How do you feel?'

'Like I was hit by a locomotive.'

'It was a car.'

'So I hear.'

Pen wiped her eyes with her left hand.

'So what's *your* excuse?' Whit asked, glancing at her cast.

'I fell down some stairs.'

'Klutziness must run in the family, huh?' Bodie saw a glint in the old man's eyes. 'Any negligence involved?'

'Just my own.'

'Awwww. We'd have some great personal injury suits, both of us, if only . . .'

'Those are the breaks,' Pen said.

'No pun intended, huh?' Then he said, 'Owooo,' an echo of Pen when Bodie had pulled the tape from her chest.

'Dad, I want you to meet Bodie.' She smiled over her shoulder at him. Tears were shimmering in her eyes.

'I thought Bodie was a town in Wyoming. You don't *look* much like a town.'

'Welcome back, Mr Conway.'

'You banging my daughter?'

'Dad!'

'Hell, I know you are. I can tell by the look of you. You look okay to me.'

'Thanks, sir.'

'Make it Whit.'

'Whit.'

'You drink?'

'I polished off most of the beer in your refrigerator.'

'Make sure you restock it before I come home. Recuperation is thirsty work.'

'Right.'

'Speaking of home, how come you're both here and Joyce isn't?'

'She doesn't know you came out of it,' Pen said. 'Not yet. We'll tell her as soon as we see her.'

'You do that. Tell her to get her sweet buns over here.'

'I will.'

'What about number two daughter?'

'She was here for a few days right after the accident. It looked like you might be the same for a while, so she went back to school. She has her classes . . .'

'Well, that's all right. I'm glad she thought enough to come over.'

'She was awfully upset, Dad.'

A smile drifted over his lips. 'That's good to hear. Melanie . . . we've had our share of troubles since your mother passed away.' He shook his head. 'She doesn't care much for Joyce, I'm afraid.'

'She loves you a lot.'

'Hell, I think I'll go out and pay her a visit once I'm on my feet again.'

Bodie held Pen's hand as they left the hospital. The morning sun was bright and warm, and he watched the way Pen's gleaming hair stirred in the breeze.

There was sorrow in her eyes.

'Are you all right?' he asked.

'I hated lying to him.'

'He doesn't need the truth. Not right now.'

303

She shook her head. 'It'll really knock the wind out of his sails.'

'Wait a few days.'

'That won't make it any easier.'

'I know.'

'He's in for a world of hurt.'

'When he finds out what his wife and Harrison did to him, he might not be all that upset they're dead.'

'Just a different kind of pain.'

'He wouldn't have had to go through it if he'd stayed in his coma. Better this way, isn't it?'

'Yeah.' A smile tilted her lips. She looked at Bodie. 'A lot better this way.' Her hand tightened in his. 'I'll have to stick around for a while, though. He'll need me.'

'I know.'

'I'm sorry.'

'Summer break is coming up. In the meantime, I'll come every weekend. If you want.'

'Of course I want.'

'Don't let anyone else change those bandages. They're mine.'

'Whatever you say, sir.'

'It'll be a fine summer.'

'We'll go to the beach.'

'Let's go to the beach, now,' Bodie said.

They stopped at a corner and waited for the traffic light to change.

Bodie felt a little sad. He knew he would be leaving Pen in a few days and he knew there would be some hard times ahead for both of them – pain and sorrow and loneliness.

But they were together for the moment. She was with

him, a missing part of him that had been found and must never be lost.

The light changed.

The traffic stopped.

Bodie waited on the curb, holding Pen's hand, and looked both ways to be absolutely sure it was safe. Then he stepped off the curb with Pen at his side and they started across.

CHAPTER TWENTY-FIVE

At the intersection of Crescent Heights and Sunset Boulevard, Phil Danson stopped for the red traffic signal. He looked both ways. Not a car was in sight, so he gunned the Jaguar XKE and sped across Sunset.

It gave him a little rush.

A small risk, a small rush.

Keeping the gas pedal to the floor, he shifted and picked up speed. The road up Laurel Canyon was steep and twisting. He took the curves fast, grinning at the way the low car hugged the road. The quick turns pushed him from side to side. If he'd had the safety harness on, he wouldn't have felt the force so much. That's why he had it off.

Ahead of him, a traffic signal turned red. He kept his foot on the accelerator as he approached it.

Not much of a risk. It was two o'clock in the morning, after all, so what were the odds of a car swooping down from one of the sides and nailing him? Slim to none. Phil hoped for a spurt of adrenaline as he shot across the intersection against the red light. He didn't get it.

He crossed the center line.

Oh yes.

His heart quickened, his stomach knotted.

'All *right*,' he gasped.

This is good, this is fine.

Hands slick on the steering wheel, he sped up the downhill lane.

'Bat outa hell!'

He killed the headlights. Enough light came from the street lamps for him to see the road ahead. Almost. The pavement was a vague runway bordered by dark slopes, curving and twisting upward.

He steered around a bend one-handed as he turned on the radio. 'This is KLFC bringing you mellow sounds from midnight till dawn.'

'Shit on it.' Phil turned the knob and got Bruce Springsteen. 'The Boss!' he yelled, and twisted the volume high.

A ghost of light swept across the darkness ahead. With a whoop, Phil flicked the steering wheel. The Jaguar lurched to the right as the glare of headlights hit his eyes. A horn blasted. A Mustang flew by, very close but missing.

Phil laughed.

He had a green light at Mulholland. He shot beneath it so fast that his tires left the pavement when the road dropped away on the other side.

The road down from the crest was wide and, he knew, often heavily patrolled. He turned on his headlights and slowed down to the speed limit.

The fun was over. He still felt a little light-headed and shaky, and he held onto the good feelings for a while by thinking back to his wild trip to the top and his close one with the Mustang.

It had been bitchin', definitely bitchin'.

When he reached the intersection with Ventura Boulevard, he turned the radio off. He waited out the traffic signal, then made a left and drove to Earl's Body Shop.

He swung into the driveway, stopped in front of the closed double doors of the garage, and honked his horn.

Moments later, one of the doors rolled upward. Earl, the stub of a cigar jutting from a corner of his mouth, waved him in.

Phil pulled the Jaguar forward. Behind him, the door rumbled down. He shut off the engine and climbed out.

Earl squinted at the car through a gray screen of smoke. 'Looks like a beauty,' he said.

'She *is* a beauty,' Phil told him. 'Handles like a dream.'

Earl walked around the car, puffing and nodding. 'You were gonna have this to me last week.'

'Don't sweat it, Earl.'

'I ain't sweatin'. It's only just I told the guy he'd get it, know what I mean?'

'Well, now you've got it.'

'Takes time, the paint job, changin' the serial numbers, all that . . .'

'Takes time,' Phil retorted, 'finding a Jag in mint condition.'

'Thought you had one all lined up.'

'I did. I *had* the baby. Snatched it over in Beverly Hills, but it was raining like shit and some old fart walked right out in front of me and I creamed him. Creamed him real good, and I think some gal saw me nail him so I had to bail out. Who needs that kind of heat? Not me. Hey, this is a better car, anyway. That other one didn't have brakes for shit.'

More Terrifying Fiction from Headline Feature

Richard Laymon

THE BEAST HOUSE

'A BRILLIANT WRITER' *SUNDAY EXPRESS*

'IN LAYMON'S BOOKS, BLOOD DOESN'T SO MUCH DRIP, DRIP AS EXPLODE, SPLATTER AND COAGULATE' *Independent*

Author Gorman Hardy is hot on the trail of another bestseller. His last account of gruesome murder made him a fortune and, if half what's said about Malcasa Point is true, he's bound to make another killing . . .

Petite and pretty Tyler and her sexy friend Nora visit Malcasa full of expectation. Tyler is hoping to repair a broken romance and Nora is aiming to strike lucky – with her looks she usually does . . .

But Malcasa Point is not a place to discover fame, fortune and wild ecstatic loving. On the other hand, it's just the place to find pain, bestiality and death in . . . THE BEAST HOUSE!

'If you've missed Laymon, you've missed a treat' Stephen King

'No one writes like Laymon and you're going to have a good time with anything he writes' Dean Koontz

FICTION / HORROR 0 7472 4781 1

More Terrifying Fiction from Headline Feature

Richard Laymon

IN THE DARK

'THIS AUTHOR KNOWS HOW TO SOCK IT TO
THE READER'
The Times

Nothing much happens in Donnerville, at least not in
the public library. Then the new librarian, Jane
Kerry, receives an envelope containing a fifty-dollar
bill and a note instructing her to 'Look homeward,
angel.' Mystified, Jane pulls Thomas Wolfe's novel
of that title off the shelf and finds a second envelope.
This contains a hundred-dollar bill and a clue to
another pay-off. Like the first, it is signed 'MOG
(Master of Games)'. Suddenly Jane is hooked, this is
one game she must play to the end.

The Game requires more and more of Jane's strength
and ingenuity. It forces her, more than once, to
defend her life. It pushes her into actions that she
knows are crazy, immoral, criminal. And when she
tries to quit, MOG has other ideas . . .

RICHARD LAYMON

'A brilliant writer' *Sunday Express*

'If you've missed Laymon, you've missed a treat'
Stephen King

'A gut-crunching writer' *Time Out*

FICTION / HORROR 0 7472 4509 6

If you enjoyed this book here is a selection of other bestselling titles from Headline